# UNDER THE VEIL

## Underwood

## SHAWNA COLEING

## Free Bonus Chapter

GET **a bonus chapter**

Simply by signing up for the (no-spam) newsletter, I'll send you a bonus chapter - Find out more at the end of the book.

## Chapter 1

THE DARKNESS in the forest was almost complete, but stray beams of moonlight broke through the canopy to coat a few spindly tree branches in white. They tore at Eva's skin as she darted through the forest. But despite the obstacles, and even though her lungs burned, she wouldn't stop. She was trained for this and trusted her body to her instincts, which meant she was fast in the night-drenched woods.

The black mass that appeared ahead alerted her to the fallen tree in her path. Eva felt it more than saw it.

After leaping at just the right moment, her feet reconnected with the soft earth. But she ran only a few paces farther before a bulk slammed into her from the side, crushing her into the ground.

Her long legs twisted around her assailant as her reflexes responded to this new development. The man grunted as she dragged him to the side with a powerful jerk.

He grabbed her ponytail, yanking on it, but she'd

gained enough space and swung her elbow up, connecting with his cheek. The force loosened his grip, and she jumped to her feet to continue her sprint.

There were three men, she knew. One was far away by now. He could never keep up. His expertise wasn't in the chase. The second man she left behind in the leaf litter was no longer a threat, but the last…

She changed her angle, aiming for the river that she could hear flowing nearby, and quickly left the safety of the woods.

Rushing water blinked beside her as the peaks of waves caught the muted moonlight, then disappeared into the flat expanse beside her.

The riverbank left her exposed, but it also afforded greater speed with the longer loping strides she could affect in the open. And if she stayed on this course, she could get ahead of her last pursuer and make it into town by the time the sun rose.

She was focused on the path before her when an explosion of light erupted behind her eyes, followed by a shock of pain on the side of her head. She tripped forward, then staggered sideways as the looming shadow of the third man appeared. But before she had time to react, her mind numbed, and she dropped into the raging water beside her.

A dull whoosh filled her ears, and the world went black.

"It's dead. I'm tellin' ya." The voice of a grown man. Deep.

"Poke it." Another voice. This one the thready sound of a woman.

"I'm not gonna poke it. You poke it."

"I ain't touchin' that thing."

"You afraid it'll bite ya?"

Eva grunted and lifted an arm against the light filtering through her eyelids.

The woman shrieked. "I knew it wasn't dead!"

"Holy mother of Jesus. It's a girl, see?"

A muffled curse. "Franklin R. Palmer, you get on your knees and repent."

"Stop it, Ma. I'm a grown man. I'll do what I want. Besides, I was just sayin'."

"But that ain't a girl. It's a woman. And you weren't just sayin'. You were lookin'. And lookin' is the same as doin'."

The man grunted. "What are we gonna do with her?"

"We can't leave her here. She's not dead, but she will be soon—Look at that."

"What?"

Eva felt the press of fingers on her wrist.

"That tattoo," the woman said.

"Just some small squares. Could be anything."

"Doesn't need to be big to mean a lot. Looks to me like she's been branded. Son, I believe we've been called to the Lord's work. Give me your bag."

"What for?"

"'Cause you're gonna carry her—But don't touch nothin'!"

"How am I supposed to carry her if I can't touch her?"

"You know what I mean."

Pain shot through Eva's body as she was lifted. But despite the fog that remained over her thoughts, she maintained control in her half-consciousness.

She didn't know she was trained to remain silent under duress. She couldn't remember anything at all.

As they went, each bounce sent a shock of agony through her body, and it wasn't long before she lost consciousness again.

---

It was a coughing fit that brought Eva around the second time. The electric shock that ripped across her forehead and tore at her ribs pulled her from oblivion.

She blinked her eyes open, and a heavyset woman filled her vision. The woman had a face like a frog. Her fat lips pushed out in a scowl that confined her eyes to slits.

"You're awake," the woman said. "You're lucky you're not dead."

Eva changed angles so she could sit up.

"You sure that's a good idea?" the woman said.

Eva didn't care. Lying down made her vulnerable, but it was still several minutes before she could get upright. She pressed a hand to support her ribs as she lifted herself, but her head spun when she was finally sitting, and she had to breathe slowly through her nose, bowed over until it settled.

"Where am I?" Her voice came out a croaking whisper.

"My house." The woman tipped her head sideways, her eyes roaming down Eva from head to toe. "You're a determined little thing, ain't ya?" She held out the cup she was carrying. "Can you drink this? Or am I gonna have ta feed ya like a baby on the teat?"

Eva took the cup, but frowned down at the brown liquid. She swished it in a worthless attempt to identify the contents. The smell was pungent, but not bad.

"What is it?"

"It's not poison, if that's what you're worried about."

"That's not—" Eva coughed again.

The woman scooped the cup from her hand to keep it from spilling. "Jesus, Mary, and Joseph," she mumbled.

"Sorry." Once the coughing stopped, Eva held her hand out to take the cup back.

The woman's face softened from suspicion to pity as she handed it over. "Oregon grape root, echinacea, ginger. I could go on, but I won't waste my time or yours. Just drink it. If I wanted to kill you, I'd have left you at the river."

"River?"

"Yeah, that's where we found you washed up like a drowned rat. Thought you were dead. You looked dead. If I'm being honest, you still look dead."

Eva took a sip, but choked on it. It burned down to her stomach, where it threatened to bring up whatever juices were stewing in there.

"I'm sorry," she said again after regaining her breath. "Maybe I should get to a hospital."

The woman snorted. "You must really have a death wish, darlin'. God brought you here to save ya. Don't know why yet. May never know. The Lord works in mysterious ways."

"What does that have to do with the hospital?"

"If you go back out into that wilderness they call civilization, you won't last a second."

Eva set the cup on a small table by the bed. She couldn't remember anything, but those words triggered a sense that she wasn't someone who trusted many people either. But she couldn't stay here. "Then I should get home."

"Home? You really want to go back to that miry pit you came from?"

"What?"

"Don't you remember?"

"I can't remember anything. Except—" Dark images swam through her head. She was running in the dark.

"'Cept what?"

"I was being chased. I got hit. That's all I can remember."

"I knew it. I knew I was right. I could feel it in my bones. You escaped from a cult."

"What?"

"You were part of a cult. You escaped. It was very brave."

"How do you know all that?"

"Where else would you have come from? You said yourself that you were chased and attacked. Not to mention you've got that mark on your arm from them to prove it."

Eva looked at her wrist. She ran a finger over the squares there that were slightly raised on her skin. "This is from a cult?"

"What else would it be from?"

"Do you know which one?"

"There are so many to choose from. But does it really matter? All I can tell you for sure is that God has work for you to do. That's why he sent you to us."

"Us?"

"My son and I live here. But I can't keep lookin' after you. Once you start feeling better, you're gonna have to pull your own weight if you want to stay. I have no patience for freeloaders."

"Stay?"

"You a parrot, girl?"

"A parrot?"

The woman hooted. "You keep repeating everything I say. Guess I should go easy on you. They would have trained you to repeat after them. Do as you're told. Lord knows I do as I'm told. But only when God speaks, and God needs to give you a home. You have nowhere else to go and mine is as good as any. Probably better than most."

"So I have no home to go to?"

The woman's face dropped into a frown and she sat on the end of the bed, putting a hand on Eva's knee. "I'm sorry, child. I really am. But the life you came from was a nightmare. It was no home. But we will open ours to you if you'll have us."

"That's...generous of you."

"Just doing my part. My name is Clara, by the way. My son is Franky. He doesn't say much, but he's a good boy. I think you two will get along just fine."

"And Franky is okay with me staying?"

Clara waved the comment away. "You let me worry about him. You're welcome here."

"Thank you." Eva was not settled on the matter, but she didn't have the energy to get into it further. If she came from a cult, then she must have a family out there somewhere looking for her.

"I am always obedient to the Lord's command. Now, you rest a little longer and try to drink more of that tea. I've got a few things to do, but I'll heat some water and bring a basin for you a bit later so you can clean yourself up."

Eva reached her hand up and scrunched a handful of stiff hair. She could feel it was a tangled mess.

"Yeah, it's a mop," Clara said. "Not sure what we're going to do about it besides give it a good soak. I could cut it all off, but I think the Lord would rather we keep it long if we can. You rest up now. I'll be back later to check on you."

After Clara left the room, Eva looked down at the gray shirt and plaid boxers she was wearing. They were much cleaner than the rest of her body. She searched the room with her eyes and saw a black mass of filthy fabric draped across a wooden chair near the door. Clara must have changed her clothes. She shivered at the thought of someone touching her while she was unconscious but pushed away the revulsion. She would have been more thankful for what Clara had done if she could ignore the sense of self-reliance that came more naturally to her than being cared for.

With her eyes still roaming the room, she studied her surroundings properly for the first time. The walls were rough hewn and the little wooden table next to her bed was basic pine and homemade. A small window high up on the wall offered a little light and judging the size, it was probably too small to climb out of.

A crease formed between her eyes. Why would she even think about climbing out? Clara had been nothing but kind and no threat had been made. But when Eva looked at the door, she had taken it for granted that she wasn't locked in.

Slowly, she lifted herself from the bed and took tentative steps across the room until she reached the other side, where she used the door handle to steady herself. It gave way under her weight and opened a crack. She peaked down the empty hall, then back up at the window.

Even if she couldn't remember anything, she knew for sure that she wouldn't allow herself to end up caged. But because of her injuries, she had no choice but to cooperate with Clara and gain back her strength until she could better assess the situation she now found herself in.

She took a step back toward the bed, but her head spun, and she dropped into the chair. Pressing a hand to her head to ease the spinning, she felt a tender spot near her temple where she'd been struck. It was the only thing she could remember from her past. She was running, and it was dark. Then she was attacked. Someone must have been chasing her and they got to her before she could escape. But who was it and why?

She reached to the back of her neck and squeezed. It could have been a cult as Clara had said. But whoever it was, they were dangerous. And if they were still looking for her, Eva could be putting Clara and her son at risk after they'd saved her life and offered her a place to stay.

Or perhaps it was like Clara had said and it was God. But Eva had no concept of who God was in her life. She understood the idea of a higher power, but whether or not she had a connection to him in any way, or if she even believed a god existed, was hiding behind a veil she couldn't penetrate.

After resting for several minutes, she stood and stumbled across the floor, falling onto the thin mattress where she collapsed into a cocoon of pain and exhaustion. Her eyes fluttered for a moment as she fought through her lapsing consciousness to discover where it was she had been running to. But her mind would not concede, and in the end she fell asleep with no answers.

## Chapter 2

BEN ADJUSTED his grip on the heavy suitcase as he looked up at the building that loomed ahead. It was unremarkable to look at from the outside and appeared identical to those around it with its plain brick façade. It should be filled with stock standard offices and florescent lighting. But what went on inside the building was far from ordinary.

He had begun working for the Underwood Foundation not long after leaving the special forces. After serving for seven years in the military running secret missions, he'd spent many months agonizing over what to do next. He was approaching thirty years old and found it impossible to settle into what those around him called a normal life. It wasn't normal for him. So when Julian offered him a job as security for an organization whose sole purpose was to bring about a genuine change for the better, it felt to Ben like an assignment straight from heaven.

But he was wrong.

That lapse in judgment meant he ended up working for a man bent on controlling a country for his own power and greed, and Ben lost all confidence in his ability to hear the God he thought he'd been serving. Today was his chance to make up for that.

He approached the guard who monitored the front door. The first of a host of security.

"Here again?" the guard said, taking Ben's pass and marking his entry. "That's three days in a row."

"I know," Ben said. "I'm waiting on my next job. In the meantime, I'm stuck running back and forth."

The guard shook his head. "That must be killing you, running errands."

"It's not so bad. You know what Julian says: We are each an important part of the greater purpose."

"Yeah. That's what we're all here for, I guess."

"You're not happy with the part you play?"

"No! Don't misunderstand me. I love my job. It's a privilege to serve Julian's vision. I just meant—"

"I know what you meant." Ben laughed. "This wasn't a test. I was just giving you a hard time." And making sure he was more focused on himself than on Ben's peculiar visits.

The guard let out a quick breath that carried a fake laugh of partial relief. Ben couldn't blame him. Julian ruled with a powerful mix of love and fear.

The guard handed Ben back his pass and fired off his next words in quick succession suggesting he would be more comfortable once Ben moved on. "Right. Okay then. Should I expect to see you tomorrow?"

"No. This is the last of it here for me. I've got a new assignment tomorrow."

"Well, good luck."

"Thanks." Ben nodded to the guard, then crossed the gate into the building.

The entry hall was empty, and he stopped to take a breath before moving to the next door.

He positioned his face in front of the eye scanner and waited for the pop of the lock and the green light before entering a long corridor.

His steps were even and steady, but they belied the fast pounding of his heart. He had come to despise this place and would be relieved to never set foot in it again. To Ben, it represented evil at its core.

After turning the corner, he noticed the door ahead was open, and as he approached, the hair on the back of his neck raised. He didn't stop, but glanced into the dark room as he passed, sensing the shadows that watched him from inside. Or was that his imagination? He never knew anymore.

It used to be a gift, being able to discern the spiritual environment. When he'd worked in the special forces, his insight proved to be an invaluable asset. With God's help, Ben had saved a lot of lives and received the medals to prove it. But back then, he'd gotten lost among the praise of his peers and forgot that without God, it was all worthless.

He never saw the demons themselves. It was more like being in a dark room with other people and feeling their presence. He didn't have to see them to know they were there. But now, he'd been in the dark too long.

When he'd first agreed to work for Julian, he had no sense of their presence. He'd felt a warning that they were there, but by then, he trusted too faithfully in his gift. And by the time the demonic forces finally revealed themselves, it was too late, and he'd done things he couldn't undo.

His fingers squeezed the handle of the case to keep his hand from shaking. He might have gotten lost along the way, but now was his chance to make things right.

He swiped his pass in another door and continued through to the next hallway.

Julian didn't often make mistakes, but he'd made one with Ben by trusting him with too much. Now, Ben would use that error to stop him from hurting anyone else.

He turned into a large, windowed room.

"Ben," said a young woman wearing a white lab coat. "I didn't expect to see you in here today." She tucked her hair behind her ear, self-conscious in Ben's presence. He'd been assigned to protect Trish a month ago when they were tweaking the program. They'd heard that a traitor was among them and Julian wanted to make sure nothing interrupted their progress.

At the time, Ben was sure he'd been discovered because he'd already begun planning what he was carrying out today. But when he confirmed that he was safe, he used Trish, who it was clear had a crush on him, to gain valuable information. Perhaps it was cold-hearted of him to take advantage of her, but it didn't feel much like he had a heart anymore.

"Hey, Trish," he said. "I won't be around long. Julian's got me running all over the place for him today."

"I guess I'll have to make myself indispensable again to see much of you anymore." A blush colored her cheeks.

His smile was close-lipped. "Can you do me a favor?"

"What do I get?" When Ben hesitated, she waved her comment away. "I'm kidding. Tell me what you need."

"Can you unlock the data room for me?"

"What's Julian got you doing in there?"

"I'd like to tell you, but I'm afraid it's confidential."

"I'm not supposed to let anyone in there without proper authorization."

Ben looked down, ignoring the pang of guilt and focusing on the toe of his shoe. It had a smudge on it. "I'll tell you what. If you can just ignore protocol for half a second, I promise to give you all the details of my next assignment over dinner."

"Really?"

"Unless you don't—"

"No, I'd love that. All right. I'll open the door, but don't tell anyone."

"Not a soul. Thanks."

Ben headed down another corridor toward the data room. He'd spent the last two days placing explosives strategically around the building in order to set off a chain reaction after he destroyed the data. It was the only way he knew how to stop Julian.

He entered the room that was the heart of the AI

program that had given Julian a dangerous amount of information. If Ben hadn't seen the students with his own eyes and observed what he'd done to them, he never would have believed it was possible. Now, he'd put an end to it.

He opened the suitcase, set up the bomb at the back of the room, and armed it.

This was it. On his way out of the building, he would set off the fire alarm to make sure the building was evacuated. There were a lot of people in the building who deserved to die for what they'd done. But there were too many others, like Trish, who were deceived. Most of them hadn't chosen to be a part of this. Julian hadn't given them the option, and Ben wasn't willing to take their lives for that.

He double-checked the bomb and the remote before he walked back out into the hall.

Callum, one of Julian's personal bodyguards, stood at the far end of the corridor.

"Hey, Cal. What's happening?"

Callum rested his hand on his gun. "I was looking for you. Rick wants to have a word."

"I'm in the middle of something. Can we do it later?"

"No."

"But I'm on an assignment from Julian. You really want to make him wait?"

"I'm not too worried about it."

"Okay, it's your head." Ben walked casually toward Callum, but as he passed him, he punched him in the stomach. It was only half a second of incapacitation.

Callum was highly trained, but so was Ben. He pulled his gun and hit Cal over the head with it, knocking him out.

He raced down the hall, but when he turned the corner, two more men were there waiting.

"Ben!" One of them shouted as they both pulled their guns. "Stop."

Ben retreated back past Callum, who was beginning to stir, and into the stairwell.

An alarm went off as he jumped the railing and dropped a flight of stairs.

He entered the floor. Pausing long enough to judge which hallway he should take before heading left. He didn't know the floor, but he knew the building's exit was east.

When he reached the end of the hall, he found another stairwell that he tried to enter, but the door was locked.

He ran back the way he came, but when he opened the door, he could hear the shouts of men coming from below and above. The building would be crawling by now. It would be impossible to get out unnoticed.

He closed his eyes. If he got caught, he was a dead man anyway.

Turning slowly back down the hall, he entered the closest room. It was full of filing cabinets.

He went to the back of the room and sat on the floor before pulling out the transmitter that would destroy Julian's work.

He stared at it, then he lifted his eyes to the ceiling. He didn't pray, just looked.

There was no turning back now. This was the only way he could stop Julian. He had no other choice. He couldn't let the program continue. So many kids had already lost everything to Julian.

He thought of Samson in the book of Judges sacrificing himself after he'd screwed up. He had gotten himself into a bad situation because he made terrible choices, and Ben had done the same.

Samson had been willing to do what he needed to stop the enemy and make things right, and this was Ben's opportunity to do the same.

Ben blew out a thin stream of breath as he considered the end. It wasn't that long ago that he'd been certain of so many things, but now he wasn't sure of much as far as his soul was concerned. He still had faith. He still believed everything the Bible said about Jesus, but he couldn't begin to imagine what Jesus thought about him right now.

He squeezed his eyes shut and pressed his thumb on the button to blow the bomb.

A loud, cracking explosion followed by a white light filled his senses, and heat seared his skin.

---

Ben shot up in bed, gasping for air. The dark stillness in his room accentuated the sound of his whimpering. He gulped down air and took several minutes to steady his breathing.

"It was a dream. It's not real." Except it was. The

memory was seared into his mind, intent on replaying itself in his dreams.

He swiped at his sweaty forehead with the back of his hand, focusing on slowing his pulse, but his heart pounded like a relentless drum.

He glanced at the clock. It was three in the morning. That was his night gone.

After throwing back the covers, he slipped out of bed and padded to the bathroom, where he splashed water on his face, trying to remove the heat that pretended to be there, blistering his skin. That part of his memory, at least, was a lie. He hadn't been burned in the flames, even if his mind insisted that he had.

He looked at his bloodshot eyes, the red veins a sharp contrast to the deep-blue iris. Then he blinked.

"You're stronger than this. Come on, Ben." He slapped his face. "Dreams can't hurt you." But they did. They wouldn't let him escape what had happened. He had survived the blast, but inside he was dead.

His heart was still racing when he moved into the living room and turned on the light. With faltering steps, he wandered the space, unsure what to do next. Finally, he sat.

His Bible was in reach beside him, but it took him a moment before he drummed up the courage to pick it up.

After opening to a random page, he slid his finger down line after line as he read the words, but the sick tightening didn't abate and he knew why. God's word was alive, but he read with dead eyes. It was impossible to trust those words anymore. He wanted to. He knew they were real because he'd experienced the power in his life more times that he could count. But in the early hours of the morning when he woke to the same nightmare that wasn't a nightmare, he found it impossible to escape the truth that he didn't know how to live anymore.

When the explosion engulfed him that day, he gave himself over to whatever eternity awaited him. He let it claim him. But when his consciousness had remained long after it should have, he opened his eyes and saw a man standing in the fire. The man reached out and took Ben's hand, pulling him up from a floor that was no longer there.

For a moment, Ben thought he was being escorted to heaven and couldn't decide if he was surprised or not.

But the angel didn't remove him from the earth. Instead, he'd brought Ben through the rubble. They walked through twisted metal and smoke and Ben came out completely uninjured. His ears weren't even ringing.

The man, dressed in plain clothes, steadied Ben on his feet.

"He's not done with you yet," the man had said.

"Who?"

"You know who. He has work for you to do."

"No." The word had come from his lips unbidden, but he knew he had nothing left to give. He didn't try to deny that it was a miracle that saved him. But after escaping, he found he didn't know how to live again and all he could think to do was hide. So he moved to a small town in a meager attempt to conceal himself from God.

It was only a couple of weeks before the angel had visited him at his new home. Ben pleaded with him to leave. But the angel stayed long enough to give warning that he would one day return.

Now Ben waited in fear. Part of him looked forward to escaping from this existence of the living dead. He was a trained soldier, after all. He knew how to go into battle unafraid. But the fear was somehow stronger than his will. So even though he went through the motions of training daily so that he would be prepared when the time came, he knew he would never be ready.

He spent the rest of the early hours of the morning staring at the wall, but when the rising sun sent light through the curtains, Ben closed his eyes in relief. The daylight would wash away the memory of the dream.

But as the remnants of the nightmare melted from him, something sparked in the memory of it, and he sat up straight in the chair. Among the cracking steel, flames, and heat that he'd endured again, something was different.

He leaned forward, squeezing his eyes closed in an attempt to recall the alteration, but he couldn't bring it back. He could only feel it.

There had been a shift. The sense of hopelessness that had always fastened itself to him through the dream was still there. The fear of death, and then living, squeezed him from the inside out. But there had been a change in the battle itself. The only sense he could make of it was that the enemy had lost footing. He pushed aside his anxiety and went back through the dream to try to find the moment, but it was gone.

He went to the window and looked out at the woods that were still heavy in shadow and put a hand to his chest, rubbing a hand across his muscle there. He had the strength and skill to match the best, but living as a hermit made him afraid of his own shadow most of the time.

The sun hit his face and he considered the possibility that God would realize he was unfit for service, and the angel wouldn't return. That thought filled him with relief as well as agony that he couldn't dwell on for long without spiraling into depression.

He went outside, taking deep breaths of the still morning air, then trotted down the steps, walking in bare feet through the dewy grass around to the back of the house.

He put his hands on his hips pretending that the animal that had been digging in his garden was a nuisance. But worrying about regular things, being annoyed by a hassle, was exactly what he needed to release the knot of tension around his heart. He'd never wanted a normal life, but it was the only place he could hide.

## Chapter 3

EVA WOKE and found the angle of light streaming through the window had changed, but she had no idea if it had been hours or days.

A fist hammered on the door and she jumped, her ribs protesting.

"You decent?" Clara yelled, but she didn't wait for an answer before opening the door, hefting a basin. When she set it down, water sloshed onto the floor. "It's only room temperature, but it's better than living in the filth that's coating your skin. We have a proper shower when you're up to a full wash. I wouldn't expect you could stand that long right now."

The smells that flooded into the room with the door open made Eva's stomach both grumble and boil. She pressed a hand to her belly, trying to cover the growl.

"Sounds like you've got your appetite back. Food's on the table when you're ready."

Clara took a quick glance into the cup she'd left earlier and tsked when she saw it was still full, but she didn't comment further. Instead, she leaned out of the room, scooping a pile off the floor in the hall. She dropped a couple of towels and soap next to the basin and tossed a heap of clothes on the chair.

"They won't fit, but it's the best I can do on short notice. You mind if I throw those out?" She pointed to the black clothes hanging on the back of the chair. "They're beyond repair."

"That's fine. Thank you."

Clara swiped them up, then paused at the door and frowned. She opened her mouth to say something, but then slammed her lips shut before nodding and closing the door.

Eva pulled off her clothes and knelt beside the water, shifting several times to find a position where she could sit comfortably with the least amount of pain. Then she leaned forward and scooped the water up, splashing it on her face. It felt so good, she plunged her head under, as deep as she could reach. She twisted her head around to give her matted hair a good soak. It was long and thick and she'd probably only make it worse, wetting it without washing, but she didn't care.

Once her hair was all under, she stilled and waited, holding her breath until she ran out of air. After a minute, with no urgency in her lungs for more oxygen, she let out a pocket of breath. The bubbles floated to the surface, the sound of which fired off a memory. Someone had a hand on her head, holding her under the water. Eva struggled to rise. Water sloshed out of the bucket as her legs kicked out.

With a yank, she snapped back and jumped up away

from the basin, falling back against the wall, where she remained leaning while she gulped down air. Water streamed down her body from her laden hair.

Her eyes darted around the room to confirm what she already knew: She was alone. It was a memory. But she could still feel the weight on her head.

"It was a test," she said, breathing hard—more from the fear than a lack of oxygen.

She didn't know what had happened other than someone had held her head under water, but not to kill her. If it had really been just a test, then why could she remember being afraid? She ran a hand across her face to wipe away the water, then reached for the towel to wash the rest of herself as best as she could before she put on the oversized floral-print dress that she cinched with a stiff brown belt.

She had to rest before drying the floor with another towel, but the memory had shaken her and she decided the best thing she could do was to get away from her own thoughts. She needed a distraction and something to eat. The sick emptiness in her stomach made her head spin again, and being weak meant she was at risk.

When she reached the door, she stopped. Every thread she recalled from her past spoke of horrors she would be better off forgetting. Clara thought it was best for her to forget about where she came from and with this new revelation, Eva didn't disagree, but it was hard to ignore the person she was and the experiences she'd had.

A wave of nausea swept through her and she took a moment to let it pass before opening the door, rubbing at the tattoo on her wrist as she shuffled down the hall. Whoever she was, she wasn't normal. Clara was right. Civilization was a scarier wilderness than the trees she could see out the window. She stopped and stared out at the tree line. She knew the forest. It was safe out there. She'd trained there.

A flinch twitched through her body and she shook her head, afraid that any memory that surfaced wouldn't be a good one. She squeezed her eyes tight as her head began to pound. There had to be other memories besides the bad ones. But she couldn't stand in the hall and dwell on it. Her strength was draining and if she didn't hurry, she wouldn't make it to the kitchen.

Using the wall to prop her up, she continued down the hall and entered the kitchen where she paused, noticing a heavy wooden table that filled the middle of the floor.

A man was sitting there, whom she assumed was Franky. He was a strong, good-looking, dark-haired man with a wide chest. Probably aged somewhere in his twenties, but it was hard to tell under the thick beard that had a little bit of red in it. He was shoveling what looked like stew into his mouth but hadn't seen her yet.

"You're up," Clara said from the stove. "Good. Sit. I'll dish you up some soup."

Eva nodded, then pulled out a chair, scraping the floor. She smiled uncomfortably at Franky, who was watching her, chewing slowly with his mouth full.

"You must be Franky," Eva said, out of breath from her trek. She tucked her hands into her lap. The way he looked at her made her edgy.

Franky grunted and focused on his food again, but shot glances up at her now and then.

Clara set a bowl on the table. "See how you go getting that down." She grabbed a handful of Eva's hair that was worse than before. "We're really going to have to do something about that."

"Yeah."

Clara flicked it aside and went back to the counter.

"Thank you for this," Eva said. "It smells delicious." She dipped her spoon into the broth and blew on it before sipping a little. It was salty and when Eva swallowed, her stomach wasn't sure whether to accept the offering or not. She'd have to take this slowly.

After dipping her spoon again, she left it to cool in midair while she took closer note of her surroundings. The front door was closed but didn't look locked. Outside the closest window, she could see the line of trees beyond an overgrown field. A knife rested on the counter next to the sink.

She didn't know why those things were important, but she knew they were. "Where are we?"

Clara turned and leaned on the counter. "Where do you think we are?"

Franky stopped mid-chew and watched Eva.

"I don't know," she said.

"Still nothin', huh?"

"No." She didn't want to sound crazy by informing Clara of her near drowning.

"Can't remember the compound you came from? Where it was?" Clara said.

"Compound?"

"Where the cult is located."

"Oh. No. You sure I came from a cult?"

"Unless you can come up with a better explanation of why you were being chased and fell into the river. But what difference does it make? You were in danger, child. You ran away and ended up here. You should be dead, but you're not. You should forget about all that and count your blessin's."

"I just wish I could remember something good."

Clara harrumphed. "Don't count on it. You were probably brainwashed, tortured, and worse. Better you can't remember a thing. Start fresh."

Eva shuddered. Clara might not know where she came from, but she couldn't be far from what the truth must be.

"Try not to think about it too much, Eva. Right now, you need your strength. There's a lot of work to be done 'round here."

"Eva?"

Clara shrugged. "You were half-conscious when I asked you. That's what you said your name was. Could be wrong, but that name didn't come out of thin air. Doesn't ring a bell?"

"I guess it's as good a name as any. But no. I don't know what my name is."

"Eva it is then."

"You still haven't said where we are."

"Does Virginia mean anything to you?"

"Yeah, it's a state."

Franky's head jerked. "I thought you couldn't remember anything." It was the first words he'd spoken.

"I can't remember anything that's a memory, but there are other things that are clear. Like, I know where Virginia is, but I don't know if that's where I came from." She looked at the stove. "I know how to cook pancakes, but I couldn't tell you when or where I learned."

"Anything else?" Clara asked. "You know what skills you have?"

Eva stiffened as the memory of being held under the water resurfaced. She could hold her breath a long time, but that skill wouldn't help.

She looked around the room and saw a rope hanging on the back of a chair. "I can tie at least ten different knots. But again, I don't know where I learned it."

"Knots." Clara nodded approvingly. "Knots come in handy out here. Can you remember anything else?"

Eva chewed on her lip. She glanced at the knife at the sink but quickly averted her eyes. She knew how to use one and not for cooking. "Not that I can think of."

"You let me know. You could be a big help around here. But you won't be any help if you don't eat up and regain your strength."

Eva took another small sip of broth to appease Clara, but almost gagged.

"You don't like it?" Clara said, obviously offended.

"It's delicious. It's my stomach. I've gone too long without eating, I think."

"Here." Clara pulled out a loaf of bread and sawed off a chunk. She tossed it and Eva caught it one-handed. "Try to get that down. Dip it in a little broth."

Eva did as she instructed. Her stomach was happy with the change, and Eva closed her eyes as she chewed. That was what she needed. When she opened her eyes, Franky was watching her, his mouth opened slightly. He pushed his empty bowl back and stood, heading out the door without a word.

Clara joined her with a bowl of her own and Eva relaxed.

After swallowing another bite, she said, "Have you tried contacting the police? See if anyone is looking for me? I mean, if I was in a cult, I probably have a family somewhere."

Clara snorted, then shoved a chunk of potato into her mouth. "Police," she said before chewing. "We're going to have to teach you everything. But at least you're a clean slate. We can start from scratch with you. Your first lesson is that you can't trust law enforcement."

"Oh. Right."

"If we tell them about you, then they put you right back where you escaped from. They're not here to protect the innocent. They're here to enforce the demands of the overlords. Same reason we can't risk taking you to the hospital. Not that you need to go to that butcher shop anyway. This world is so full of heathens and murderers. You go out that door and your life is in danger. But you don't have to worry about any of that. You're family now."

Eva nodded, unsure what else to say about it.

"By the way, I've got a little job for you to do if you're up for it in the next couple of days. An easy one."

"I'd like that. I need to get busy doing something. I

know I'm still recovering, but I'm finding it hard not to be busy."

Clara smiled. "Good."

"What is it I can do?"

"There is a small town nearby where we get our supplies. Unfortunately, there are those there who have discovered our way of life."

"What's wrong with living in the woods?"

"Exactly, but when they found out that we aren't willing to submit to the powers that be, that makes them uncomfortable. We believe in a free society where folks can be left in charge of their own affairs."

"And they don't agree with that?"

"No way."

"I'm not sure how I can help with that."

"We can still get most things. We put up with the sideways glances we get, but Franky's been bugging me about getting his hands on some more fertilizer. He's been threatening to break into old Roger's place, but that'll make trouble."

Eva waited for her to continue, but she didn't. "That's it? You just need fertilizer?"

"And a bottle of bleach."

"And…why can't you get fertilizer and bleach?"

"Roger, the guy who owns the store, he won't sell it to us anymore. He thinks we're making bombs with it."

"Are you?"

Clara squinted. "What difference does that make? It's supposed to be a free country. What we do with it is up to us. We have a right to protect our way of life from those who want to steal it from us. From those who want us to conform like lemmings."

"What makes you think he'll sell it to me?"

"Because he don't know you. We'll stay out of sight. It will be easy."

"Sounds simple enough. When do you want to go?" Maybe getting out of the confines of the house would help stir up some better memories.

"We'll wait until tomorrow, at least. Make sure you have some strength. Don't want you to go fainting in the middle of the store. Today you eat and get plenty of fluids. I'll take you for a walk around the property so we can see how your legs are working and we'll go from there."

"Clara, can I ask you something?"

"Sure."

"Do you think I was a bad person?"

Clara's nostrils flared, and she thumped her elbows on the table. "What on earth would make you think somethin' like that?"

"I don't know."

"Have you remembered somethin'?"

"No. Not really. I guess I'm just worried."

"We have all sinned and fallen short of the glory of God. But if you were a truly bad person, it was all down to that cult. You're free of that now. You can make your own decisions now about how you choose to live your life."

"I guess."

"No."

"What?"

"No, I don't think you were a bad person like you're thinkin'."

"Why?"

"I can feel it in my bones."

Eva wished she could be as sure as Clara. But at least she did have control over her choices. Assuming that any memories that returned wouldn't turn her back into the person she used to be, she could spend the rest of her life making sure to make the right choices from now on.

# Chapter 4

JULIAN UNDERWOOD LOOKED out the window across the yard. The fading light sent long shadows across the grounds. It was his favorite time of the day, and normally he'd be enjoying a drink, but he had an important meeting. And he was looking forward to it with great anticipation.

He turned at the knock, then strode across the large study, pausing at the door before opening it. A large portrait hung on the wall nearby. It was a painting of his great-great grandfather, Harold Underwood, who had begun the work that Julian carried on now. The men who'd followed, including his own father, had been greedy and short-sighted. Julian was the only one who had resurrected the majority of his ancestor's mission that had been left to fall into ruin. And while circumstances lately had been disappointing, that was about to change.

He slid the door open.

"Mrs. Beaman. How lovely to see you. I've been

looking forward to your visit this afternoon." He looked down at the eight-year-old girl who clung to the plump, elderly woman's arm. "Please, won't you both come in?"

Julian moved back to give them room to enter and Mrs. Beaman gently tugged on the girl as they entered.

"Julian, I'd like you to meet Kaitlyn," the older woman said.

He smiled at the girl but didn't move closer. He didn't want to scare her. This was a fragile stage. A wrong move could set things back months. "Hi there, Kaitlyn. Have you been having a nice time with Bea?"

The girl nodded but kept herself hidden behind Mrs. Beaman's meaty arm.

"Don't let her shyness fool you," Bea said. "She's a plucky little thing. She just needs time."

"Of course she does. I wouldn't expect anything different. This is an extremely difficult time for her."

When Kaitlyn's face emerged from its hiding place, Julian took one step closer and crouched down so he was eye level with her. "I know this is hard, but I'm glad you're here. Right now you're feeling sad, and that's okay."

The girl's lips bunched up to keep her tears at bay. "I want my mom."

"I know you do, sweetheart, but Bea's been looking after you, hasn't she?" He looked up at Mrs. Beaman, then back at Kaitlyn. "I know it's hard to lose family. I've lost family of my own. It's heartbreaking."

Tears spilled over onto her cheeks and she tucked her face against Bea, who squeezed her tightly. "Shh. It's okay, little one. I know you're upset."

"You can take as much time as you need," Julian said. "But I want you to know that you're not alone. That's why you're here. We're going to look after you now. We'll be your family and you'll have everything you ever wanted."

The girl sniffed. "I want my mom."

Julian stood, pressing a hand to his heart as though he grieved with her. "If I could give her back to you, I would. Truly, I want nothing else." He turned, walked behind the leather couch, and lifted a wrapped box. "With all my heart, I wish I could give you your mom back. But even though I can't offer you what you want the most, what I can do is help take your mind off your pain." He held out the box to her.

Kaitlyn wiped a hand across her nose. "What is it?"

"Open it."

After a tentative step forward, she sucked in her cheeks and took the gift. Her fingers scratched at the paper, searching for the edges.

"It's okay to rip it open." Julian winked. The girl bit her lip and scratched a couple more times before tearing at the paper, pulling it away faster once the toy was revealed. Her eyes widened, and she ripped until the doll was free.

She clutched the box in both hands and stared in awe. "I always wanted this one. My mom said I couldn't have it 'cause it cost too much."

"Here, nothing ever costs too much. I hope it helps make you feel a little better."

Kaitlyn stepped back and took Bea's hand, hugging the box to her chest with the other.

Julian took a deep breath. Satisfied. It was always the small, thoughtful things that pulled them in at the start. She would need time to forget her life before. It always took them time to stop grieving their parents, but he was continually surprised at how easy it was to wash away the grief of the past when they think they can have anything they want.

Challenges were part of every new introduction, but Julian was an expert at this. It had always been easy for him to draw people to himself. But now that he'd been doing it for so many years, it had become something of an art form.

He looked forward to molding Kaitlyn into more than she could have ever dreamed of for herself. He had big plans for her. With her old family, she wouldn't have amounted to much. But Julian had the power to position her for power.

There were those who considered him a monster, but even his enemies couldn't deny that he brought out the best in these kids. He took them from an ordinary life and unlocked gifts and abilities that would have laid dormant their whole lives. He deserved their unquestioning devotion. He earned it.

"Mrs. Beaman, would you like to show Kaitlyn to her new room?"

"Katy," the girl said.

"Pardon?"

"You can call me Katy. Everybody does."

"Katy. That's a lovely nickname. Why don't you go have a look at your new bedroom?"

Katy looked up at the high ceiling. "I'm staying here?"

"You sure are."

"But this is a castle."

Bea smiled down at the girl. "You deserve the best, sweet one. You're a very special girl."

"I am?"

"You certainly are. But we'll have plenty of time to talk about that. Right now, I think we should go settle in. Your new bed has a canopy and everything."

"Really? I've always wanted a bed with a canopy."

Bea looked up at Julian with a grin. "Is that so? I never would have guessed. Looks like you'll fit right in."

Julian followed Bea and Katy out of his office. He waved when Katy turned to smile at him, then he nodded at the man who had been waiting outside the room.

"She's a lovely little girl," Julian said to the man.

"You would have seen her scores?"

"Yes. Very good."

"Higher even than Eva, from what I understand. Although we used different testing methods back then."

Julian sighed deeply and dropped his eyes to the floor. "Eva was an unfortunate loss. You still haven't been able to recover her body?"

"No, sir. We haven't been able to locate it yet."

"So it's possible she's still alive?"

"It's been days, sir. I don't think—"

"Need I remind you of her expertise? She's a survivor and you know as well as I do what she's capable of."

"Sir, she fell in the river unconscious. There's no way she could have lived."

Julian took an aggressive step closer to the man. A knife flicked out of his sleeve and he pressed it to the man's throat. "If I were you, I would not presume to tell me she's dead unless you've seen a body. If there is any chance she is still alive, which there is, you will not stop looking. Do you understand?"

The man flinched when he swallowed and the blade of the knife poked into his skin. "Yes, sir. We'll keep looking."

"And if she is still alive, you had better hope and pray that we find her first."

"Yes, sir."

"That will be all." Julian waited until he walked away before returning to the window. He still felt Eva's loss keenly. He would never show that weakness to any of his people, but she had always been his favorite and was one of the most extraordinary woman he'd ever known. But she wasn't the first thing he had lost, and she wouldn't be the last.

In a war, there would always be sacrifices. That was the price he was willing to pay to build the utopian society he dreamed about. Even setbacks were an important part of progress. Mistakes strengthened you and opened up new opportunities. He had learned that lesson well when his facility was destroyed last year. He thought it had set him back decades, but it only forced him to consider new possibilities. The project he was now establishing would never have come to life without that loss. There is no progress without death, and Eva's loss, too, would define his achievements.

He looked back at the door. He hadn't expected to find Kaitlyn so quickly. They still had ways of identifying the children with the right attributes. It just took more time. Progress was slower than it used to be, but that would change in the future. When one door closes, another opens.

Kaitlyn would be things Eva never could be. He had studied her results carefully. What Eva had lacked, he'd found in Kaitlyn. Even at eight, she was formidable. Once she began her training, she would become unstoppable. He even dared dream she would one day be his successor. At the very least, she would usher in a new season. He may not live to see all of his hope come to completeness, but she would.

# Chapter 5

EVA WOKE the next morning delirious with fever. Clara sat by her bed all day giving her sips of water and cooling her face with a wet towel.

But Clara's soft tones and her gentle fingers that brushed the clinging hair from Eva's sweaty forehead were a foreign sensation. The kindness felt more like a dream than the recurring vision she endured as she slipped in and out of consciousness. Those images hidden in her mind held an intimacy with her past that seduced her to remember. But even in her delirium, Eva knew they were a siren song and if she gave into them, it would mean her destruction.

Clara's touch slipped away and Eva found herself standing in front of a man tied to a chair. His gray T-shirt was drenched in blood or sweat—she couldn't tell. But the smell, she knew. It was the smell of fear and death, and it was intoxicating. The things you could do to a person when they were afraid of you...

Her consciousness ached to be heard. "Who are

you? Who am I?" she tried to whisper. But her mouth would not submit. Instead, the corner of her lips drew up into a smile as she studied the face of the man in the chair. It was bruised and cut, but his eyes bore into hers in defiance. Eva felt the satisfaction knowing that this man was restrained, and she wasn't. She'd soon watch the confidence drain from him.

As she circled around the chair, a murderous intent strengthened her stride. She wanted answers from him, and she'd do what it took to get them.

But she continued to fight against the desire to hurt this man. Somewhere inside the recesses of her mind, a pocket existed where Clara cooed softly. In that space, she did not want to kill him. She wanted to set him free. Scream at him to run. *She* wanted to run. If she could make her legs obey her, she would flee. But escaping this dream would be impossible until it had its way with her.

When she stopped in front of the chair again, something cold weighed heavily in her hand, but she had no memory of picking anything up. Her first time through the dream she didn't know what it was. But this was no longer her first time cycling through these images.

"No," she whimpered in her mind. She knew what came next. "Don't make me do it."

"Shh, Eva, it's just a bad dream," Clara's words pulled her back, but threads of the nightmare laced with madness remained attached. She thrashed in the bed to throw off the burden until the momentary burst of consciousness sucked her back in and the world fell away, beginning the dream all over again.

A man, his shirt drenched, watched her. She

strained, desperate to get free of the sickening carousel. There had to be a way to stop it.

Before circling his chair, she strained to speak, but it was no use. She wasn't able to control her body and when she moved to orbit the chair again, bile rose from her stomach. She tried to bring it up if only to disrupt the scene, but her body continued to resist just like her vocal chords had, and she came around again with the cold weight in her hand as her eyes focused on the man's face.

She gave up trying to control her muscles. Instead, she concentrated on her peripheral vision, where she could make out the darkness beyond the wreath of light she was in. Faint outlines formed, and she could discern a long table and two other people, their faces in shadow.

As her arm lifted, her attention was dragged back to the man. Her fingers tightened around the knife in her hand. She tried to uncurl her fingers even though she knew it was useless. But as the seconds ticked away, desperation took hold. Panic tightened inside of her. But she remained a prisoner to the scene.

All she could do was watch in horror as she leaned toward him. His eyes, a deep blue, opened wide. There was no fear there. It was something closer to surprise.

She tried to look away, pleading with herself to stop, but her mind in the dream was empty and unyielding.

The man shook his head. "You don't know what you're doing," he said.

Her heart hammered as her arm lifted higher and the pit of her stomach writhed as she attempted to ignite muscles that didn't exist except under the dream's control.

She pleaded with the man in her mind. She wanted him to look away or close his eyes, but those blue eyes remained focused on her. They were sad and seemed to say to her he was the one who was sorry.

Her head turned up to the large knife she held and the muscles in her arm tightened.

"No," she mewled. The word stuck in her throat before the tension in her arm released and the knife thrust forward.

"No!" She shot up in bed, shouting.

Her forehead connected with something hard, and a voice cried out in pain. She didn't know if it was her own or someone else's until the sound continued and she recognized it as Clara's.

"I've had just about enough of this. I know you're sick, but this is beyond me." Clara stomped around the room with her hand on her face.

"Clara?" Eva panted.

The light switched on and Eva covered her eyes until they adjusted enough that she could squint at the woman across the room.

Clara dabbed at her bleeding lip with the sleeve of her shirt. It was already puffy. "You really connected that time. I hope that got the last of it out."

"The last of what?" Eva breathed out the rest of her panic.

"You tell me."

"I'm sorry. I had a bad dream."

"I know. You've been repenting of it all night."

"Repenting?"

"Yeah. Mostly you thrash around in bed for a minute and then mumble 'sorry' repeatedly, followed by 'I'll never do it again' and then you quiet back into sleep. That is until that last time. Not sure what's going inside that head of yours. That cult must have really done a number on you. Maybe that fever is the fire of God. He's cleaning you out."

"You think that dream was a memory?" It was the thing she feared the most, that she could be that person.

"If I were a bettin' woman, which I am not, I'd say yeah. That fever's been purging somethin' inside a you."

But Eva was sure if Clara knew what she'd dreamed, she wouldn't be so casual about it. Eva certainly couldn't be casual about it. Those emotions of revenge and anger were as real as the anxiety she felt now. They had burned her insides and left blisters she couldn't ignore. If she ever got her memory back one day, it was conceivable that she could become that person again. She wouldn't ignore that there had been the wisp of exhilaration. She had been terrified in the dream, but other emotions had gotten through as well. Something dangerous and savage lived inside of her.

Clara stretched toward Eva, and she flinched.

"No need to be jumpy," Clara said. "I'm just checking your temperature."

"Sorry."

Clara frowned, but reached forward and pressed the inside of her wrist against Eva's forehead. "I think that may have done it. You're much cooler now. Thank the Lord."

"I'm sorry about your lip."

Clara waved her hand. "I've had worse. You should try to get some sleep now your temperature is down."

"Isn't that what I've been doing?"

"That wasn't sleep. But with the fever gone, you shouldn't be hounded by that dream no more."

Eva laid back on the pillow. "I don't know if I can."

"You want to talk about it?"

"Not really."

"Suit yourself. Here——" Clara opened a drawer in the table next to the bed and pulled out a Bible, resting it on Eva's stomach. "Read that. If you have anything that needs repenting of, you'll find the way in there."

"Thanks."

After Clara left the room, Eva sat up and opened the Bible to the beginning. It was a big book with small writing, but she must have had a familiarity with it because she wasn't surprised by the flimsy pages.

"Genesis. In the beginning, God created the heavens and the earth. Now the earth was formless and empty, darkness was over the surface of the deep…"

It was too much. Her mind was too tired to squeeze comfort from those words. They didn't have the power to free her from the memories of the dream. Nothing did. If she was truly capable of hurting another person, the only way she'd stay free of it was to hope it never caught up with her again. She had to make sure that she never remembered the person she used to be.

After setting the book aside, she rubbed at her head where it had connected with Clara's lip.

She had been offered a home here, and if she

couldn't come up with another solution, hiding out with Clara and Franky was the only way she could keep her sanity and make sure no one else died at her hands.

———

Ben pushed himself hard. As he wound through the course he'd created for himself in the forest, he ran as though he were being pursued by death itself.

He'd been slacking off for a couple of weeks, but after the change to the dream, he needed to make sure he was ready, at least in his body, even if his mind wasn't.

Sprinting along a path, he darted to the side and leaped for the tree branch he knew he'd only reach if he gave everything he had. Half the time he missed it, but today his hand grabbed hold, bark biting into his skin. He kicked his leg up, hooking it before he hoisted himself on the branch.

The next move was to spring to another tree, but as he went for the leap, he hesitated, and that cost him the jump. He tumbled to the ground and rolled.

Sitting in the dirt, he picked up a rock and hurled it away, then dropped his head into his hand. He had no idea what he was preparing for, but now he was afraid it wasn't enough. It would never be enough.

In the special forces, second-guessing wasn't an option. That's what kept them alive. But now he couldn't do a simple course without indecision. If he couldn't find a way out of this uncertainty, the enemy would eventually catch him. The hair on his neck lifted at the thought, so he jumped up, dusted his pants off, then sprinted the last mile of the course until he entered a clearing that signaled the finish.

He paced around with his hands on his hips while he recovered from the run. The sun was high and hot and he lifted the bottom of his shirt to wipe the sweat away.

That's when he felt it. His blood chilled and he spun around, peering into the trees. He could sense them watching him, and they were inching closer.

"Get outta here!" he yelled. The birds chirped in response and a soft breeze rustled the trees. He turned in a slow circle as though he'd be able to see them coming. "I said go," he yelled again. The hair on his arms bristled.

He hadn't felt the darkness like this in a long time— like it was coming for him. Shapes swirled behind his eyes as he shook his head. He scrubbed his face, telling himself it was a drop in blood pressure. But it felt more like he was losing his mind.

Blinking against the fog, he tried to get a clear view of the path where he'd entered the clearing. He could make a run for it. But that would be a waste of energy. He couldn't outrun them.

"I can't be losing my mind," he mumbled. Fear pricked at his shoulders, tightening the muscles in his neck.

Maybe he was. All that time he'd spent on his own waiting for something to happen could have pushed him over the edge. Or what if that angel wasn't sent from God to save him? What if he was already in hell and the devil has been waiting for the right moment to spring the truth on him as a cruel joke?

He stumbled backward, looking for an escape, but he couldn't find one. Someone someday would find his body out here because he'd finally cracked and there was no one around to help him.

*No one?*

The thought was so small that he almost missed it. "No one?" he repeated out loud. He looked up, squinting at the sun. The heat burned his face.

There was one. Maybe.

But if he was already lost, what was the point? Everything he'd done in his life was useless. He'd let himself slip. He'd been alone for too long with his own thoughts, and now he'd finally cracked. Everything he'd believed had turned into shifting sand and he couldn't—

*Fight it.*

"What? Fight what?" Spots floated before his eyes. If he was already gone, then what difference did it make if he called out to God? It couldn't hurt him.

His mind scrambled for the words he needed. There had to be right words. His mind was numb. He dropped to his knees in the grass and squeezed his head between his hands.

"How do I fight it if it's my own mind abandoning me?"

Dizzy, he fell backward onto the ground. He could feel his sanity draining away. He could close his eyes and let the darkness take him. He wanted to give up. It felt as though he'd been fighting for so long, it would be easier to give in.

His eyes fluttered.

*Fight it.*

"I don't know how." But that wasn't true. There was one thing he hadn't tried. It was a long shot, but he couldn't let go until he'd exhausted all options. And this was it. This was all he had left. And then he'd give up.

"Jesus." His mouth was dry. "Jesus. I call on the name of Jesus. Help me." The spinning continued, but it didn't worsen and the drowsiness that he thought would consume him lifted.

"Jesus." His voice strengthened. "Holy Spirit. Help. I need help."

A sensation like fingernails down a chalkboard radiated through his body. He couldn't hear it, but the writhing seared his skin. Then a warmth filled his chest, and a song rose from the pit of his stomach.

He opened his eyes and found he was standing, although he couldn't remember getting up.

His arms lifted and with his eyes squeezed tightly shut, he began shouting at the forest. "Holy, holy, holy is the Lord God Almighty." If someone came upon him now, they really would think he'd lost his mind, but he didn't care. He could feel the madness lifting.

"Holy, holy, holy…"

The birds chirped, the wind whisked among the trees, and his mind cleared. He breathed in the smell of wildflowers that he hadn't noticed before and blinked his eyes open.

Turning in a circle, he confirmed they were gone, but a hint of fear still lingered. "I belong to the Lord. I belong to Jesus."

The fear flared up, but Ben pushed his shoulders back and stood straighter. "Jesus is king here, not you. Go." The fear abated and Ben's mind strengthened.

He'd experienced a lot of crazy things over the years, but that was a first. "What—was that?"

He waited for an answer but only got a hint of something that felt like, *"You already know."*

Ben wiped the sweat off his face. There were only two reasons he could think of why the darkness would try something like that. It was either because he was ripe for the picking or because they were afraid.

He began the jog home, considering these two positions. He wouldn't lie to himself about that experience. He had come close to losing. But in the end, God had given him the power to hold on. To act on the things he already knew. He might be weak, but he knew too much about who God was to be easy prey for them. There were other times in his life when they could have found him ready and willing. He recalled darker times that he'd walked through when they could have taken him easily. But that only left the one option. That the enemy was afraid. But afraid of what? What could Ben do that would get them so agitated?

One last thought flitted through his mind when he reached his house.

*You're not the only one they're after.*

## Chapter 6

A WOMAN IN HER FIFTIES, her white hair tied away from her face in a loose bun, was hunched over the ground. She thrust a spade into the dirt and added it to the pile beside her.

After sitting back on her heels, she used the back of her wrist to scratch an itch on her forehead, then she carefully lifted a marigold from its cup and deposited it into its new home.

Tires crunched on the pebbled driveway at the front of the house, but she couldn't hear it. Her earbuds filled her head with a hymn that made her eyes glisten with tears. She'd made a lot of mistakes in her life, and she'd lost all of her friends and family, but none of that mattered anymore because she'd found a peace she didn't know could exist. It didn't make everything better, but without her newfound hope, she never could have survived.

She pressed the dirt around the flower to secure it, then sat back to admire her handiwork. She smiled. It was God's handiwork, really. And this morning in particular had been special. It was a gift. God was closer to her in this moment than she thought possible. She had discovered over and over again that his mercies were new every single morning, but today was unique. Today he held her close and whispered into her ear that she had nothing to fear because there would come a day when she would be with him in paradise. On that day, she would never cry another tear.

She longed for it. After the hell she'd lived through, she couldn't wait to be free of fear and regret. But she would endure the rest of the days God had for her on this earth, and hold close the treasure she looked forward to, knowing that one day, she'd get to stand before him. What a day that would be.

She jumped at the touch on her shoulder. When she looked up, squinting at the sun that put the man in shadow, she fell back, crushing her newly planted flower.

She ripped the earbuds from her ears. "Julian?" Her peace shattered in a moment. "What are you doing here?"

Julian smiled warmly. "Sorry to startle you, Deborah."

"What do you want?"

"What makes you think I want something?"

"Because that's what it always is with you. You take until there's nothing left."

Julian looked around. "I don't know. This place is small, but it has a certain charm. And look, you've even gotten a new hobby. I hear gardening is good for the soul."

"I've rebuilt a little of my life, yes."

"But it's a far cry from the White House."

Her heart twisted. She had loved working in politics, but she loved the peace she had now so much more. "I'm happy here. Now I've got something you can't take from me."

"Oh really? Interesting riddle, but we can come back to that. What if I told you I was here to give you a gift?"

"There is nothing you could give me that I want."

"Not even your daughter's love?"

"You've got to be kidding." *Lord, give me strength.*

"I'm not much of a kidder. I find it doesn't suit me."

"I think you should go."

"You don't even want to hear what I have to say?"

"Why would I? You destroyed my life. You're the reason my daughter won't speak to me."

"Oh my. Passing the blame. That's very unbecoming of a stateswoman such as yourself."

"I'm not passing anything. It's the truth."

"As I recall, you had your chance. But you turned your back on me and paid the price."

"I didn't want to be one of your minions if that's what you're referring to."

"Michael, would you come over here for a moment, please?"

A young good-looking man with a strong jaw and a perfectly tailored suit approached.

"Michael, I'd like you to meet Deborah."

"Pleasure." Michael held out his hand, but Deborah only frowned at it.

"That's childish," Julian said. "My apologies, Michael. She didn't used to be this cold."

"No harm done," Michael said as he slid his hand into his pocket.

"Michael is one of my protégés. A far cry from a minion, I'd say."

Michael laughed. "Is that what she thinks of me? Sounds like she's jealous."

Deborah scoffed.

"All I want is a great society," Julian said. "Is that so terrible?"

"A great society for you and no one else." Deborah crossed her arms. "I did believe in you once."

"What changed your mind?"

"I realized that humanity is naturally selfish. It's who we are. You can talk about utopia all you want, but deep down you're a prideful beast."

Julian laughed. "I hardly think that's true. What do you think, Michael?"

"I'm quite looking forward to the future myself."

"You would be," Deborah said. "You're just like him."

"Why thank you."

"We're not here to trade blows," Julian said. "I don't want to argue. Like I said, I'm here to offer you your daughter back."

"In exchange for what, my soul?"

"Maybe, but it would be worth it."

She smiled. She'd been afraid of Julian once, but now she saw him for what he was and she had God to thank for that. "Not interested."

"Oh, I see, so you enjoy being alone? It satisfies you?"

"Yes, actually."

"I don't believe you. Just hear me out. It's a small thing that I need from you. And it means all of this misery would go away. I've got a new plan in action and I need you to execute one tiny little part of it."

"And how will that get my daughter back?"

"Oh good. I'm glad you're listening now. I would like to offer to pay off your daughter's student loans and also create a trust that will pay for her children's educations. Whatever school they want. And I'll tell her it's all from you."

"You think I'm interested in buying my daughter's love?"

"Your sacrifice means her family has a big future ahead of them."

"My sacrifice?"

"Yes, you won't make it out of this one alive, I'm afraid. But from what I understand, you've considered ending it all on more than one occasion, am I right?"

"How do you know that?"

"I have people—minions—everywhere."

"I won't do it."

"You really want to test me a second time?"

"There's nothing you can do to me."

Julian's head dipped, covering his eyes in shadow. "You have only seen a portion of what I'm capable of."

Deborah scooted forward, keeping her chin high. "I'm not afraid of you."

It happened in slow motion. Deborah had no time to comprehend as Julian nodded to Michael, who pulled the gun.

Fear had no chance to whisper lies into her ear. Jesus was there and then Deborah wasn't anymore.

---

Julian tsked as Michael wiped his prints off the gun and curled Deborah's fingers around it.

"That's a real shame. I thought we had a chance with her." He shrugged. "Oh well, can't win them all." He headed back for the car as Michael followed. "Who else can we get? I need some low-hanging fruit that won't cause me any trouble. I've got too many wrapped up elsewhere that I can't afford to lose. Do you have anyone we can use?"

"I do, actually. I've been saving him for the right occasion. Looks like this is it."

"Who is he?"

"He was a teacher. Had an indiscretion with a student before we got to him."

"Excellent, so he should go unnoticed among other teachers."

"No. I'm afraid not. He'd gotten pretty rough, but that shouldn't matter too much."

"That was one of the reasons I wanted to use Deborah. But you're right. It shouldn't make too much of a difference. How long have you been working with him?"

"It's been a couple of months. Actually, it's perfect timing. If we don't use him now, I think we might lose our window."

"Why's that?"

"I've so thoroughly convinced him of his own importance, I'm afraid he'll do something drastic on his own. It's better if we can steer him. I've got his pride swelled up so big, he'll think it was his own brilliant idea to blow up the library."

"Wonderful. What's his name?"

"Ray Thomson. No friends. No family. Nothing to lose."

"But everything to gain."

"That's his understanding, yes."

"Perfect. And if things go wrong?"

"I've stored away some extra lapses in judgment that we can lay at his feet so no one will believe a word he says as far as we're concerned."

"Excellent. Get it set up."

---

Eva sat in the rocker on the porch. It was the first time she'd been outside. It was a nice change, but she was drained. She hadn't even had a shower yet. Her eyes were heavy and her muscles ached.

Clara joined her. "One of the things I'll get you to do once you're able to stand for more than a couple of minutes is feed my chickens." She nodded over to the pen. "I think you'd like that."

"I think I would too."

"They're mostly egg chickens, but if any of them stop laying, we have a nice roast for dinner."

Franky exited from the shed at the back of the property. When he saw the other two, he stopped, looked at them both with what Eva interpreted as a threatening glare.

"Franky, for crying out loud," Clara called out. "No one cares what your business is in there. Stop lookin' like the entire universe is out to get ya."

He secured the large padlock hanging on a chain to seal the door shut. "That's rich comin' from you, Ma. You tellin' me it ain't?"

"Not here it ain't. Stop lookin' at us like we're the enemy."

Franky grumbled under his breath as he approached the house. He pushed passed Clara without a word and went inside.

Clara whispered, "Sometimes I think that boy's gone too far and lost a screw somewhere along the way." She shook her head. "He's a good boy deep down, but I worry about him."

"I guess it's normal for a mom to worry." But Eva had to agree. He made her uncomfortable, and he made it clear from the glares he gave her on a regular basis that he didn't trust her.

Clara had opened her home, but Franky looked like he was waiting for her to slip up and looked forward to rubbing it in her face. He wasn't often in the house so she didn't see him much, but she avoided him when she could.

"I wouldn't worry too much," Eva said. "It must be

hard having a stranger living in your house."

"Maybe, but that shouldn't stop us from following the example of the Good Samaritan. That boy's got war in his blood like his pa."

It was the first time Eva had heard mention of Franky's dad. "Where is he?"

"Blew himself up."

"You mean…literally?"

"Sure do."

"Oh, Clara, I'm so sorry."

The frown on Clara's face had more frustration in it than sadness. "He got so wound up about the coming apocalypse, he had a lot of bombs put together. One day, one went off. I'm worried that's what Franky's got going on in that shed."

"You don't know?"

"He won't let me in there. Says he needs his privacy. Which is right."

"I thought you said you didn't care what he was doing in there?"

Clara patted Eva on the arm. "One day when you have kids you'll understand. If I act like I care, that opens up a whole other can of trouble."

"Well, I'm sorry to hear about your husband."

"Nah. It was years ago, and Simon was a beast. I got the broken bones and scars to prove it. I see his father in him." She nodded backward at the house. "It scares me sometimes, but he's my son and I love him."

"You're afraid of Franky? Has he ever hurt you?"

"Not like that. He would never lay a finger on me.

But the thoughts in his head are wild sometimes. I'm afraid he'll do somethin' stupid one day."

"Like blow himself up?"

"Exactly. Now, you see that little openin' in the woods over there?"

Eva looked but couldn't see anything. "Where?"

Clara leaned toward Eva and pointed with her arm next to Eva's face. "Next to that thick tree there on the left. There's a bush, then another one, then a space."

Eva squinted. "I guess I see it."

"I guess that's good. It's not meant to be obvious. It leads to a small clearing just behind that line of trees."

"What's in the clearing?"

"The one good thing that Simon left me before he left this earth. If you wandered back there, you wouldn't even know it exists."

"What?"

"Under the ground is a bunker that Simon built. Took him years. There's a secret tunnel running from the house all the way out here. Anything happens here and we're safe."

"Why are you telling me this? You don't even know me."

Clara screwed up her face. "Can't really explain it. I'm not the trusting type, but you're different. I can feel it."

Eva flinched. Clara had no idea what she was talking about. Eva was not a woman to be trusted, but she still felt overwhelmed by this woman's care for her.

"If anything should happen to me," Clara continued,

"I want you to know where you can hide. The entrance is in my closet. Looks like a regular floor, but you can lift it up. Then just follow the tunnel. There's enough food in there to last a solid year if you're careful. Or, there is an emergency hatch. Can't get in that way, only out."

Eva looked at the ground. "Thank you, Clara."

"For what?"

"Everything. For caring enough to look out for me. To share your secrets in order to keep me safe."

Clara screwed up her mouth like she was chewing on something. "It's nothin'. Let's get you inside. You look like you could use a rest."

# Chapter 7

THE NEXT MORNING, Eva sat up with an energy she hadn't had in her short memory. Her ribs were still tender, but she didn't notice them much when she stood.

She'd had a dreamless sleep, no longer haunted by memories she refused to let surface. And she was confident that the longer she went without them, the safer from them she would be. If there was a chance of leaving her past completely behind her, she would take it.

After standing in her room for a few minutes to test her strength, she went into the bathroom for her first shower.

She stood under the lukewarm water and let it cascade down her body, cleaning away dirt and soothing her mind. It took all her self-will to move on to washing her hair, a task she hadn't been looking forward to.

Clara had given her homemade shampoo, and she used most of it, scrubbing it through her hair until she was satisfied that she'd sufficiently tackled the dirt. It wasn't until the water had gotten chilly that she finally turned it off.

A half hour of picking at tangles finally gave Eva the ability to slide the comb through her hair. She'd moved back into her room so she could sit on the bed and rest between attempts. Her arms ached, but it was worth it when she got rid of the ratty nest.

With her stomach protesting for something to eat, she twisted her hair in a braid before heading for the kitchen with a clear head. She found the room empty and there was no food out.

Clara had always given her meals, so she wasn't comfortable helping herself.

A loud thwack came from outside, followed by another. She walked out to the small porch and looked around the side of the house where she found Franky chopping wood. He had his shirt off and as he swung the ax again, it was clear that he was incredibly strong. His broad chest had been chiseled by the hard labor he carried out every day.

As he reached to retrieve a split log, he caught sight of her and stood up straight. "Eva?" His eyes drifted to her bare feet and then back up again. "What happened?"

Eva put a hand to her braid and pulled it across her shoulder. "I had a shower."

"You look...different." His eyes roamed again. "Feeling better?" That was the first time Franky had showed more than a suspicious interest in her.

"Yeah." She didn't like the way he was looking at her now. When she'd seen herself in the mirror after fully washing off the grime and fixing her hair, she was surprised to find a beautiful woman staring back. Now, she wished she hadn't bothered cleaning up. "Is Clara around?"

"Out back. Feeding the chickens."

"Thanks." Eva nodded and hurried around to the chicken coop. She felt Franky's eyes on her all the way.

"Morning," Eva said as she approached Clara, who was tossing seed on the ground.

The woman lifted her eyes and sucked in a breath. "My goodness. Look at you. I had no idea you were hiding under there. You look like a grown woman now."

"I hate to ask what I looked like before."

"A confused sewer rat. And after that fever drained your color, you looked like a dead sewer rat. But your cheeks have pinked up. I take it you're feeling better?"

"Much. But I was hoping for some breakfast. Is there anything that's okay for me to eat?"

"You think you need permission to eat?"

"I didn't want to take something that was spoken for."

"Help yourself to anything in the kitchen. Whatever you like. And if you're still up to it this afternoon, we might take that trip into town."

Eva frowned.

"You don't want to go into town?"

"No, it's fine. I know you need my help."

"Then what's with the frown?"

"I was just thinking that it could trigger something in my memory."

"And that's a bad thing?"

"It is if they're bad memories."

"You poor lost soul. I see your point. But you can't hide from it forever. If you're going to remember, may as well get it over and done with. Franky and I will be there with you. And don't forget, even if your memory comes back, that doesn't change anything."

"Doesn't it?"

"Why should it?"

"But if I slip back into the person I was…"

"You think you might get rebrainwashed by your memories?"

"I don't know. But what if the person I was—I mean, what if I was a bad person?"

"You weren't. I told you I can tell. I can feel it in my bones."

Eva nodded. Arguing with Clara was pointless. She couldn't understand, so Eva let it drop and went back to the kitchen, keeping her head down as she passed Franky.

Her stomach growled when she opened the fridge and removed a block of cheese. After laying it on the counter, she pulled open several drawers before finding a knife. As she reached for it, she stopped. With her hand poised over the knife, she just breathed. Her instinct was to take the knife and hide it among her things. It turned her blood cold. What would she need with a knife? Nothing good.

With her hand hovering over the drawer, she made a fist, then released her fingers and pulled out the knife. She noticed the weight of it in her hand and knew how she needed to wield it. She knew how hard she should throw it to stick it into the wall next to her.

Swallowing back the bile that threatened to erase her appetite, she focused on cutting a few slices of cheese. There had to be a way to gain control back from her past. She pushed a thin stream of breath out of her mouth. This was an opportunity for a new beginning for her. With Clara, she could live a simple life with minimal contact from the outside world. It would be safe here, and she could choose the type of person she wanted to be.

She would resist every old instinct she had, suppressing it until she smothered it into nonexistence. Nothing could force her to use whatever terrifying skills she'd learned once upon a time. Clara had offered her a rare opportunity. She'd take it and never let go.

With the cheese ready, she cut two slices of bread from a fresh loaf, but stiffened when the floorboards creaked with heavy footsteps. She knew who it was without looking, but she turned to face Franky anyway because she didn't want him to think she was unaware of his presence.

He was pulling on a plaid shirt, but stopped when she looked at him, then smiled and buttoned the shirt slowly.

"You mind bringing me some of that?" he asked.

"Sure." She grabbed another plate and cut the bread before setting it in front of him.

"Butter?" It was in front of him on the table.

"It's right there."

"I know."

She gritted her teeth and slid it closer to him.

"Knife?"

She retrieved a butter knife from the drawer and laid it on the table. He grinned.

She got her plate and headed for the door. "It's a nice day. I'll sit outside with mine."

"I'd rather you didn't." She stopped. "We haven't had much time to get to know each other, and I'm afraid I've been a bit rough on you. I know Ma likes to remind me of that daily. Why don't you sit down?"

Eva didn't want to make an issue of her discomfort, so she pulled a chair out and sat.

"So, still no memory?" he said, taking a large bite.

"Nope." She nibbled on the crust. She wanted to look him in the eye and challenge the strange smile he had on his face, but she couldn't shake the intimidation. She was sure the woman hiding inside of her—the one who knew how to throw a knife—would know how to deal with a guy like Franky. But she'd rather endure Franky than risk letting out whoever that woman was.

She ate as fast as she could.

"It's good you have your appetite back. You need to put some meat on those bones."

"Yes, I guess being injured and sick will do that to you."

"Mind you, I'm not saying you look bad. In fact, I was quite surprised to see the beautiful woman hiding underneath the filth. How old are you?"

"No idea."

He nodded. "'Course you wouldn't know. I'd say we're around the same age."

"Could be." She cleared her throat. "I've been meaning to say thank you. You and your mother taking me in like you did was very generous. I want you to know that I don't expect anything from the two of you. I'll help where I can and I'll keep out of the way."

"There's no need for that. You're welcome here."

"No, I insist."

Franky let out a small puff of air that sounded like a laugh. He leaned forward. "I don't get the opportunity to meet people my age. Especially someone like you. Your being here is a gift, really."

"Did you find something to eat?" Clara asked, stomping the mud off her boots at the door.

Eva's eyes fluttered in relief. "Yes. I feel much better now." Clara had opened up about how she felt about her son. If Eva got the chance, she'd make sure Clara understood that she wasn't looking for a relationship with him. Surely Clara would understand.

"I thought that we should take that trip into town today," Eva said. "I think I'm up to it."

"Great," Franky said. "I'll come too."

"We can get you some new clothes," Clara said.

"Good idea. Pick out something that fits her figure better."

"Never you mind her figure, young man. But he's right, Eva. You could use some clothes of your own. If you're ready, we can go now. I've got my chores out of the way for the morning."

"Hold your horses," Franky said. "She'll need protection."

"From what?" Eva asked.

Franky stood and headed down the hall without responding.

"You really think that's necessary?" Clara called after him, then mumbled, "That boy."

"What's he doing?"

"The belt."

"This one fits fine."

"Not that kind."

"Here we go." Franky said as he came back into the kitchen.

"What's that?" Eva eyed the chunky belt.

"Security," he said. "Arms up." He stood in front of her, waiting.

Eva crossed her arms. "No thanks."

Franky scowled at Clara. "You gonna put up with this? She's a guest in our home."

Clara pressed her lips together, but said, "You should put it on. It's important."

"Well then, give it to me. I can put it on myself."

"It's a bomb," Franky said.

Eva stepped back. "What?"

"Give it here." Clara took the belt. "Come on, Eva, it's for your own safety. We can't be too careful."

"I'm not comfortable with this."

"We've been threatened in town before. And since we can't be with you in the store to protect you, this should do the trick if anyone gives you trouble."

"Why not give me a gun or a knife?"

Franky snorted. "You don't give guns and knives to people who don't know how to use 'um."

Eva swallowed. "Right. But wouldn't it be better if I

have no weapon at all? Then I'm not a threat. Like you said, they don't know me."

"I also said they're brainwashed," Clara said. "And brainwashed people do crazy things. If you're worried about it going off, don't be. It's only for show in case you get into trouble. All you have to do is show them the belt and tell them to back off or you'll blow everybody up."

"You want me to blow myself up if I'm threatened?"

"What, do you think we're monsters?" Franky said.

Clara sighed. "It's not armed. There's no chance of it going off. You only have to bluff."

"What if they don't believe me?"

"Tell them you're with the Palmers," Franky said. "They'll believe you."

Clara held out the belt. "Come on. Arms up."

Eva obeyed this time, but the breakfast she'd eaten rolled around in her stomach. "You're sure it won't go off?"

"You've got nothing to worry about, child—There. It's a little loose but it'll do. Now, let's get going."

# Chapter 8

IT TOOK an hour to drive into town. Every bump on the road sent Eva's heart into her mouth. The press of the belt on her hips kept her afraid the whole drive so that by the time they arrived in town, she was sweating and anxious.

She wiped her top lip as Franky pulled the truck to the side of the road.

Clara turned to her from the passenger seat. "You okay? You're pale again."

"I'm not used to having a bomb tied around my waist."

"It's not armed."

"But it's a real bomb?"

"No point using a fake one," Franky said.

"Why not? I'm not going to use it."

"Yeah, but they can tell."

"Who?"

"Them." His hand gestured in a wide sweep.

Eva looked out the window at the street. "That woman pushing her baby in the stroller?"

"Are you bein' smart with me?"

"Franky," Clara said. "Cool off."

Eva opened her door. "Let's get this over with."

Clara got out, too, but stayed behind the door. "Can't be too careful out here. You never know who's watching. Now, you see that store there, on the corner?"

"Yeah, the hardware?"

"That's the one. All you need to do is to walk in there, grab the bleach and fertilizer, and walk out. That's it. You don't have to talk to anyone. Although a smile wouldn't go astray. You've got nice straight teeth. And people 'round here like a friendly grin. They don't care if you mean it or not."

"But don't say more than you have to," Franky said.

Eva let out a slow breath. "Bleach and fertilizer. Got it."

"Here's some cash to cover it. Good luck," Clara handed her several bills.

Eva stuffed the money into her pocket, then made sure the belt was hidden before stepping onto the sidewalk.

No memories came to her, but terror still touched the edges of her thoughts. She didn't expect it to be this hard. If she lingered too long, she'd never get moving, so she put her foot out for that first step and kept going.

The belt was heavy on her waist as she crossed the street and she swiped the sweat off her forehead, not pausing when she reached the hardware store.

A bell dinged over her head when she entered and she cowered.

"Afternoon," came a voice from nearby.

She looked around but couldn't see anyone. Straightening, she walked stiffly past a counter where she found a man who looked like he could pass for Santa. He had a fleshy, warm smile and rosy cheeks. "Oh," he said when he saw her. "Haven't seen you in here before." He leaned on the counter. "Welcome to my store, miss."

She smiled, gritting her teeth. "Hi." Her eyes lifted to the small TV on the wall. It was playing an ad for fabric softener. She looked back at Santa. "I'm new in town."

"Oh yeah? You staying with anyone?"

"No. No one."

"Staying long?"

"I don't know. I hope so."

"In that case, welcome to town. My name's Roger."

"I'm Eva." Her lips slammed shut. She shouldn't have told him that. The less he knew, the better.

"Nice to meet you, Eva. You're not staying with anyone. Does that mean you bought a house in town? Was it that two-story over on White Oak Drive? Seems like a big house for one person. You have a family?"

"No, I—uh. Yes. That's the house. No family. Just looking for a change." She needed to stop talking. It wouldn't take much instigating to discover she was lying.

"I hope you like it here and can find whatever it is you're looking for. Or are you trying to forget?"

"Forget? No. I've got nothing to forget."

"That's good to hear. There are a few people in town who came here to forget, but the past has a way of hunting you down whether you want it to or not."

She sure hoped he was wrong. "That's not me. I'm just here for a change. That's it."

"Good. What is it you do for a living? It's nice when you have a job that gives you the freedom to go where you like. Didn't used to be that way, but the internet has opened up new possibilities."

"Um. I'm in between jobs."

"Oh. You won't find much around here."

"It's fine. I'm good. Uh, I'm kind of in a hurry, so I'll just—" She jutted her thumb behind her, then turned to escape the questions.

She looked up the aisle and noted the door at the back. It would most likely open to an alley that would exit onto a side street, judging by the way the shops were set up.

"No," she said under her breath.

"Do you need any help? Can I help you find anything?" Roger said.

She was too busy pushing aside the uninvited surveillance to hear him. She didn't need an escape route. It was a regular door at the back of a store for whatever purpose Roger needed it for. That was all.

"Miss?"

"What?" Her hand jerked for the belt, but she didn't touch it. It didn't matter that she'd been assured it wasn't armed. It was still a real bomb around her waist.

"Anything I can help you find?"

"Uh, yeah, where is your gardening section?"

"Head to the end of that aisle and to your left. You need a hand?"

"No. I've got it, thanks." She wandered toward the back, trying not to study the shelves and what she could use the contents for. But when the bell above the door dinged, Eva glanced at the row of sledgehammers she was passing. She stopped and squeezed her eyes closed before moving forward without another glance at the potential weapons.

"Ben," she heard Roger say. "It's been a few days. It's good to see you. How're you doing?"

"I'm okay. Had a rough day yesterday, but I'm better now. Thanks for asking." The man had a deep, strong voice.

"Glad to hear it."

"But there is the matter of the raccoon. It's been digging in my garden again."

"I told you." Roger chuckled.

"Yes, you did."

"Does that mean you're finally giving in and building that fence?"

"I sure am."

"You know what you're looking for?"

"I think I got it covered, yeah. That raccoon is going to be sorely disappointed when he sees the barbed wire fence and security gate I'm erecting to keep him out."

"Hmm. Good luck finding barbed wire fencing in here. Might have to try the army surplus store."

"It was a joke."

"Oh. 'Course it was. Sorry."

"No need to apologize. I'm not a tender reed ready to break as much as you might think so."

"No. I know. Let me know if you need a hand."

"I will. Thanks, Roger."

Eva stopped at a shelf that had a set of six long-reach hooks. The thin metal tools were good for picking locks. She shuddered and turned, spotting the aisle with cleaners. She'd grab the bleach first.

Halfway down, she found an empty space on the shelf that had a tag indicating bleach was usually displayed there.

After a quick search, she found a box stored on the top of the shelf. The word *Bleach* was visible. She reached for it, already knowing it was too far.

Placing one foot on the bottom shelf, she put a bit of pressure on it to test the strength. It should hold, but she couldn't afford to draw attention to her by pulling a whole shelving unit down.

She gripped the shelf at waist height that she could use to take some of the weight while she reached again, but when she stretched up, her fingers only brushed the bottom of the box. She went for another reach and levered the box forward an inch, but it wasn't going to work. While she debated whether she should try jumping, a figure appeared beside her, brushing her shoulder as an arm reached past her.

Without thinking, she grabbed the intruder's hand and twisted sideways before she threw a punch toward his face.

He jerked his head back and blocked it with his free arm. "Whoa," he said, keeping hold of her. He spun his other arm out of her grip and held her wrists tightly. "Settle down."

Her mind had hyper-focused, only processing the threat who now had control of both her arms. But not for long.

She pitched her head forward to connect with his face, but he anticipated it and arched to the side.

The movement loosened his grip on one of her hands and she freed it, swinging again. But he caught her.

"Hey, whoa. I wasn't trying to hurt you." He let her go and took a step back, holding his hands out to deflect a further attack. "I was just trying to help."

"Help?" She was panting.

"You were reaching for that box, right?" He glanced quickly to the shelf, but then back at her. "Couldn't reach it?"

"The bleach?"

He laughed. "Yeah, the bleach. I was trying to be a gentleman and help you out. Sorry if I scared you. I guess I should have asked if you needed help first."

She looked up at the box. "Sorry. I didn't think."

"May I?" he asked.

She stepped back. "Yeah, thanks." He pulled down the box, ripping it open. "Just one bottle?"

"Yeah."

He pulled one out and put the box on the ground, but didn't hand her the bottle.

"I'm sorry," she said again. "I don't know why I did that."

He tipped his head to the side. "I guess if you've got the skill, you're entitled to use it to protect yourself. That was a mean right hook you were going for there. It's a good thing I've had some training of my own, otherwise I'd be hurting pretty bad."

She pressed a hand to her head. "I can't believe I did that."

"Don't worry about it. No harm done."

But there was. She'd done harm to herself. Now she knew she couldn't even trust herself. She'd have to be more careful.

"Can I have the bleach?" She reached out a hand for the bottle, but he still didn't give it to her.

"I haven't seen you here before."

"No, I'm new."

"Really?"

"Is that so surprising?"

"You just don't look like you fit in here, that's all."

"Neither do you."

He nodded slowly. "That is true. Does that mean you're running from something too?"

"Too? I'm not running from anything. Why does everyone in this town think everyone is running from something?"

"Most people are. I didn't mean to pry. My name's Ben."

She nodded but didn't offer her name.

He held out the bleach. "You want this?"

"Yeah." She reached for it and they both held it for a

second. Ben looked down at the bottle. The sleeve on Eva's shirt had pulled back and his eyes locked on the marks on her wrist. She resisted the urge to cover it. A couple of squares didn't mean anything to anyone, but his fingers flexed off the bottle like it burned him and he shrunk back. "It can't be."

She looked at her arm where his eyes were still glued. "Wait? Do you recognize this? Do you know what it means?"

"How'd you find me?" He bumped into the shelf behind him.

"I don't know what you're talking about. Do you know me?"

"How did you know I was here?"

"I don't even know who you are. You came up to me, remember?" She looked at the tattoo again. "This tattoo, is it a cult?"

"A cult?"

"Yeah. Do you know what it means?"

He shook his head. "Just leave me alone."

Roger came around the shelf. "Hey, what's goin' on back here? Ben? What's going on? Are you okay?" He looked at Eva. "Ben, you're not bothering this lady, are you?"

Ben kept his eyes pinned on Eva. "No. It's nothing. Sorry, Roger. Just a misunderstanding." He spun around and raced from the store.

Roger watched his retreat until he heard the bell, then he looked back at Eva. "You okay?"

"Who was that?"

"Sorry about him. Don't pay any attention."

"But who is he?"

"That's Ben. You know how I said people move here to forget? He's one of those people."

"What's he trying to forget?"

"Who knows? All I can tell you is that he's had a rough life. Nice guy, but I have noticed he gets agitated from time to time. He told me once that he was part of some special forces team."

"But not anymore?"

"No, now he's just a broken man. War's done that to a lot of men over the years. He's mostly harmless, but I think sometimes it gets to him."

"He thought he knew me."

"Don't take any notice. He's probably having a flashback or something. Did you find what you needed?"

Eva held up the bleach. "Almost. I'll grab some fertilizer and meet you at the counter."

"Sure thing."

Eva looked back at her arm. She could fight, and a man who was part of the special forces was afraid of her. Clara might believe in her, but it was clear now that she was a dangerous woman. What she'd do with that information, she had no idea.

Keeping her head down, she headed to the back of the store trying to discern which part of that interaction bothered her the most, that she'd attacked a man whom she could have hurt very badly, or that he knew something about where she came from and was terrified.

She'd have to steer clear of town. Franky would have to find another source for fertilizer. She couldn't afford another slipup like that. Next time, she might not be so lucky and she couldn't live with herself if she ever hurt anyone.

Hiding out in the woods was her only option now. If she spent her days feeding chickens and cleaning the house, she might get through life without another encounter like that. And she'd have to make sure she never ran into Ben again.

Eva laid the items on the counter. "So, uh," she said, "he lives in town, then?" She pulled out the money.

"Who?"

"Ben."

"You worried you'll run into him again?"

Yes. "No, it's not that. I was just wondering."

"Just outside of town. Near the river. He's got a tidy little blue cabin considering."

"Considering what?"

"How messed up he is. He keeps his house looking nice and looks after his garden, but you never know what's going on inside his head."

"I guess that goes for all of us, really."

"Maybe, but not all of us were once killing machines."

Eva's head dropped a fraction. "No. I guess not."

"That'll be seventy-two fifty-seven."

She handed him the money and took the change. "Thanks."

"He doesn't come into town much."

"Okay."

"In case you're concerned."

"I'm not." She wouldn't be coming into town again herself, so it didn't make any difference.

She lifted the fertilizer in one arm and carried the bleach in the other, careful not to bump the belt.

"Have a good one." Roger waved as she left.

Because Eva's back was to him as she walked out the door, she didn't see his gaze lift to the television set or the small *O* his mouth made when he saw her picture on a missing person's news broadcast.

# Chapter 9

BEN PACED the floor for a solid twenty minutes, arguing with himself about what had happened with that woman at the store. She acted as though she didn't know who he was, but she'd attacked him. She made it appear as though it was a reaction to being surprised by him. But Ben knew how manipulative those involved in the Underwood Foundation could be. It was impossible to tell the truth from the lies. But could it be that she truly didn't know what the marks on her wrist represented? He couldn't see how that would be possible.

Ben had finally settled into the armchair when a knock came at the door. He reached for the gun that he'd removed from the safe as soon as he got home.

He never had guests. And if it wasn't a guest, then there were only two visitors it could be. It was either the woman or it was Felix. He wasn't sure which would be the better option. Then an odd moment of calm settled over him. Either way, his time of hiding was up. As he stood from the chair, his gun still in his hand, he understood now that it was the waiting that had been the worst part for him. Hiding from the enemy wasn't in his blood. He had always been a man of action.

The knock came again, and Ben went to the door. He couldn't avoid the inevitable.

After turning all the locks, he pulled the door open. A man in his forties, maybe a little older, stood on the porch with a smile on his face. He wore a plaid shirt that Ben was surprised to see suited him.

"Felix," Ben said with a tremble in his voice. He had hoped it was the woman. Even her unknown presence in town would be easier to handle than having an all-powerful God send his messenger. Seeing the angel again brought back things Ben had been trying to forget, and the calm he'd had moments ago was replaced by a rising anxiety. "You look good. If that's an appropriate thing to say."

"I don't mind a compliment. I thought this attire would fit the surroundings."

"I guess you should come in."

"You're not surprised to see me?"

"I don't get many visitors. Besides, you said you'd come back."

"I thought maybe you'd convinced yourself I was a bad dream." Felix stepped across the threshold.

"I tried."

"Well, it's still good to see you."

"Sorry I can't say the same."

Felix's smile widened, if such a thing were possible. "That's what I always liked about you, Ben. Straighttalker. No flattery. You never tried to get in my good books."

"I didn't have time. I was too busy almost dying." Ben fell back into his chair with a huff. "I'd offer for you to sit, but you won't."

"You weren't as close to death as you thought."

"It sure felt like I was."

"What about the second time I visited?"

"What about it?"

"You weren't dying, you were hiding."

"Your point?"

"Has anything changed?"

"Is that why you're here? To find out if I'm done hiding?"

"Last time I visited, you said you wanted more time, and He knew you needed space. You're not the first, you know. Elijah was the same."

"You're comparing me with a great prophet from the Bible?"

"You're both men who He has called. What's the difference?"

"For starters, Elijah got to hand over to his predecessor when he ran from the fight."

"You're right. His story differs from yours. It's your time now."

Ben closed his eyes for a moment to prepare himself. "For what?"

Felix leaned back onto the edge of the kitchen table and crossed his arms. He didn't sigh, but it was written all over him. "He told me to come and see if you were ready."

"He doesn't know?" Ben shook his head. "I don't even know why he's bothering with me. I'm still not even sure why God sent you to save me in the first place. Why not let me go down with the building?"

"Because it's not your time yet. He's not done with you."

"But why?" Ben's voice rose, and he moved forward on the seat. He almost stood, but the angel's presence was intimidating.

"Why not?"

Ben scoffed. "Maybe because I disobeyed him? I joined up with that maniac and look at the mess I made."

"That's true. It didn't need to happen like that. But He always meant for you to work for Julian. Destroying that building was not your idea."

"What?"

"You went about it the wrong way, but ultimately you were in His will. You were right where He wanted you to be."

"You can't be serious."

Felix's eyebrows rose. "What an odd thing to say."

"Okay, maybe you are, but I can't see how that's possible."

"Julian does not hire outsiders, Ben. The fact that he brought you on board was a miracle."

Ben leaned back into his seat, his eyes shifting back and forth as he thought back to that time. "No. No, I made a mistake. I didn't see the darkness until it was too late. God warned me and I didn't listen."

"You made mistakes, yes. But He didn't warn you

about the darkness because He wanted you to stay away."

"That makes no sense."

"He knew you were trusting more in yourself than in Him, and He needed to change that. He wanted you to look to Him in order to discern the darkness, not to trust in the gift He had given to you."

Ben shifted uncomfortably in the chair, trying to absorb Felix's revelation.

"He wanted to be there with you while you walked that path. The biggest mistake you made was not letting Him close to you. You're paying the price for that now, but that changes nothing. He can still use your mistakes for His good. He's not done with you, Ben. He'll never be done with you, but He won't force you."

"So you're here to see if I'm willing to do it all over again."

"The problem isn't *will*."

"It's not? Then please enlighten me as to what could possibly hold me back."

"Fear. The darkness found a loophole and has filled you with fear since that day."

"Loophole?"

"You believed a lie, and that gives the enemy permission to taunt you to his heart's content."

"What about what happened in the forest earlier? Do you know about that?"

Felix smiled. "I was there."

"You were? Would you have let them devour me if I hadn't cried out for help?"

"My reason for being there was not to give you strength."

"But you did in the end. I felt it. You helped me when I asked."

"That wasn't me. That was Holy Spirit."

"So you were just there to watch?"

"No, I was awaiting orders."

"Whose?"

"Yours."

"You mean all I had to do was give you orders? I wish I knew that at the time. I could have given you some. "

"You did. When you gave us our directive, we responded."

"We?"

"I wasn't the only angel there."

Ben pressed his fingers into his eyes. "But I never gave you any command."

"Yes, you did. You told the darkness that Jesus was king and they had to go."

Ben remembered the wave of fear that had left him at that moment. "That was you?"

"Sure was."

"So doesn't that mean I should be free of the fear?"

"No, the lie is still there."

"What lie?"

"I could only guess."

"You don't know?"

"No, only He knows that. I'm just His messenger."

"Look, Felix, I appreciate everything you've done for

me, but this is all too much. The lies, the fear. I'm just not the right man for the job."

"Oh yeah? And what job would that be?"

"The mission you've come here to send me on. You'd be better off doing it yourself."

"I suppose I could."

"Perfect."

"But how would that help you?"

"So that's what this is really all about? Making me a better person? There are easier ways."

"No there aren't. There is only one refining process, and it involves fire."

"So this whole thing is about burning off the chaff?"

"Not completely, but why else would He ask for your help specifically? You think He needs you? You already know how this ends."

"Exactly. My involvement does not change the fate of mankind."

"But that's not what this is about, changing the outcome. The end is sealed. It will come no matter what."

"Then why are you here?"

"Like I said, He wants you to grow, but there's so much more. So many more lives. He's numbered each hair. He doesn't want anyone to perish. There is still work to be done before the end comes."

"That's a rather broad assignment."

"One step at a time."

"What's the first step?"

"Does that mean you're on board?"

"I'd like to hear the step first if I can."

"You think it will make a difference to hear it before you commit?"

"I won't know until you tell me."

Felix paused and looked at the floor. His head tilted slightly to the side as though he'd heard a sound, then he looked back at Ben. "Okay. She needs your help."

"She?"

"Pretending you don't know won't change anything."

"Don't tell me it's the woman from the store. Do you know who she is?"

"You don't think I do?"

"I don't know. You're just the messenger."

Felix smiled. "Her name is Eva."

"I don't care what her name is. She's the enemy."

"I won't insult your intelligence by correcting you."

"You don't have to. I can read your mind."

"Oh yeah?"

"You were going to say that God knit her in her mother's womb. We were all enemies, etc. I don't need to hear that."

"That's why I didn't say it."

"But you were thinking it."

Felix chuckled. "I missed this. You were always one of my favorites."

"You have favorites?"

"Not in the way that you might understand it. Each of you has a unique quality that I enjoy."

"I can't begin to imagine what mine is."

"You're the one who makes me laugh."

"You're kidding."

"Nope."

"But we've only met two other times."

"Each time was a delight."

"I'm glad you find me amusing."

"Someone has to. You certainly can't find joy yourself. Although it's available to you."

"Ah yes, the joy of the Lord is my strength. I still have all the scriptures memorized."

Ben noticed a flex in Felix's cheek as his face hardened.

"Good. You'll need them." He pointed to his head. "But not up here. You'll need to find a way to move them into here." He rested a hand on his chest. "You haven't delighted in your Father for a long time."

Ben tsked. "I don't need this. Is patronizing humans in your job description?"

"You're in pain, Ben. He doesn't want that for you."

Ben stood and walked to the window. "Then why doesn't he come down here and tell me himself?"

Felix didn't respond and when Ben turned around, it appeared as though the angel had grown taller. A glow ringed his body, creating a shadow in the space around him.

"You still don't get it," Felix said. "After everything you've been through, you still don't understand. You want to know why I'm here and not Him?" He took a step closer to Ben. "He's been here speaking to you the whole time and you won't listen. He shouldn't need to send me to tell you at all. Not after everything you've been through. Not after everything He's done. He should be able to tell you himself, but you've closed your ears, and it's almost too late."

Shame reddened Ben's face, and he sat back in the chair, his energy completely drained.

He should know by now not to argue with an angel. But Felix was right. Ben had heard God's voice over and over, but he wouldn't listen.

"I haven't felt up to it," he mumbled.

The shadow diminished and Felix took another step closer. His voice was barely audible. "The scripture is clear that your heart is deceitful above all else and yet, repeatedly, you trust it over the truth." Ben didn't respond. "If you want the answers you're looking for, then you're going to have to be obedient."

"And what if I'm not?"

"That's your choice. Sit here and stay the same. Let the fear eat a hole in you until all that's left is a shell."

"Maybe I will." Ben couldn't resist the urge to collapse into a fatalistic approach to Felix's goading. "What then? Am I damned?"

Felix wouldn't rise to Ben's provocation. "Too late for that. Your name's in His book. I've seen it myself. But being helpless is not what was written for you in this lifetime. It's not what was written for any of you. Still, it's your choice. Help her or don't. It's up to you."

Ben pinched the bridge of his nose and squeezed his eyes tightly against the headache that was coming on. "You brought me an impossible choice."

"I didn't bring you anything. You already knew what you had to do. Didn't you?"

Ben wanted to say he had no idea, but he had

known somehow deep inside. He knew when he looked at Eva in the shop. When he held her hands to stop her attacking him, before he'd seen the tattoo, God had spoken deep into his heart, but he had ignored it. And now, the thought of helping someone connected to Julian turned sour in his stomach.

"I don't know if I can do it. You know what I went through. You were there. You pulled me out of it. And now I'm just supposed to go help a woman who's a part of that…that…plague?"

"*He* uses plagues, too, you know. If you'll let Him, He'll take what the enemy uses for evil and use it for good."

"And if I can't face it? What then?"

"He's not asking you because you can do it alone. He chose you because you need Him."

Ben rested his face in his hands. "I don't know," he mumbled through his fingers.

"If you don't go, He'll choose another. But I strongly advise you to submit to His leading. All that's left for you here is your fear." He walked over to Ben and knelt down in front of him, resting a hand on his knee. "Ben, there is more for you in this mission than you realize. More than you can ask or imagine. It's time for you to step into the light."

Ben lifted his head. The threat of tears tightened his throat. He bit his lip to hold them back as Felix reached a hand up and touched Ben's forehead.

"Your mind has been clouded for a long time. The enemy has had a grip on you, weighing you down and whispering lies you've believed. You've been praying to be set free. I'm here to answer that prayer in part. It's up to you to complete it, but I can give you space."

Ben felt a warmth spread through his chest and the anxiety that had choked him continuously for the past year, eased.

"What did you do?"

"You've still got a journey to go on, but He's given you an open door to enter into His rest in a way you haven't been able to for a long time. You can sleep in peace. The dream won't haunt you anymore. But I'll leave you with this warning. You will need to seek Him. What I give you now will only be temporary if you don't look to Him for more. You're not completely free from it yet, but you can be."

Felix stood and Ben pressed the heels of his hands against his eyelids. A new peace met him in the dark there, but he was afraid to believe it was real.

"I don't know." He pulled his hands away and found the room empty. He tipped his head up to the ceiling. "I hate when you do that."

He stood and went to his room, where he lifted down a box from inside his closet. It was full of mostly his own scribbling, trying to make sense of what he saw and felt.

After his time in the special forces, after the things he'd seen in desolate places, he thought he knew what evil was. But it wasn't until he got mixed up with Julian that he found out how deceptive the devil really was. To call him the father of lies was an understatement.

He pulled out an article that spoke about the explosion that should have killed him. It said he had died in the blast, but Julian was safe and he was rebuilding, and Ben had been helpless ever since knowing that the work Julian began would continue. And now he was being asked to save a woman who was a part of that.

Even without the dream tormenting him, he could still feel the heat from the fire and he could remember the moment he thought his life was over.

His head lifted in revelation. That was the lie he had believed. When he gave his life in that moment, it wasn't an act of heroism, it was an act of defeat. He embraced the idea of death not because his salvation was secure, but because it would be the end. It had only been for a moment, but because he survived, the choice to give up life had lived on with him. From that point, he'd carried around the lie that he was meant to be dead.

He stumbled to his bed and fell onto it. Tears formed behind his eyes and his throat tightened, but he didn't cry.

Felix said his time wasn't up yet. God wasn't finished with his life on earth, but for the last year, Ben had been finished with it.

"God, I'm sorry I've ignored you. But I don't know how to be alive anymore. I don't know how to want to be alive anymore."

His breathing slowed, and he didn't fight the sleep. He'd take whatever came to him in his dreams. It was like Felix had said: He paid a price for his disobedience and it was time to face it. He wouldn't know until he awoke that the sleep he was about to fall into would be dreamless.

# Chapter 10

FRANKY TOOK the fertilizer and bleach into the locked shed as soon as they returned home.

Eva watched him, but Clara didn't give him a second look. She didn't want to know what he was doing, but if she wasn't careful, he'd ruin the life they had here. Eva wondered if there was a way to bring it up. There had to be other places he could take the weapons that he must be constructing in there.

"You want to feed the chickens for me?" Clara said as she lifted an empty sack and balanced her shotgun against her shoulder.

"Sure. You going somewhere?"

"Yeah. I'm heading into the woods before it gets dark."

"Hunting?"

"If an opportunity presents itself, but mostly I'm looking for edibles. We like to be good stewards and use what's freely given to us."

"Okay—Hey, Clara."

"Yeah?"

"Are there others around who share ideals with Franky?"

"What do you mean?"

"What he's doing in the shed. There must be more who feel the same as he does."

"Yeah, there's a few around."

"I thought maybe he might like to spend some time with them. Away from here."

"You want him to go?"

"I'm concerned that his activities are going to make life difficult for you."

"You let me worry about him, okay? You've had enough troubles without getting involved in mine." Clara sounded hurt and mildly offended.

"Sorry, you're right. It's not any of my business."

"I better get moving. I'm running out of light." She marched toward the woods, but when she got close to the shed, she yelled out, "Hey, Franky, you still haven't fixed that gate. If we lose any of those goats, you're the one who's not gonna eat."

"I told you I'll fix it." His muffled response came through the shed wall.

"I'm going collecting." She paused, waiting for a response, but none came. She shrugged and disappeared into the woods.

Eva rubbed at her waist as she went to collect a bucket of cracked corn. She was glad to be rid of the bomb, but a shadow still followed her around.

After scooping up the feed into a small bucket, she

dug her fingers into it. The corn sliding across her fingers was an oddly soothing sensation.

She leaned on the fence, scratching through the chicken feed before scattering it the way she'd seen Clara do.

When the bucket was empty, she stayed where she was watching the animals pecking at the ground. This had to be the first time she'd ever fed a chicken. Nothing about the simplicity of this lifestyle had a connection to her past, and that knowledge filled her with hope. There might be issues that came up, like Franky making bombs in the shed, but a life like this was perfect for her future. She could easily avoid confrontations like the one she had with Ben at the store. This was her life now, and she'd do anything to protect it.

She twisted her arm around and dropped her gaze from the chickens to her tattoo. She'd find a way to remove that, too, or better yet, change it into something else. A design that represented a new beginning.

When she stepped back from the fence, she bumped into something and a weight rested on her hip. She spun around, pushing away the hand, but she was conscious of holding back any further aggressive action.

"No need to be so jumpy," Franky said, standing his ground. "You're the one who bumped into me, remember?"

Eva pressed her lips together and stepped around him, heading for the side of the shed, where she dropped the bucket into the feed barrel. "Sorry, I guess having that bomb around my waist has gotten me wound up. I won't wear it again."

"That's okay. There are other ways to keep you safe. I could teach you a thing or two 'bout handling a knife, if you like."

"I'd rather not know." She walked toward the house to put an end to the conversation, but he followed.

"Things aren't always easy 'round here. The world don't like people like us. It's important you know how to defend yourself."

"I'll take my chances." She reached the porch and turned to make sure he wasn't going to follow her inside. She would spend the rest of the evening in her room until Clara returned.

"I could teach you some self-defense," Franky said. "You know, just in case you get into trouble." His eyes traveled the length of her body. "Girl like you could find herself in trouble if she's not careful."

"I'll take my chances. Don't you have a fence to fix?"

"Those goats are stupid animals. They'll never figure out that freedom is only a few steps away. I can leave 'um. What I'm interested in right now is the fact that my ma has finally left the two of us alone."

Eva's hands tightened into fists, but she held them in place at her side. "Don't know why that makes a difference. I'm going to my room for a rest."

"You want me to come?"

"What? No."

"You don't think I've seen the way you look at me?"

"I don't know what you're talking about."

"I saw you watching me while I chopped wood."

"When?"

"This morning. I was hot, took my shirt off. You noticed."

"I didn't notice anything."

"You want me. Don't bother denying it. I've been to a few bars around the place. I know how ladies respond to me."

"The last thing I'm interested in right now is a relationship."

"That's okay. We can save that for later. But you are a beautiful young woman and we're here alone together. You can't tell me that's not fate."

"That's not fate."

Franky smiled. "Let's call it good luck, then."

"I'm not interested."

"Let me be straight with you, Eva. When my ma wanted to bring you home, I was put off. I mean, who wants to bring a dingy rodent into their house, but I was wrong. They say you can't judge a book by its cover and they were right. I should have waited till you cleaned up proper before I decided whether or not I wanted you hanging around. Turns out, I like your company."

"I'm glad to hear that you're okay with my being here, but nothing is going to happen between us."

"Oh, I see, so you think you can come in here and run the place like a fancy princess with no thought about those around you?"

"I am more than willing to work hard and earn my place."

He took a step closer. "I know you will. But look at you. You're so uptight. You have been the whole time you've been here. If you let me look after you, I can take care of some of that tension."

He reached out to touch her shoulder, and she slapped his hand away. "Clara will be back soon."

"No, she won't be back till close to dark. We have plenty of time."

He reached for her again, but she moved out of his reach. "I said no."

His face hardened. "I didn't mind hard-to-get at first, but it's running thin. You want to be one of us? You want to have a home out here? Then you need to learn obedience, woman."

He lunged forward, grabbing for her, but she jumped out of his way and sprinted toward the woods, ignoring the pain in her ribs.

She focused on the safety of the trees. It wasn't in her nature to run. Her instincts screamed at her to face her enemy, but she wouldn't give in to the dark part of herself that wanted to tear Franky apart. If she could reach the forest, she knew she could escape, maybe even find Clara. Her skill in the woods might be tied to her past, but it was a less terrifying option than staying to fight.

The heavy shadows of the lowering sun were already thick behind the trees. Only a few more strides to safety.

But Franky dove, catching her ankle, and she tripped, falling hard on the ground. He pounced on her and she jammed her elbow behind her, but couldn't connect hard enough. She bucked, pushing him sideways, giving her room to turn.

Wrenching her knee up, she nailed him in the side. It was enough to force him back an inch or two, but not enough so she could get to her feet before he held a knife out in threat.

"I told you not to play hard to get." He was breathing hard. "But we can do it your way if that's what you want. It's growing on me, but you might get a little hurt." He twirled the knife around in his hand.

She could only guess that his display with the weapon was an attempt to intimidate her, but she could do the same thing with it. In fact, she could do better. But now she knew there was no way out of this without a fight. If she didn't surrender to her ability, she wouldn't make it out unharmed and might not survive the day.

Giving in to her instincts sent a shock of adrenaline through her body. "You should let me go," she growled.

Franky responded by thrusting the knife toward her. It was an aggressive move, but she could read the intention in his motion. He wasn't trying to cut her. He just wanted her to submit to him without any more fuss.

This was her prime moment, when her opponent underestimated her skill. Shifting her hips, she swung her leg up and around, kicking the knife from his hand. He fell back onto his haunches, stunned.

Running for the woods was a forgotten possibility. Eva had committed to the fight, and the exhilaration of allowing the dormant part of herself to emerge was a tide that could no longer be held at bay.

Franky was big and strong, which meant she had little time to incapacitate him. She sprang forward, tackling him backward, and began punching him in every vulnerable place on his face and body that she could reach quickly.

He lifted his shoulders to throw her off, but she hit him in the jaw, stunning him so he fell back again. All she needed was a couple more punches and he'd be fully unconscious. That would be the time to make a break for the forest, when he had no ability to follow. She wouldn't kill him. He deserved to die, but she wouldn't do that to Clara. What she could do was make sure he couldn't make bombs for a long time.

She pushed off him and lifted her leg back to finish off the job with a few kicks when a gunshot echoed through the air nearby. Eva knew the sound of the reload without needing to look up.

She jumped back with her arms lifted and turned to face Clara.

"You want to tell me what's going on?" Clara said, keeping the gun aimed steadily at Eva.

"Franky attacked me."

Franky grunted as he rolled over and pushed himself up on his hands and knees. She watched in surprise as he stood slowly to his feet. He should have been out cold.

He wiped blood from his swollen face. "No one's going to believe that load of crap," he said, then spit blood on the ground

Clara stepped closer. "I know what my son is capable of. If he attacked you, you'd be the one bleedin'. Not him."

"I'm sorry, Clara, but it's the truth. I was only defending myself."

"By punching Franky senseless?"

"I had no choice. I told him no. I told him to let me go, but he wouldn't listen."

Clara's steady gaze flicked to Franky. "Is that true? Did you try something with her?"

"Ma, this is me we're talking about. Have you ever known me to attack anyone like that?"

"I've seen the way you look at her. You don't think I do, but I see everything."

"Okay, so punish me for appreciating a beautiful woman. Can you blame me? How many girls have I had the opportunity to know while being caged out here with you?"

Clara lowered the gun a fraction. "You feel caged here?"

"No—Ma, that's not what I mean. I'm just saying, I'll ask forgiveness for being attracted to her. I just thought, since she was stayin', maybe I could make her my wife."

"What?" Eva said.

"You got a problem with my boy?" The gun lifted. "He's a handsome young man."

"It's got nothin—Shouldn't I have a say in it?"

"It's not a terrible idea. I've always wanted a daughter."

"Look, let's not move away from the main point here, which is that Franky attacked me."

"No," Franky said. "The main point here is that you have abilities that you should not. You should have seen it, Ma. The way she moved. She's not some weak girl who fell into a river and ended up on our property by accident. She acts all innocent, but she ain't."

"Is that true?" Clara said to Eva.

"I didn't know I could do that. I must have been trained by the cult, but I don't want to fight. I was just defending myself."

"Sure you were," Franky said. "Makes me wonder what you would have done if we put a live bomb around your waist. Maybe you would have seen an opportunity to take us out then and there."

"What are you talking about? Why would I do that? Why kill myself?"

"I don't know," Franky said. "It depends on what your objective is."

"Franky, we found her by the river, remember? She didn't come to us. We brought her here. And she was hurt bad."

Franky shook his head. "Ma, you are so naïve sometimes. Why don't you give me that gun, and I'll take care of things from here?"

Clara warned Franky with a glare, then looked at Eva. "Why don't you just tell us who you are?"

"I don't know. That hasn't changed. It must be that cult. They've taught me things, but I don't remember learning them."

"If that's true, why didn't you tell me sooner?"

"I didn't really know."

Franky spit. "You don't do what you did without knowin' about it."

"I was only protecting myself."

Clara sighed. "How can we even trust you anymore?"

"I don't know. But you were willing to risk it before, remember?"

"That was before I knew what you were capable of."

"Clara, you said you felt it in your bones that I wasn't a bad person. You offered me a place to live, and all I want is to live a peaceful life. I don't want to be that person."

Clara bit her lip and Franky saw it. He walked over, snatching the gun from her hands. "Don't listen to her."

"Then you come clean about why she attacked you."

"Because I figured out her secret. That's why. I became a threat, so she tried to take me out."

"He's lying."

"You keep your mouth shut. Ma, you really think that sob story she's given you is true? Come on. You're no sucker. She is a master of manipulation. They all are.

"You think it was your idea to bring her back from the river? They study people like you and me, and they would have known that if you found a broken woman at the river, you'd take her in. That's how they work. They know how to make us think it was our own idea. Ain't that right, Eva? Or whatever your name is."

"This is ridiculous." Eva crossed her arms. "You're saying that I allowed myself to be almost drowned in order to infiltrate your family? For what purpose? To discover how many chickens you have?"

"You been eyeing off that shed of mine the whole time you've been here."

"Yeah. You've got bombs in there. Congratulations.

You can blow some stuff up. Listen, Clara, if you're worried about me being in your house, then I'll go. I never wanted to hurt you. I'm only grateful for everything you've done for me. Just let me go."

"No way," Franky said. "There is no way I'm giving up this opportunity."

"To do what?" Eva said. "I've got nothing I can give you."

"Nothing but valuable information. You're a gold mine."

"I don't know anything. I have no memories. All I have are skills that I don't remember training for."

Franky stomped toward her. She waited for him to push the gun into her face. Just a couple of inches closer and she could get it from him. But he stopped out of reach.

"You're lying and I can prove it," he said. "Let's go. It's time to find out what's really going on. You're going to tell us who you are, who you work for, and what your mission is, or I'll make your life a living hell."

"You can interrogate me all you want. I've got nothing for you."

Franky grinned. "Not interrogate, Eva. I've been trained in many torture tactics."

"Franky," Clara said. "Stop this nonsense. We're not going to allow her to turn us into monsters."

"Ma, in a war, there are always sacrifices. You don't like it, you can sleep out with the goats." He waved the gun toward the house. "Let's go."

Eva looked at Clara, her eyes pleading, but Clara

bunched her lips together and dropped her head. She walked obediently into the house.

# Chapter 11

BEN JERKED AWAKE, then lay still as he realized he hadn't woken as a reaction against his nightmare. Felix was true to his word.

Of course he would be. But Ben had been afraid to hope that he could have peace while he slept. He rubbed his eyes, then lifted his gaze to the ceiling. "Thank you," he said up to heaven.

Out the window, the shadows were long. He'd slept most of the day away and knew it was time. He had a decision to make. He could be obedient to his fear or to God. He was tired of being bound by fear. It was time to do things God's way for a change.

He had a quick shower, then headed for the door, but stopped when he reached his truck. He knew that Eva was the person he was supposed to help, but what exactly was he supposed to save her from? Herself? Felix had never said. And when he met her at the store, he only had a vague sense that something wasn't right, but his discernment hadn't gone further than that.

He waited a moment, trying to listen for any instruction, but there was none. "Am I just supposed to ask her what she needs?"

Nothing.

"Okay," he mumbled as he got in the truck, "guess I'll have to find her and ask her." His hand froze on the key before turning the ignition. "Unless she really was pretending at the store that she didn't know me. What if she really is here for me, God? What then?"

Still no response.

He wanted to be indignant. He could go back in his house and slam the door on the way. If God wanted his participation in this, then he'd have to speak up.

But Ben didn't move from his seat. Instead, he rested his forehead on the steering wheel. He was a trained professional. He might not have the whole picture, but he already knew what he could do next. He didn't need God to hold his hand through this part. And as much as he'd like to use that as an excuse, it would be a childish move.

Once he discovered where she was, he'd do some reconnaissance. He could hypothesize about what God wanted from him, but he'd make a more informed decision if he used the skills he'd gained, until he heard otherwise.

He started the truck and looked at his watch. Roger was the only one he knew who'd had contact with her, but the store would be closed, which meant Ben would need to pay a visit to Roger's house.

There was nothing wrong with that idea in theory, but he wasn't keen to show up on Roger's doorstep unannounced. The store owner was always nice to him. But it was *nice* in the way you might treat a stray dog. Maybe throw out a bone now and then, but ultimately, he was sure that Roger was afraid of him. And unfortunately, that was Ben's own doing.

When he had first moved into town, he was still reeling from his experience with the factory explosion, and he'd had a minor meltdown that Roger had seen. It was only once, but it was enough. Ben was now regarded as a bomb in danger of going off if you weren't careful. Or at least, that's how most people around town tended to look at him. Most would offer him a tentative smile or a wave, but Roger was one of the few who really engaged with him, if only at arm's length.

But until Ben knew what God required of him, Roger was the only one who could tell Ben where Eva was.

He turned on the radio as he headed toward Roger's house, turning the music up loud. His thoughts were spinning in circles and he needed a clear head, so he focused on the music and let everything else slip away for a few precious minutes.

---

The flash of police lights had Ben slowing to a crawl before turning onto Roger's street. He pulled over immediately when he saw police cars parked in front of his destination. The absence of ambulances or firetrucks, along with the presence of other unmarked vehicles, suggested the FBI were in town. Whatever Eva was doing here, she'd brought trouble with her. That was clear.

He might not get the chance to talk to Roger, but he could attempt to confirm details with the officers he saw standing outside.

Ben got out of his truck, tucked his hands in his pocket, and headed toward Roger's house like he was a regular guy out for a stroll.

"What's going on here?" he called out as he approached.

One of the officers walked toward him. "Sir, I'm sorry, but this is official—Ben?"

"Hey, Allan. I didn't even recognize you." Allan was probably the only person in town who respected him. Maybe because he wasn't from town. He was based in a larger town nearby but offered support here when they needed it. Ben had met him accidentally about six months ago. It had to be God's doing that he was out here tonight.

"Is Roger okay? Has something happened to him?"

"No, it's about the missing woman."

"Missing woman?"

"That's right, I forgot you steer clear of the news when you can."

"Haven't seen it in months."

"A young woman went missing recently."

Eva. But Eva going missing didn't make sense. "No. I didn't hear anything about it. So what's going on? Have they found her in town? Is she okay?"

"Roger served her at his store."

"Roger? No kidding? Wow."

"He saw her on the news report and called it in."

"But you said it's a woman who was missing? You don't think maybe she ran away? Can't she go where she wants?"

"Of course she can, but the circumstances here indicate differently."

"Circumstances?

"Looks like the Palmers are involved."

"Franky and Clara? Really? Have they caused trouble before? I mean, I know they're a bit crazy, but kidnapping a woman?"

"You may not be aware, but they are known to the FBI."

"I didn't know that, but I'm not surprised."

"After Roger saw her on the news item, he followed her out to see if she was okay. He wanted to let her know that her family was looking for her. She had indicated that she bought a house in town, but he saw her get into a vehicle that belonged to the Palmers. Said she looked frightened."

"Wow. Good thing Roger followed her." If she was trained by Julian, it was more likely she had kidnapped them, not vice versa. Although he couldn't imagine why. Julian might be looking to acquire weapons from them, but that didn't make sense either. He wouldn't be interested in the homemade variety. It was more likely he was using them for a suicide mission. "You're sure she's been kidnapped?"

"Sure looks that way. She comes from a wealthy

family. Not the type who would naturally make friends with people like the Palmers."

"Who is it that's looking for her? The one who reported her missing?"

"Her father. We're waiting for a ransom demand."

Ben wondered if Eva's father knew about her connection to Julian. More likely, she'd been living a double life. Hiding her association from them. Probably using his money too.

"I don't know how they got their hands on her," the officer continued. "But they'll have the full weight of the law breathing down their necks. They picked the wrong woman to mess with."

He didn't know how right he was. "So what's the plan? Does her dad know she's been found?" If her dad knew, it was likely Julian did too. And if he'd sent her on an assignment, he'd want to see it finished.

"I don't know much more. And really, I've told you more than I should."

"You know I'll keep the information confidential."

"I know you will."

Ben had gotten what he needed so he didn't waste any more time. "I'll leave you to your work then."

"Hey, what were you doing here anyway?"

"Had a question for Roger, but it can wait. "

He knew where the Palmers lived, but he'd have to move fast if he was going to get there and discover anything further before the FBI arrived. Once they were on site, things would become much more complicated. And he still had no idea what he was supposed to be helping Eva with. Unless she really was kidnapped. But if by some miracle—if he could call it that—the Palmers had somehow abducted Eva against her will, there would be a lot of firepower to contend with from their end.

"Good luck," Ben said, waving as he went back to his truck.

He'd only run across Clara and Franky twice, but it was enough to know they were totally convinced of their position and would do anything to defend their way of life. Having the FBI turn up at their doorstep could send them over the edge. But maybe that was the incident that Julian was after. He wouldn't put it past Julian to use Eva to his own ends. Any one of Julian's followers could be dispensable if it meant he got what he wanted. If he had sent her on a suicide mission and used her own father to instigate the event, then it was up to Ben to dismantle his plans.

---

"So, I'm here, God. I'm being obedient, except I don't know what I'm meant to do," Ben prayed as he headed for the Palmers. All he could come up with was to keep putting one foot in front of the other.

Felix had told him that God wanted him to be reliant on his leading, but so far, God hadn't offered any direction.

"Okay, so maybe I'm better off not knowing, but can you at least give me a hint about what it is you'd like me to do here?"

*You'll know when you get there.*

"How did I know you were going to say that? So let's say, for argument's sake, that Eva has been kidnapped by the Palmers and I rescue her from them. What then? Do I hand her over to the FBI? Do I take her to my place and get information from her? Or do I walk away like nothing has happened?"

Silence.

"Great. I guess what's the worst that could happen? I die and things are as they could have been a year ago."

But he didn't want to die. He'd only just chosen to live.

"Can you promise me one thing? Can you promise me I won't have to face Julian? I'll save this woman from whatever she needs saving from as long as I never have to set eyes on that man again."

Silence.

"I'll take that as a yes." He cringed. He was being an idiot. He'd face whatever he needed to when the time came, and he knew God would help him do what was required. Whether he liked it or not, he'd chosen to be obedient to God and that meant accepting everything that went along with it.


Ben had spent a lot of time roaming the woods around the town. Mostly in the acres around his own house, but he'd explored farther when necessity called for it. And even though he had never been to Franky and Clara's house, he knew where it was. He had visited the outskirts of their property after recognizing them as a potential threat the first time they'd crossed paths. All he could do at the time was gather intel. He liked to be prepared, even when attempting to hide from the world.

He pulled into a small turnoff about a mile from their house, where he had parked the first time he'd been there. His truck would not only go unnoticed by the Palmers if they went out, but it wouldn't be discovered by the FBI either.

With no moon to light the way, it took time for his eyes to adjust, but moving through the dark in the forest gave his mind and body time to assimilate into the reality of what he was about to do. The training had kept his body in shape, but beyond that, a mental stability was needed when executing a mission and he was rusty. His thoughts kept drifting to a myriad of scenarios that didn't help him keep his focus, but it was still better than the anxiety that had built up on the hour drive it had taken him to get here. Having an action to focus on had the benefit of releasing some tension. Beyond that, he'd have to force his thoughts to stay focused on his need to remain invisible as he neared the house.

When he arrived at the edge of the forest, he stopped and listened. His eyes roamed the property looking for any movement. The small noises that carried across the yard alerted him to the fact that animals were present on the other side of the house. The Palmers had chickens the last time he was there, but this was a new sound, larger than chickens. Probably goats, if he was judging correctly.

A series of shouts erupted from inside the house, followed by a crack that echoed across the yard.

He waited another moment to ensure it was safe to approach the house, ignoring the itch in his chest that reminded him that Eva was his enemy. If they were holding her captive, she would get what she deserved. Or worse was the stronger possibility that this was planned by Julian. If they had her, then it might be on her terms.

*God, I sure hope you know what you're doing.*

A warm breeze drifted between the trees and cleared Ben's mind of fear. He straightened and looked up at the few stars he could see from breaks in the clouds. "I don't know if you're here with me, Felix," he whispered. "But if I can still order you around, then I want you in there with me." He wasn't sure it was the type of order that Felix would even respond to, but it was worth a shot. "Okay, I'm going in. But I don't like it."

*My ways are higher than your ways and my thoughts higher than your thoughts.*

The scripture that drifted through Ben's mind carried a lightness that suggested God wasn't chastising him. He was urging Ben to trust.

"Okay then. Let's get this over with."

He crept along the edge of the trees to the back of the house.

A bell jangled and Ben froze until the small muttering of a goat sounded nearby as it approached.

"What are you doing out here in the open? Shouldn't you be behind a fence?" He scratched its head. "I'd head out into those woods if I were you." It didn't move. "Who am I to talk? I'm about to walk in there myself." He gave the goat one last pat, then crept up to a darkened window at the house.

He looked through into the kitchen where he could see light coming from down the hall.

Moving along the back of the house, he snuck around the corner to the other side where he found a small window high on the wall. It was lit up. He stood under it. The only way to see in would be to pull himself up.

He jumped lightly, his fingers catching on the edge of the window frame, and he pulled until his eyes got a view of the room for a quick scan before dropping silently back to the ground while he processed the scene.

All three of them were in the room. Clara stood back against the wall near the door. Franky paced in front of Eva, who was tied to a chair with her back to the window. Her head was hanging, and he was pretty sure the dark marks on the floor were blood. A woman like Eva could withstand a beating, but if Franky had it in mind, she wouldn't be able to withstand a bullet.

"I could go all night." Franky's voice drifted out the window. "I'm only getting started."

"Come on, Franky," Clara said. "Maybe it's time to let up. I don't like this."

"Then leave. I never told you to stay."

"This isn't like you."

"Maybe you don't know me as well as you think you do. Besides, someone has to do what is necessary to protect this family."

"Then just give her a break."

"I'll give her a break when she tells us something useful."

"I already told you," Eva grunted. "I don't know anything."

"Eva, please," Clara said. "Just tell him something. Anything. Whatever you know. This will all stop if you tell him."

A sound like fist hitting flesh, a scream, and a crash. Ben couldn't tell if the scream belonged to Clara or Eva, but judging by the crash, Franky had hit Eva hard, sending her and her chair toppling to the floor.

A faint rumbling hit Ben's ears, and he tipped his head to the side listening. He shook his head. It was the feds. He was running out of time and the only option he could see was to rescue Eva to either save her or stop whatever plan she had. Once she was safely out of the house, he'd trust that God would give him the next step.

## Chapter 12

EVA SPIT blood onto the floor, and that earned her a slap across the face.

"Mind your manners, girl," Franky said. "Ma's gonna have to clean this up when we're finished here. Didn't they teach you any decency? No, I suppose they wou—What's that?"

A hum filled the room.

"Son of a biscuit. Sounds like it could be the calvary."

"What'd you do?" Clara said to Eva. "Who'd you tell?"

Franky pressed the rifle against Eva's chest. "You shouldn't expect her to fess up."

"Why would you do this to us, Eva?" Clara said. "After everything I did for you. How could you do this?"

"I didn't do anything."

"This is easy for you, ain't it?" Franky said. "It's easy when you're one of them. When you have no soul. Isn't that right? You don't care if we die. That's the rules, ain't it? Comply or die? Well, we'd rather die and we'll take you with us."

"Franky, we could hide—"

"No! I won't hide from them. They can't make me cower. They don't know that I've been preparing for this day, and I'm going to take as many of them with us as I can."

"Hidin' ain't the coward's way, Franky. It means we can live to fight. This doesn't need to be our last stand."

"'Course it does. Don't you see, Ma? This is what my whole life has been leading up to. Let's go."

They left the room, and Franky locked the door behind them. Eva almost retched, but she took a breath and swallowed it back. She had let the fight inside give her strength while Franky beat on her. It had worked, but now that she was alone again, it had shifted into the background and a stirring deep inside her wondered if Franky was right. If someone was coming for her, then they were coming for the person she used to be.

What if losing her memory hadn't been part of the plan, but ingratiating herself to this family was? But to what end? Why would anyone want anything from these two? There had to be more dangerous people out there. It was her presence here that had brought out the worst in Franky. If she had never turned up, they'd keep living life the way they had before.

She couldn't dwell on that now because she had no answers in here. The only thing she was completely sure of was that if she didn't escape, Franky would see all three of them blown to pieces.

But there was only one way out, and that was to

continue to surrender to the person she used to be. It was a horrifying thought. The whole time she'd been tied up and beaten, when she'd allowed the other part of herself to protect her, she'd felt not just normal, but energized. All she could do now was hope that if she came out the other side of this, she'd be able to find peace again. But she had no guarantees.

Closing her eyes, she pushed away all her fears and shifted on the chair. It was solid, but it was wooden. And after the falls she'd taken when Franky knocked her to the ground, it had already been weakened.

Tipping her weight forward, the back legs of the chair lifted. She got her weight on her feet and raised the entire chair off the ground before thrusting backward as hard as she could. After two more times, it finally cracked. Moving her body from side to side, she could feel the give that was now present in the joints.

She rocked, weakening it further before it finally split enough that she could stand and shimmy to the post at the end of the bed. Bracing herself, she swung around hard, catching the side of the chair on the post with another crack. The ropes burned on her wrists and pain shot up her arm, but it wasn't long before the chair collapsed and she got free.

She went straight for the door to check the lock. If she had listened to her instincts at the store, she would have already hidden something in the room to pick the lock. But it didn't matter. She'd find a solution. It wasn't a complicated lock and almost anything would do to get it open.

Dropping to the floor to look under the bed, she stiffened when she heard Franky yell out, "Ah, hell."

"Watch your mouth, boy. We may be in strife, but this is no time to lose your cool."

"I'm not the one losing it, Ma. You're the one who's grown some sort of depraved conscience about tryin' to save anyone who wants to destroy us."

"That's not true and you know it."

"Then get down here and help me get the rest."

Eva reached an arm under the bed and dragged it across the floor, but there was nothing there.

She moved to the table beside her and checked the drawer. It was empty except for the Bible.

A scratching sound came from the door and Eva stopped to listen.

The door handle shook, and she grabbed a piece of the broken chair to use as a weapon. She'd only have one chance at this. But that's all she needed.

Her hands were steady as she moved to stand behind where the door would open. She blocked her mind when she became concerned that it was Clara. She couldn't afford to care. That wasn't who she was right now.

As the door opened, Eva sprung around, swinging, but the surprise at seeing Ben made her hesitate enough that he was able to block her attack. She would have pounced, but he had a gun pointed at her. He lifted a finger to his lips, shushing her.

"You're not tied up?" he whispered.

"What are you doing here?"

"I'm here to get you out."

"Why?"

"You don't want to leave?"

"How did you even know I was here?"

Ben looked back down the hall. "We don't have time for this conversation right now. You're coming with me. I don't know what it is you're trying to accomplish, but if we don't get out now, we're going to die."

"I think I'm handling it okay on my own."

He gave the gun a jerk to bring attention to it. She lifted her hands. She could make a grab for it, but he'd expect that. "You're here to rescue me by pointing a gun at me?"

"If that's what's required."

"Put it away and I'll come with you."

"I'm not comfortable with that."

"I could scream if you'd rather."

He looked at her for a moment, but slipped the gun into the back of his pants, then lifted his hands, flipping them back and forth in an exaggerated show that they were empty. "Can we go now?"

She could tell by his stance that he expected her to attack. Why would he save her if he didn't trust her? She'd have to broach that subject later. Right now, she had no choice but to trust him. "Okay, let's go."

They slipped out the door. She might be unsure of why he was here, but the good thing about accepting Ben's help was that she could leave any savagery to him. If she didn't have to kill anyone while escaping, perhaps she wouldn't lose herself in the process.

*That was too easy*, Ben thought as he hurried down the hall, keeping one eye on Eva. Saving someone you expected to turn on you at any moment created an extra set of dilemmas.

"This way," he said, leading her into the kitchen where he'd entered the house.

When a shout came from behind, Ben grabbed Eva, dragging her past him so he was between her and Clara, who was standing at the end of the hall. "You stop right there," she yelled, lifting her rifle.

Ben jumped sideways, pulling Eva with him right before a slug embedded into the wall. Clara should have been a good shot, but that hole she left would never have struck him unless he'd jumped for it. He returned the favor, firing back high enough that he wouldn't hit her.

"Jump out the window. Now," Ben said to Eva, who he was surprised to see was cowered against the corner cupboard. "Eva?" Maybe she'd gotten in over her head.

"The window. Right." She stood, then sprang up onto the counter like she'd done it every day of her life, and dove out the window. That woman was a conundrum.

He fired another couple of shots to keep Clara where she was, then followed Eva out.

After landing with a roll, he grabbed her by the back of the shirt and shoved her into the darkness beyond the house.

Clara shouted from the window, and Ben dove on Eva, flattening her to the ground. Clara might not hit them with a bullet, but she wasn't the only one firing anymore.

After Clara let off her shots, return fire came from the trees at the edge of the property.

"I've got Eva," Ben shouted to the dark forest.

"Identify yourself."

"Special Agent Johns." Ben wouldn't expose himself unnecessarily. "I'm off duty. I've got Eva with me."

"We'll cover you," came a shout back, along with more gunshots.

Ben and Eva, backs bowed, raced to the trees as two men, covered from head to toe in black, converged on them and pulled them to safety.

"Agent Johns?" one of the men said.

"Yes, and this is Eva. She has some superficial injuries, but otherwise, she appears okay."

"So, my name really is Eva?"

"You don't know?" the same man in black said.

"That's what Clara said she thought my name was. She and Franky found me at the river. I have no memory before that."

"Wait," Ben said, "You don't know who you are?"

"No. I can't remember anything except…"

"Except what?"

She looked at him and he could see she was fighting to find the right way to respond. "Nothing."

"I'll radio this in," the man in black said.

Ben pulled Eva aside. "At the store, when I saw your tattoo, you asked me if I knew what it meant."

"You recognized it."

"I did. But you're saying you don't know what it represents?"

"No, I have no idea. What's it from?"

"It's...um...probably not the right time to get into it."

"So it's bad. Clara said she thought I was branded by a cult. Franky thinks I'm part of some evil organization trying to infiltrate them. But he thinks everyone is evil." Ben flinched and she saw it. "You know the truth. Don't you?"

He cleared his throat instead of responding. He didn't know what to think, but there wasn't much they could do about it here. God still hadn't given him direction. "The best thing we can do is get you back to your family."

"My family?"

"Yeah. Your dad's been looking for you. Whatever you've been mixed up in, this is your chance to get out of it. If that's what you want."

Eva sighed. "That's what I want more than anything. I wondered if anyone was looking for me."

The man in black interrupted. "Eva, I'm going to need to bring you around to the front. Thanks for your help, Johns. They didn't tell us we had one of ours inside. That could have gone pear-shaped."

"Yeah, sorry. I didn't know you guys were coming so quickly. I just knew we needed to get her out of there. I'm glad it worked out okay."

"Well, that was good work. Now we've got to get Eva back."

"I'll take her around. You guys should stay here in case Franky or Clara make a break for it."

"They've got an ambulance waiting and I've been informed that Eva's father has arrived."

"Did you explain her mental state?"

"My what?"

"Your memory loss," Ben said.

"Yes, they know."

"Okay then, let's go get you back with your dad." Ben said, hoping he had the right idea.

Eva hesitated when he tried to pull her forward. "I don't even know who he is."

"They'll walk you through the reunion."

They started back through the forest, but Ben stopped her before they were close to anyone. "You really don't remember anything?"

"I've had some bad dreams, but other than that, no. Do you think the dreams could be part of my memories?"

He didn't want to have any part in telling her about Underwood. He didn't want to be responsible for her remembering.

"Stick close to your family. And if you do recall anything…" What could he tell her to do? Julian probably had people inside the FBI, so telling them could be a death sentence for her. Her only option was to go home and hope Julian left her alone and none of her memories came back. "Just try not to remember anything."

Her lip quivered. "I don't—"

"Whoa, hey, sorry, I didn't mean to upset you."

"I don't want to remember."

"Good."

"But you won't tell me?" She held up the arm with the tattoo.

"It's better if I don't."

"And you won't tell your team in the FBI?"

"I'm not connected to the FBI."

"Then who are you? Roger said you used to be in special forces."

"Let's go." He turned and continued through the trees. "We need to get you back."

They waited where they wouldn't be spotted, and Ben looked through all the faces he could see. It was a useless exercise. He wouldn't be able to tell who belonged to Julian.

"Wait here."

"Why?"

"Trust me."

Ben approached a woman in an FBI jacket who looked like she had some authority. "Excuse me," he said to her.

"Yeah?"

"My name is Agent Johns."

"Oh yeah. I'm Agent Baker. You've brought Eva around?"

"Yes. You've been informed about her memory loss?"

"I have. Where is she?"

"She's waiting back there in the woods. I was told her father is here."

"He's coming in now."

"She's stressed about seeing him again. She can't remember anything."

"Nothing at all?"

"It appears that way. You'll need to go slow with her,

but make sure her dad stays close. Don't let anyone else take her home."

"Agent Johns, you said your name was?"

"Yes."

"I'm aware of how to conduct myself in these types of situations."

"Of course you are. Let me take you to her."

They trudged back through the underbrush.

"Eva, this is Special Agent Baker. She's going to look after you. Make sure you don't get overwhelmed by everything."

"How are you feeling, Eva? Besides the memory loss."

Eva put a hand to her bloody face. "A little bruised, but otherwise okay."

"Did the Palmers do that?"

"Yeah."

"Why don't you come with me? I'll take you directly to the ambulance, then have a word with your dad before he sees you. He's very keen to make sure you're okay, as you can imagine, but I won't let anyone near you until you feel safe."

"Thank you." She reached back and took Ben's hand, pulling him along with her.

He looked down at their hands. *God, please don't let her remember. Let her go home to her family and be safe.* God was still silent, and as much as he wanted to hide her away, he knew he couldn't hide her forever. She had to face what was next as much as he did.

As Baker led them toward the ambulance, Ben

noticed a man in a trench coat standing off to the side with his head down.

"Have a seat here, Eva." Baker pointed at the ambulance. A paramedic was waiting.

"Agent Baker." Ben indicated for Baker to step closer.

"Yeah? What's up?"

He looked at Eva, who was watching him. He kept his voice low. "There's a guy standing across the way over there. Off to the side."

"I see him."

"Can you keep an eye on him? Maybe send someone over to check him out."

"Is there something we should be looking out for? The Palmers are still inside the house."

"We don't know if any of the Palmers' associates have gotten word about this."

She looked at the man again. "We'll check up on him."

"Thanks."

A Lexus pulled up at the edge of the gathering. Ben nodded to it. "Looks like Eva's dad has arrived."

The driver got out. He had a long blond ponytail, and he went to the back door and opened it. A man with white hair got out and looked around.

Ben took a step backward, then another, and faded into the darkness behind him.

# Chapter 13

EVA WATCHED Ben as he talked to Baker and wondered what it was that Ben didn't want to share with her about her past. When he looked up the driveway, she followed his eyes and saw the car that had arrived. A man with short white hair got out of the back seat.

Agent Baker approached Eva. "We have a doctor here who can have a look at you," she said. "I'll go get him."

"Is that my dad?"

Baker looked over. "Yeah. Don't worry about him. The paramedic will assess you while I go get the doctor."

Eva watched the white-haired man who spotted her. A strange look crossed his face that had elements of both a smile and a frown, but she couldn't read it beyond an expression close to confusion. He started toward her, but Baker intercepted.

Nothing about him looked familiar. She wondered if he knew about her skills or the group that had given them to her. If she really had been involved in some kind of cult, he could have no idea of the person his daughter had become.

As Agent Baker spoke to him, he put his hand up to stop her and spoke into the ear of a man with a long blond ponytail who stood nearby. The ponytail man nodded lightly, then walked away from the scene, out of her line of sight.

The man she assumed was her father turned back to Baker, but kept his eyes pinned on her. She couldn't hear what Baker was saying to him, but it was only another moment before his face softened and his forehead crinkled. She'd just informed him of his daughter's current state.

They spoke for a few more minutes, then the man nodded. He looked up at Eva, although his eyes seemed to look beyond her. He tilted his head in an odd way, then he turned and went back to his car.

"Eva?"

She turned to the paramedic. "Yeah? I guess everyone keeps calling me that, so that's who I am." Weariness settled heavily on her chest. Now that she was safe, she could be just Eva, the woman who had almost drowned and had lost her memory. And that woman had run out of strength.

"I can't imagine how hard all of this has been for you. My name is Dylan. Besides the stress of what you've been through, how're you feeling? Do you need any pain relief? I'll need to check you over for injuries, but is there anywhere I need to check first?"

She put a hand to her face. It was sore, but the

headache bothered her more. "I don't think anything's broken, but do you have something for this headache that won't make me drowsy? I've got enough of that without any help."

Dylan climbed into the back of the ambulance and collected what he needed.

"Here you go." He handed her a couple of white pills and a small cup of water.

"Thanks." She swallowed the pills, then looked around to find Ben. She hadn't noticed he'd left her side. She searched the surrounding people, but he wasn't there.

"Where'd he go?"

"Who?" Dylan asked. "Can you sit still for a second? I'm going to put something on those cuts. They shouldn't need stitches, but we don't want them getting infected."

"Did you see the guy who brought me over?"

"Uh, I did see you come over with a guy. Don't know if he's the one you're talking about."

"Yeah, that would be him. Did you see where he went?"

"I'm afraid not, but he's probably gone to report to the agent in charge."

"Who's that?"

"I don't actually know. They all look the same to me."

"Eva," Baker said when she approached again. "I spoke to your dad."

"I saw that. Thank you."

"I explained the situation, and he's agreed to stay

back until we give him further instruction, so you have as much time as you need. He's very sympathetic to your situation and said he'd do whatever was necessary."

"Thank you."

"The doctor is on his way over, but can you tell me, is there anyone else in the house besides Clara and Franky? Is there anyone else we need to be looking out for? There hasn't been any further movement since you left the house."

"No. It was just the three of us." She thought of the bunker Clara told her about. Franky wanted to fight, so he wouldn't hide in there, but Clara might and she couldn't forget all the kindnesses Clara had given to her. "What are you going to do?"

"Well, they kidnapped you, so we're going to do our best to bring them to justice."

"They have a lot of weapons."

"We know."

"Bombs too."

"Yes." Baker turned.

"Wait. If you can bring them in without killing them…it's just, they saved me, you know. I would have died if it weren't for Clara."

"Eva." Baker took her hand. "I know you were with those two for a while, and that can cause you to grow attachments to them, but they are dangerous people, and they probably would have killed you if we hadn't gotten you out of there."

"I know. I just—it wasn't Clara."

"Don't worry about that. We want to bring them out

alive too. We don't kill people if we don't have to. That's not the outcome we're trying for here."

"Okay."

"Focus on you right now. On your recovery. We'll get you out of here as soon as we can. There's no reason to stay here, and it's only going to make this harder for you."

A man in his sixties stepped up beside Agent Baker. He didn't have an FBI jacket.

"Dr. Smith," Baker said. "This is Eva."

"It's nice to meet you, Eva. I've heard you're having some trouble with your memory?"

"Yeah."

"Okay, we'll get you to the hospital and make sure you're physically okay, then we can run some tests and find out what's going on. I imagine you're feeling pretty overwhelmed right now?"

"Yeah."

"I bet. Agent Baker said you don't remember who you are or who your father is. Is that correct?"

"Yes. I can still do everything. I know facts and things, but I have no intimate memory of my past since waking up at the river."

Dr. Smith nodded. "So it wasn't after you were taken that you lost your memory? Are you sure it was gone before you met Clara and Franky?"

"Yes. They found me washed up on the side of the river. When I woke up, I couldn't remember anything."

"This might be difficult to remember, but can you think back to the first day or two with them? Do you recall either of them suggesting to you that you had no memory? Did they mistreat you or make you uncomfortable when they first brought you to their home?"

"No, not at first. Clara looked after me while I was injured. She was very kind. It was only Franky. He was the one who turned out to be dangerous."

"So Clara didn't threaten you in any way?"

"She did, but—" Eva pressed a hand to her face.

"I'm sorry, Eva. But I need to get a few things down in my notes as quickly as possible."

"It's just hard to process everything. Especially after what's happened today."

"That's normal. There's no need to make sense of it yet. That will come in time. And we'll do everything in our power to help you get your memory back. You know it's a miracle you survived at all. You must be a very strong woman."

*You have no idea,* Eva thought, trying not to shiver.

"Before we leave, can you tell me if you have any other snippets of memory from before you fell in the river?"

Eva thought of the man in the chair whom she threatened in her dreams. "Not much. I remember running through the forest."

"Were you running for exercise?"

"I don't think so. It's fuzzy, but I remember feeling like I was running away from someone. Like I was being chased. And I think I can remember being hit, but none of it is clear."

"Can you remember anything else about the river? Any landmarks?"

"No. It was dark. I can only remember trees and the river." She pressed a hand to her forehead.

"Okay, I think that's enough for now. We're going to get you back to the hospital and give you a proper checkup. There's some swelling on your face and a few cuts that we'll need to monitor. Dylan will get you settled in the back of the ambulance and I'll go give your dad an update. Then we'll get going. I think it would be better for you to be away from here while the FBI is finishing their job."

She nodded and watched as he went to speak to the white-haired man. Then she looked for Ben again. He was still nowhere to be seen. She would have felt better if he was still close. He was the only one who knew what was really going on with her beyond a simple kidnapping.

"Excuse me," she said to a passing agent. "Have you seen Agent Johns anywhere?"

"Who?" the man said.

"Agent Johns. He's the one who saved me. Or... Ben."

"No, I'm sorry. I don't know any Agent Johns or Agent Ben."

She looked in the direction of her dad and saw the man with the blond ponytail again. He was leaning on the Lexus, watching her, but averted his eyes when she looked at him.

The doctor returned. "Your dad's going to meet us at the hospital, but we will work with you and see how you're feeling."

"How will I know when I'm ready to talk to him?"

"Well, I don't think you will ever feel like it's the right time, but it would be good for you two to talk soon. You're going to need him for your recovery, especially if your memory doesn't return."

"Do you think that's likely?"

"I'll need to run some tests but at this point, we have no reason to believe that it will never return."

"Whatever you think is best." If she was going to get her memory back, having her dad close and being in the safety of the hospital would be the better than staying out here. She'd hate to be on her own if she remembered the horrors of her past.

She looked for Ben one last time but he was gone. But Roger had told her where he lived. If she needed him in the future, she'd know where to find him.

## Chapter 14

EVA SETTLED into the stiff bed, tugging at the sheet that was tucked tightly under her.

"Let me help you with that," said a nurse who had entered the room. "Bet you can't wait to get back into your own bed—Oh." She put her hand against her mouth.

"What?"

"I'm sorry, I wasn't thinking. You can't even remember your own bed."

"No."

She tipped her head to the side, studying Eva for a moment. "You're handling it well."

"I don't really have a choice."

"Sure you do. If you fell apart, no one would be surprised. Don't think that you need to hold it together for anyone. It's okay to cry if you need to."

A cynical laugh slipped out. "I think I'm trying to hold it together for my own sake. Falling apart won't help anything."

"Maybe not, but there is a process of recovery you'll need to go through. Don't shy away from that."

Eva pulled a bunch of flowers from the table beside her. It was only one of many that filled the room.

"Where did these flowers come from?" Eva asked, smelling the jasmine. "It's late. There wouldn't be any flower stores open."

"Your dad has a lot of sway, and there have been a lot of people praying for your return. I can't imagine it was hard for him to find someone willing to brighten up your room. Enjoy it. You've had a rough time and you could use a bit of spoiling."

"I guess."

A twist of regret twisted in her stomach. Her dad must be struggling with this terribly. He'd been through hell while his daughter was missing and now that he'd found her safe, she didn't want to see him. She was nervous about their reunion, but she couldn't put it off forever. The next time the doctor suggested it, she'd take the offer. She didn't want to cause anyone any more pain. She'd done it enough in her life whether she could remember it or not. She didn't want to hurt anyone else.

"Dr. Smith said you can't remember anything about your life before. Is that right? You have no memory at all?" the nurse asked as she took Eva's blood pressure.

"Yeah."

"Then you have a rare gift."

"Do I?" Eva was glad she had no memory of the past, but she wouldn't call it a gift.

"Your family is rich. You have everything you could ever want and you get to discover that all over again instead of being brought up in it. You can start fresh," the nurse continued. "You can be whoever it is you want to be."

Eva had been so focused on the nightmare, she hadn't really thought about it as a good thing. "I hope so. I'm not sure I like the person I was before."

"Don't be so hard on yourself. But rest assured your dad will be supportive. I heard him talking to the doctor. He said he'd lost you and he thought he'd never get you back."

"I guess he would have been afraid I was dead when I'd gone missing."

"I don't think he meant it in that way. It sounded to me like you were lost to him before you were actually lost. So this could be a chance to start over."

Eva set the flowers aside. If that was true, then her dad must have known she was involved with something, and it had estranged their relationship. That was her fault, and she hoped he didn't know about the terrible things she'd done.

"Thank you." Eva smiled. "That actually makes me feel a lot better."

"Good. Now, why don't you lie down and have a rest? The doctor will be in shortly to see you, but you have time to close your eyes. You must be exhausted."

Eva waited, sitting on the edge of the bed until the nurse left the room. Her eyes ached with fatigue, but her muscles were taut, like she was waiting for something horrible to happen.

But the nurse was right. This was her chance to

remake her life and restore a relationship that she'd lost with her dad.

She laid her head back on the pillow, tucking her feet under the sheet. Her eyes were heavy, and she let them fall closed. She could feel her mind slow as she drifted into sleep.

---

Wind howled past Eva's ears and her eyes opened onto a dark, open field. The howling came again, but it wasn't the wind that made the sound. The air was still, and she felt the eyes of a creature on her.

Her muscles tightened as her instincts took over and she ran. But as soon as her feet pounded into the ground, the scene changed and she found herself in the woods. A log appeared ahead and her body responded in reflex, jumping clear, then she ducked past heavy branches that seemed intent on catching hold of her.

Hot breath hit the back of her neck, and she pushed herself faster. Then a giant wolf appeared in front of her and she skidded to a halt. The wolf reared up on his back legs and its arms straightened at its sides so it looked both man and wolf.

It smiled. "Welcome back, Eva." The words rumbled from its throat like a growl. Then it opened its mouth, exposing sharp teeth dripping with saliva and blood before it lunged forward and Eva jumped awake.

Dr. Smith was there. "Eva, sorry if I startled you."

Eva focused on Smith's face, but his concerned smile couldn't erase the image of the wolf. "Bad dream."

"That's normal after experiencing a trauma like you've had. Here." He set a small cup on the table beside her bed. "When you're ready to sleep, take that. It will help you sleep without the dreams. It's important that you get good sleep."

"Thanks."

"Now, I imagine you've had enough of our questions, the pokes and the prods, but I appreciate your patience through all of this. You've been very resilient."

"I just want it to all be over with."

"I don't blame you at all. We'll keep you here tonight to monitor you and we will want to do some follow-up visits, but the best thing for you is going to be getting you back where you belong."

"Which is where, exactly? The nurse mentioned about my being estranged from my dad."

"Yes. He said you'd gotten involved with some people who had caused your relationship to become... somewhat hostile."

"He doesn't have to worry about that anymore. I can't remember who I was, but I've been getting a sense of it and I know that I do not want to be that person anymore."

"I'm glad to hear that. He will be too. And that may assist you in moving forward." He hugged her chart against his chest. "If you don't mind, I'd like to invite your father in so I can talk to the two of you together. But only if you're up to it. I'd stay here, of course. But I'd like to talk to you both about your memory loss and what we can do from here."

"Yeah. Okay."

"You sure?"

"I'm never going to be ready, but I feel bad."

"About what?"

"My dad. His own daughter can't remember him. I can't imagine that's easy for him."

"Eva. Your father is fine. We are both more concerned about how hard it is on you more than anyone else. Your dad is relieved to have you safe. You don't have to worry about his feelings."

"Then I guess you better bring him in."

Dr. Smith nodded, then opened the door. "She's ready," he said.

The white-haired man entered with a warm smile. "Eva." He was tentative and didn't walk farther than the threshold.

"Please come in," she said. "I'm glad we finally have the chance to talk."

Dr. Smith directed him to sit in a chair near the bed.

Eva sat cross-legged.

"Eva," Dr. Smith said. "I explained to your dad that this could be difficult for both of you, but I need you to tell me, now that he's sitting here with you, is he familiar to you at all?"

She studied her dad for a moment. She wanted there to be a flicker of something, even if it was small. But there was nothing. "I'm sorry."

Her dad smiled sadly but kept eye contact. "That's okay. You don't need to be sorry. I'm glad you're alive. Nothing else matters."

"We've done some preliminary tests," the doctor said. "And because of the injuries you sustained, Eva, both physical and mental, we believe you have dissociative amnesia."

"What does that mean?" she asked.

"Often with this type of amnesia, it's the trauma that causes the block. You said you remembered being chased through the woods, then when you woke up, you were helped and then harmed by your rescuers. If the mind can't cope with the mental stress, it will sometimes remove the memories completely."

"How long does it last?" Eva's dad asked.

The doctor hesitated before he responded. "We don't know a lot about it. There is no clear research about how to recover the memories."

"But she will get her memories back eventually?"

"There's no way to know. Some people never do."

Eva shifted. "Is that common?"

"Like I said, there isn't enough research to say with any certainty. That's why it's important for you both to prepare for it. You could get everything back in a rush. That's unlikely, but possible. If that happens, you could be incapacitated for a time by the shock. You need to be aware of that."

"You said that's unlikely that would happen to me, though?"

"Yes. More often, it comes back in parts. You'll recall different events. Having your dad to lean on will be good. You can share that with him and he can help you piece it together. If you visit with some friends who you're comfortable with as well, that can be good."

"Is there anything else we should do?" Eva asked.

"The best thing you can do is to go home and settle back into your life as best as you can."

"Do you think that will trigger my memory? Seeing things from my past?"

Dr. Smith shook his head. "It has for some people, but you have limited options. What I want you to focus on when you go home is recovery of your physical injuries. A healthy body helps you to have a healthy mind. You're a fit woman, so I would suspect you exercise regularly. It would be good for you to continue that when you are physically capable."

"That won't be a problem to organize," her dad said.

"I need you both to understand that the more time that passes, the less chance Eva has of regaining her memory."

Eva let out a breath. "But I'm okay? Besides that?"

"Everything else appears normal, yes. Like I said, we'll keep you here tonight under observation, but I would advise that tomorrow you go home with your dad."

Eva looked over at her dad, who had been sitting silently most of the time. "Thank you," she said to the doctor. "Would you mind if I spoke to my dad alone?"

"Of course. You two take as much time as you need."

Eva folded her hands in her lap and turned to the stranger sitting close. "It must be strange for you, that your own daughter can't remember you."

He smiled sadly. "It is very unusual, yes, but I can't begin to imagine how scary this must all be for you.

Having to trust yourself to a stranger." He looked down at his manicured fingers. "We haven't had the best relationship lately." Tears welled in his eyes. "It hasn't been good at all. I have a second chance with you to make up for before."

"The nurse said she heard you talking. That you felt like I was lost to you. So I guess we weren't close."

"It wasn't always that way. We used to be like two peas in a pod."

"But it was my fault that we grew apart."

"Partly. I could have handled things differently. You'd gotten mixed up with some people. I didn't deal with it very well. I've struggled to be the parent that you really needed. I'm an ambitious man and there were times I pushed you too hard. I made you do things you weren't prepared for. I regret that. Without your mom there to soften your life, perhaps I got carried away."

"My mom? Where's she? I hadn't even thought about having a mom."

"She passed away."

"Oh."

"That's terrible. I'm sorry. After everything you've been through. I shouldn't have brought it up."

Eva frowned. "I'm not even sad about it. I don't remember her at all. That doesn't seem right."

"But none of this is your fault, and it was a long time ago."

"Can I ask you a question?"

"Anything."

"This group that I was mixed up with. Were they dangerous?"

"I would consider them dangerous. Why?"

"I think they trained me to do things."

"What kind of things?"

"I know how to fight. I've had dreams about hurting someone."

"Ah well. Your skills I can explain, at least partly. And maybe your dreams too."

"You can?"

"Yeah. Since you were a little girl I've sent you to training. I wanted to make sure you could protect yourself. Being part of a wealthy family makes you a target. I wanted to make sure you were trained in everything I could think of. You were good too. I'm not saying that wasn't exploited by them, but you shouldn't feel bad about your training."

A pile of anxiety dropped off Eva. "You can't imagine how glad I am to hear that. When I found out I could do those things—I know how to handle a knife."

He smiled. "Yes you do."

"I thought it was all horrible. I was afraid to be able to do that stuff because I thought it was bad."

"Not bad at all."

"And the dreams? You said you can explain those."

"Eva, I don't know what you got mixed up with recently, but you've always had nightmares."

"Really?"

"Yeah. Ever since you were a little girl. I thought you'd grown out of it, and I don't think you had them as much as an adult, although you probably wouldn't have told me about them if you did. So it's possible you're still getting them. But I also wouldn't be surprised if your

153

trauma has brought them back. It's too bad the amnesia didn't take your dreams like they took your memories."

Eva wiped at her eyes. "I thought I was some kind of monster or something."

"No. Now listen." He leaned toward her, reaching for her, but then pulled back. "Don't ever think that about yourself. Once we get things back to normal, you'll get settled into life and make some new memories and you'll get your life back. I promise. But for now, you need some rest. The doctor said he'd bring you something to take care of the dreams."

"He already has."

"Good…There is one other thing."

"Yeah?"

"There is a man who works for me, Tyler. I'm going to leave him here to guard your door."

"Is he the man with the long blond hair?"

"Yes, you saw him?"

"Yeah."

"He's one of my bodyguards. I'm sure you're safe here, but I am a little concerned that those people who kidnapped you will come looking for you."

"I thought the FBI would have dealt with them already."

"Apparently it's ongoing. I know it's unnecessary but I will sleep better tonight knowing for sure that you're safe."

"That's fine. I'll sleep better knowing I'm protected and don't need to be on guard myself."

He frowned. "That's not all."

"It's not?"

"That group you were involved with. I want to make sure they can't get in here either."

"Do you think they would try?"

"I don't know."

"Do you know who they are? Is it related to this mark on my wrist?" She lifted her arm, and he looked at the squares there.

"I don't know a lot about them. But I do know it's my fault you're caught up with them."

"How can you say that?"

"Because they took you to hurt me."

"I'm sorry that I was on their side for a time."

"That's all over now. It's so good to have you back."

He stood and squeezed her shoulder. "Sleep well."

"Thanks, Dad."

He straightened and his lips pushed tightly together like he was fighting emotion. "It's been a long time since you've called me that."

"What did I call you before?"

"By the time they were done with you, I don't think you even wanted to speak my name."

"I'm really glad we have a second chance."

"Me too."

## Chapter 15

BEN'S LUNGS burned as he sucked in air. He hadn't run that hard in a long time. His muscles screamed at him as he shut the door, but the pounding in his head was worse. Panic was taking over, and he was close to a breakdown.

After securing every lock, he slid down onto the floor and ran his hands through his hair, groaning against the fear that wanted to take hold.

When Ben had seen Julian emerge from the back of that car, he wasn't sure his legs would have the strength to get him away.

"I'm safe. They didn't see me. He didn't see me." He had never been a man to run from a fight. He'd been avoiding it, but he didn't think when the time came he'd actually run away.

He banged his head back on the door several times, trying to dislodge the path his brain was taking. The enemy had created a rabbit hole it wanted him to fall into and he was standing on the precipice.

"Why did you do that to me, God? You must have known what it would do to me. Why would you ask me to save that woman? Did you really want things to be put back the way they were? Is that really what you wanted?"

Maybe he'd heard wrong. Maybe he'd saved the wrong "she." Or maybe he shouldn't have left her with the FBI. Was he supposed to kidnap her himself? His head swam with possibilities that didn't help his mental state.

*Trust me.*

He jumped up from the floor. "So that's it?" he yelled at the ceiling. "That's all you have to say about it? I did everything right? Because nothing about that whole scenario felt right. You sent me in there blind, telling me to trust you. But at every turn, my assumptions were flipped on their heads. Nothing I knew going in there was right. That's not how it's supposed to work."

He stomped across the floor. "I was supposed to be rescuing Eva from potential murderers. I went in there to save her, but Clara didn't shoot to kill or even hurt. Then when I got Eva out, she said she'd lost her memory—Was that true? Because if it was, I just threw her right back into the lion's den to be devoured. Doesn't that make me the murderer?"

He went into the kitchen and anchored his hands on either side of the sink. "I can't believe you had me save Julian's own daughter. I think I'm going to be sick." He stuck his head under the tap. The panic was dissipating quickly into anger—the better of the two options, as far as he could see.

He walked the length of his house before saying, "Maybe you didn't know who she was." Of course God knew. He knew and yet he still asked Ben to rescue her. Of all the things God could have asked him to do, that was as bad as it could get.

*Trust me.*

Ben threw his hands up in the air. "Trust you. Right. I'd heard about her, you know. Eva," he said to the empty room. Perhaps he was finally losing his mind, but he didn't care. "When I was working for Julian. I can't believe it didn't click when Felix told me her name. Everyone was afraid of her. She was some kind of prodigy.

"Are you aware that she's the one who's supposed to be Julian's successor? And now you've had me hand her right back to him. I will be the one responsible for seeing her put on the throne." He shook his head.

"Ben."

Ben jumped, his arms raised and muscles tight. But he recognized the voice, and when a shadowy figure emerged into the lamplight, Ben lowered his arms.

"Felix, how'd you get—Never mind. You don't bother knocking anymore?"

"You need to be on your guard, Ben."

"That's what you snuck in here to tell me? I did what God asked. Why can't you leave me alone?"

"There is so much going on right now that you have no idea about."

"So you've already heard what happened?"

"I was there."

"What?"

"I was there."

A hysterical laugh burst from Ben's mouth. "In the trench coat. That was you?"

"Yes."

"Did you do something after I left?"

"No, the purpose of my presence was only to observe."

"Right. Make sure I did my job like a good little soldier. And besides, what possible reason could there be to get in Julian's way? No, it's a far better plan to help him on his journey. God forbid anyone should stop him."

"Saving Eva was the beginning, but there is still work to be done. Julian's distracted, but it won't last long."

"Distracted?"

"He's preoccupied after getting her back."

"So—what—Eva's a pawn on the board, or a magician's sleight of hand?" Ben scoffed. "I can't argue with distraction as a tactical move. I've used it myself. I just wish I was more than a piece for him to move around on a whim."

"You think this is a game? You think all you are to Him is a cog in the wheel?"

"Why else keep me in the dark? Is he afraid I'll get in the way? Why not warn me that I was about to give Julian back his daughter? And Tyler—" He clenched his teeth to stop the memory of seeing both those men again. He wiped his hands down his face. "I can't keep doing this. You can't use me like this."

"Use you?"

"Call it whatever you want, but I've had enough. I'm done."

"And how many more will we lose because people like you won't act?"

"Oh, I see. So it's a guilt trip you're here to give me."

"If you have a guilt trip, you've given it to yourself. Don't blame Him for that."

Ben stared at the floor. He wanted to be mad at God, but he was only mad at himself. He was mad at how he responded to everything about this job. "I wouldn't have done it. If I knew who she really was, I wouldn't have saved her."

"I know."

"Then why ask me?"

"He has plans for you. Plans to prosper you and not to harm you. He wants to give you a hope and a future."

Ben expected Felix quoting scripture at him would rile him up more, but all he could do was sigh in resignation. He really did want a future, and he had nothing else to hope in besides God. "So after all of that—after my ranting and tantrum throwing—you really do have another assignment for me?"

"*He* will. I've only come here tonight to debrief you."

"That's very generous. But what more can he even want from me? I don't have anything to give. And I've certainly proven myself to be unreliable."

"In what way?"

"Running from a fight."

"You weren't there to fight. You did everything He required."

"It's not that I don't want the good things he has for me, but I——" He couldn't escape a feeling of worthlessness. "There's really no one else who can do it?"

"If you knew how many have said no already…"

Ben stumbled across the room and fell into his chair. "Are there that many of us who are afraid?"

"Afraid, tired, busy. There are a lot of reasons."

"And you choose to persecute the one who's afraid?"

"Interesting choice of word."

"You don't think it's fitting?"

"I've seen persecution firsthand. It doesn't fit at all."

"I guess I walked right into that one. Okay, how about harass? Why harass the ones who are afraid? Wouldn't busy people be more amenable?"

"Busy people are hardest. 'I'm too busy' sounds noble when used as an excuse. Believe it or not, the ones who are afraid are the simplest to bring around."

"Why?"

"Because you don't want to be afraid anymore."

That burned a hole through Ben, but he continued to resist. "I don't know. You really think you can bring me around? You really believe you have something to offer me that will change my mind?"

"I'm not here to bribe you. I have nothing to offer you that you don't already know. It's all in the Bible. Follow Him or don't. It's up to you. You already know that if you say no, there's a cost."

"Yeah? Well, there's a cost to me saying yes. And

don't tell me you know, because you don't. You're not human. You don't know."

"You're right. I'm not human and I will never understand you," Felix's voice rose. "It doesn't matter how much He gives to you, you keep holding back. The patience that He has for you astounds me, and yet I will continue to serve Him. But even if I can't understand your pain, there is One who does, and He's seated at the right hand of the throne. You want to talk to someone who knows about suffering? You go ahead and talk to Jesus. See what He has to say about it." A pop followed a flash of light and the angel was gone.

Ben wanted to fan the anger in his chest into a flame to burn away his shame, but he couldn't. A picture of Jesus hanging on the cross seared into his mind and he fell to the floor in a heap.

Felix was right. There was a cost to saying no, and he knew it. He was terrified of it, and yet he continued to hold back.

"God, I'm sorry. Forgive me my stubbornness, I just—"

*No excuses.*

He closed his eyes. "You're right. It's like Felix said, I choose to follow you or I don't." Ben gave his life to Jesus a long time ago and he knew that in the end, he could only be obedient to the one who saved him. The one who understood his pain like no one else ever could.

Julian smiled at Eva as she took the sleeping pill and settled back into the bed.

"Rest well," he said.

"Good night, Dad. See you in the morning."

He closed the door softly and found Tyler standing outside, already on guard.

"Tyler."

"How'd it go?" The frown on Tyler's face made it clear he was skeptical about what had transpired, but he still stood straight and obedient.

Julian sighed. Content. "Much better than I could have hoped. I'd call it a miracle if I believed in such things."

"She still has no memory?"

"None whatsoever. And the doctor said there's a good chance she won't ever get it back."

"How sure is he?"

"Enough to fill me with hope. But I want you to stay here tonight."

"Of course." Tyler's jaw twitched.

"Is there something you'd like to say to me?"

"It's just…Sir, I know what having Eva back means to you, but do you really think it's a good idea?"

Julian looked at the floor in thought. "My daughter was lost to me, and now I have the opportunity to have her back again. She's one of the most extraordinary woman I've ever known and if I get a second chance with her, I'm going to take it."

"I agree, sir. Her skills have always been above and beyond the others, but is it worth the risk?"

"Having her back again? Yes. But Tyler"—Julian

moved closer to his guard—"if she runs again, shoot her. And this time, make sure she stays dead."

"Sir."

"Spit it out."

"I don't understand how she could have survived."

"Frankly, neither do I. I thought I sent three competent men out to hunt her down, and yet, she still got away."

"That's what I mean. She got away."

"Didn't I tell you not to take her death for granted? She survived because she's better than all of you put together."

"Yes, sir. But what if she's faking it?"

"Faking what?"

"Her memory loss."

"To what end? If she wanted to infiltrate us, she didn't have to turn on us in the first place. Besides, the doctor ran tests."

"You can trust Dr. Smith?"

"He's one of us. So is the nurse on duty. I called them in for this. Anything goes wrong, we've got our bases covered."

"Then why am I here?"

"I don't want anyone else entering that room. I don't want any of those fanatics she got mixed up with getting to her again. All those lies about God and his order that they filled her head with have been wiped clean, and we're going to make sure it stays that way."

Tyler nodded. "Now that we are aware of the threat, it will not be difficult to keep them away from her."

"You had better hope so, because if you let me down again, you're the one who's going to pay the price."

"Yes, sir."

Julian turned and headed down the hall. Maybe it really was a miracle, or maybe it was luck, but he never would have dared dream that the universe would bring Eva back to him. It was gratifying in so many ways. Not only did he have one of his best back on his team, but there also was a satisfaction in knowing that the ideal she'd given her life over to wasn't as powerful as she had thought. She would never know the truth, but he'd know, and it gave him a greater power over her.

It was clear that she belonged to him, and the future he had planned, and it gave him hope that he'd see his work completed before his death. There was no doubting now that the society he sought to create was supported in some unexplainable way by universal forces. There was nothing to stop him.

## Chapter 16

EVA WAS groggy when she opened her eyes the next morning, but the doctor had been true to his word. She had no memory of any dreams. The only side effect was getting over the fatigue of a sleeping pill. But she'd put up with that nuisance as the much better alternative.

She glanced up at the window. Judging by the light outside, it was well past morning. She welcomed the assessment she made of her environment instead of being horrified by it. Knowing that the skills she had were well intentioned changed everything. She could embrace them, knowing she wasn't the monster she thought she was.

"It must be around ten thirty," she said, testing her abilities. The clock on the wall confirmed it was ten minutes to eleven.

"Not bad."

After scrubbing at her eyes, she slipped out of bed and went to the bathroom to splash water on her face. A toothbrush, still packaged, along with toothpaste, had been left on the sink.

She took the toothbrush out and flipped it into the air, catching it easily. "This might actually be fun." She could use a little fun. After flipping it a few times around her finger, she caught sight of the tattoo and stopped. Ben had been afraid of it and what it meant. Once she was settled, she'd go back and find him. She could give him the reassurance that she wasn't mixed up with those people, whoever they were, anymore. He'd helped her despite his fear about who she was, and he deserved more than just a thank-you for that.

If only he was here now. She would have liked him to meet her dad. Or maybe that would be too much. It was obvious he didn't want the attention, but there had to be something he wanted that she could get for him. She had to thank him for her new beginning.

After brushing her teeth, she decided it was time to go home. She was eager to see more of the life she used to have and discover who she had been.

She hummed a tune she didn't recognize and opened the door, intending to find the doctor, but she found Tyler blocking her way.

"Did you need something?" he asked. His face was stony.

"You must be Tyler." She glanced down at his hand resting on the gun under his jacket. He dropped his hand to his side.

"Sorry. Habit."

"At least I know you're ready for anything. Thank you, by the way."

"For what?"

"Being here and making sure I was safe. I took the sleeping pill and I don't think I would have woken for anything."

"I was following orders."

"Do we know each other?"

"I know you."

"Did you not like me? Was I rude to you before?"

"I'm sorry?"

"I realize being formal is probably part of the job, but you don't seem to like me very much."

"We weren't getting along recently, no."

"Is that since I got involved with that group Dad told me about?"

"Yes."

"What about before that? Did we get along then?"

"We got along quite well then, yes."

"Look, Tyler, I'm sorry. I don't know what I'm apologizing for, but whatever type of person I became recently, that's not who I am anymore. Can we start over?"

"If that's what you want."

"Isn't that what you want?"

"I work for your dad and do as he asks. It doesn't matter what I want."

"Okay, fine. Be difficult, but would you mind if I asked you a few questions?"

He hesitated before answering. "You should wait for Julian."

"You're not willing to tell me how long you've known me?"

"I've worked for your family for most of my life."

"Oh good. So there are questions you're willing to answer without my father's supervision. What do I do for a living—or what did I used to do?"

"You worked for a PR company that Julian owns."

She frowned. "Does my combat training help me with public relations?"

"I don't have enough experience in PR to answer that question."

"When I had my memory, could I tell you what to do and you'd do it?"

One side of his mouth began to lift in a smile, but he stopped it. "At one time, yes."

"But you won't now."

"Right now, I'm working strictly for your father. It's up to him to make any changes to that."

"He will."

Tyler shrugged.

"You are a fount of conversation. Did my dad say when he'd return?"

Tyler looked at his watch. "I can call him now if you like. I don't think he expected you to be up so early."

"Early? It's almost eleven."

"You went to bed late."

"Yes, please let him know I'm up. And if you see the doctor, can you send him in?"

Tyler stiffened.

"Please." Eva didn't wait for him to respond before going back into her room. She went to the window and looked down on a small grassy area that had a bench on one side. A man in a trench coat was sitting there reading a newspaper. He looked up at the sky, then to her window. She jumped back out of view, then stepped backward and sat on the bed. So someone was watching. If her dad hadn't had the money to protect her, she would be in danger. She looked at the door, grateful that Tyler was there.

The world was a scary place when you had no memory of it.

———

Julian waited outside Eva's door while she got dressed in the clothes he had brought for her.

"We're stopping at your apartment first," he said through the door. "But once you've had a quick look around and gathered some of your things, I think it would be best if you stayed with me for a while."

She opened the door. "Oh. Uh. I guess I assumed I'd be going to wherever I lived before—everything. I thought that would be best. Unless my apartment isn't secure?"

"It is secure, but I'm not comfortable with the thought of you being on your own. Not yet anyway. What if everything comes back to you all at once? There would be no one there to help you through it."

"But the doctor said I should stay somewhere familiar."

"He also said it wouldn't be good for you to be on your own. And my house is familiar to you. It's the one you grew up in. You've only lived in that apartment for a couple of years. Please, Eva. It would put my mind at ease."

"I don't want to hide from my life. I just think it would be better for me to get reacquainted with who I was before all of this. Besides, it might be good for me to have some space while I'm readjusting."

"If space is what you need, that won't be a problem. My house is large. It would be easy for you to find room for yourself. You don't have to worry about me smothering you. I have a large organization to run so I don't have a lot of free time to bother my daughter."

Eva bit her lip. "I'm nervous about getting back into life. I appreciate your offer and I understand why it would make you feel better to have me close. But everyone knows who I am and I know no one. Nothing is familiar. I think it would be easier for *me* if I could ease back into life on my own without the pressure of having anyone around."

"There's no pressure."

"But there is. It may be a pressure I'm putting on myself, but that's why I need time. At least let me try. If I can't handle it, then I'll let you know."

Julian sighed and put a hand on Eva's shoulder. "If that's what you want, then of course. Whatever is going to make you comfortable. But you promise me that if you start feeling anxious, you'll tell me right away. Let me help you."

"I will. I promise."

"Okay, now that's settled, if you wait here for a second, I'll confirm that you're ready to be discharged."

Julian nodded for Tyler to follow and he headed for the nurses' station.

"Can you make a call to the press?" he said to Tyler under his breath. "Let them know Eva's on her way home."

"Which one?"

"All of them."

"Yes, sir."

---

Eva was awkward settling into the back of the limo. "You didn't have to do all this. A normal car would have been fine."

"Perhaps I didn't do it for you," Julian said. "Maybe I want to spoil my daughter because it makes me happy. But if it makes you uncomfortable, I won't do it again."

"No, it's fine." She groaned. "This is what I mean about pressure. Everything I say is pandered to. Everyone is being so careful with me."

"I wish I could fix it for you, but I'm afraid these things take time. Everything will get back to normal soon. It's going to take time for all of us to adjust, but we will get there. We need to be patient with each other."

"You're right. I'm sorry if I'm being difficult and moody."

"Let's make a deal."

"What kind of deal?"

"Let's both promise to stop apologizing to each other."

"Yes, I like the sound of that." She looked out the window as they drove away from the hospital. "It's so strange being out here. The woods is all I know."

"That sounds like a wonderful opportunity to appreciate all the things you have. Not taking them for granted, like the rest of us."

"That's what the nurse said."

"Smart woman."

"Did Dr. Smith tell you what I remembered from before I fell in the river?"

Julian shifted in his seat. "You remember something from before?"

"I have this memory of running through the woods. I was being chased, and I got hit in the head and fell into the river. At least, it feels like a memory."

Julian frowned. "Are you sure that's a memory and not one of those bad dreams?"

"I don't know. I don't think so. It's so hard because I've been having the nightmares."

"Even with the sleeping pills?"

"No. They've helped. But after everything that's happened, I'm finding it hard to discern what's real and what's not."

"So, your memories from before could have been a dream?"

"Something knocked me into the river."

"Or that was part of a nightmare getting mixed in with reality. A bump on the head could have come from anything. Right now, I think you have to be careful about trusting your own thoughts."

"But it does feel different from a dream."

"And maybe it's not and if that's the case, then I'm sorry you remember. The doctor did mention it. I was hoping you'd forget if you could."

"Why should I forget?"

Julian let out a noisy breath. "It must be a terrifying memory for you."

"Do you have any idea what could have happened?"

"I could only speculate. You know it's possible that it was the Palmers chasing you. Maybe their plan all along was to catch you. It could have been them who sent you into the river and then they fished you out pretending to be your rescuers."

"I don't know."

"You experienced what they were capable of. You don't think they would have done something like that? People like that, they're so consumed with what they believe, they'll do whatever it takes."

"But I don't think they'd do that. I can't explain it. It doesn't feel right."

"Eva, I know this is hard, but it may be that the best thing for you to do is to forget everything about the past and move forward. Have a fresh start."

"It may sound strange, but that's exactly what I want."

"Does it?"

"I know you said I have bad dreams, but some of what I dreamed felt so real. I'm afraid I'm not a good person, or at least, I wasn't in the end."

"Eva. You're one of the best people I know. You are the type of person who has never been afraid to sacrifice for the greater good. What makes you think you're a bad person?"

"I don't know. I just wanted to make sure."

"That is one thing you don't have to worry about. No matter who you had become before falling in that river. You are not that person anymore."

## Chapter 17

EVA WAS SHOCKED when they pulled up to the high-rise apartment building. Wherever it was she thought she lived, this was not it. They were in the middle of the city with traffic and people everywhere. It was awful.

She tried to swallow, but her chest was too tight. She wrapped her arms around herself. "You said I've lived here for two years?"

"That's right," Julian said.

"Are there usually this many people?"

"The city is always busy, but no, it's never been this crowded when I've visited." He let out an exasperated breath. "I'm afraid that today it looks like the press has found out you were coming home. I'm so sorry, Eva. I thought I could keep it quiet. I certainly didn't want you coming home to this. Someone at the hospital must have leaked it." He shook his head. "Someone only looking out for themselves. I hope they enjoy their fifteen minutes."

"But why would the press care about me coming home?"

"It's not you—well, it is you. But it's me. I'm a high-profile businessman and the entire country knows that I've been looking for you. After you went missing, I made sure your face was in the news so that if you were out there somewhere, I could find you. I knew that someone somewhere would have seen you. And luckily, someone did. So now, your homecoming is a big deal. But I thought I could spare you."

"I don't know if I can do this."

"There's only one way into your apartment, I'm afraid."

"There's no underground parking?"

"Not that the limo would fit into."

Eva wiped the sweat from her lip. "Then let's get this over with."

"You're sure?"

"Yeah."

"Okay, follow me and stay close."

Eva slid out of the car after Julian, who put his hands up as the crowd swarmed.

"I will make a statement later today. Can you please give us some space? My daughter has been through a terrible ordeal and this isn't helping."

"Ms. Underwood," someone in the crowd shouted. "Can you tell us where you were being held? What did they do to you there? What was the ransom demand?"

Cameras flashed and Eva stumbled back.

"Tyler. A little help here," Julian said.

Tyler elbowed his way forward, pushing people back and making a path through to the door.

"Eva is not up to answering questions today, and we'd appreciate it if you'd respect our privacy." Julian said as they wove forward.

Eva burst into the foyer, breathless. She pressed a hand to her chest. "You taught me to fight, but you never trained me to deal with them? Seems like a huge oversight."

"Actually, you've always been excellent with the press."

"Oh."

"I expect you'll get that back one day, but I'm not surprised if your fears got the better of you today. They can be intimidating if you're not prepared. But it's not the first time you've endured their torture."

A tall, wide man approached. "I'm so sorry, Mr. Underwood, Miss Underwood. I didn't even know they were out there. Are you all right? I've called the police."

"We're fine, Silverman."

"It is so wonderful to have you home with us again, Miss Underwood." He hurried to the elevator.

"We are very relieved to have her back safe with us," Julian said, taking Eva's arm as he led her forward.

Eva smiled at Silverman when she got on the elevator, but she didn't speak. He had the expectant look of a puppy about to be taken for a walk, and she didn't know what to do with that. He knew her, but she didn't know him. The ever-present problem. She had no idea what level of friendship they had or how she usually treated him.

After the doors closed, she eased back against the railing. "Silverman said he called the police. Does that mean we can get rid of them?"

"Who, the press? I'm afraid not. That's a public street. The police can ask them to dissipate if they're disrupting the flow of traffic."

"Which they are."

"Yes, but they won't leave. They'll lie in wait for you to reemerge."

"I feel sick knowing they're out there. How long until they go away, do you think?"

"Days for most of them. Weeks for the hard core looking to score an exclusive…You know, my offer still stands. You can come live at my place for a while. Just until they're gone."

"But won't they be there too?"

"I've got an extensive property with lots of trees and wide-open spaces. But I also have a gate. They can't get anywhere near the house."

"You've got trees?"

"Big ones."

"I guess I used to enjoy living in the city."

"You don't have to do this to yourself. Don't force it. Come to my house and enjoy the wide-open spaces until everything settles down. If you stay here, it will be like living in a prison and that's the last thing you need right now."

Before Eva could respond, the elevator opened, and her breath escaped her.

She stepped out into the penthouse with views across the city. "This is where I live?"

"You like it? I helped you pick it out."

"It's huge."

"That's what you were accustomed to. How does it feel?"

Eva shook her head as she crept forward. "Weird. I lived here on my own?"

"You did. You loved it. You can't remember it at all?"

"No. It all feels foreign. It's like I've stepped into someone else's life." Eva let out a thin, steadying breath. She couldn't imagine staying here all alone. "I think I will take you up on your offer. This is too much."

"You don't know how happy that makes me. And it's a wise choice. Take your time looking around. You can collect some clothes from your room. They might not be familiar, but at least you know they all fit."

She nodded, then pointed down a hall. "Is it that way?"

Julian smiled. "Yes."

Being in the bedroom was easier. It was still large and completely alien, but it felt safer.

She sat on the edge of the bed and bounced while looking around the room, taking in every detail from the bronze lamp on the small desk against one wall to the embroidered pillow centered at the head of her bed. Then she closed her eyes. She could remember doing the same thing at the Palmers. Looking through the room and assessing it.

She had no need for that anymore. Her training had been for self-defense, like her dad said. There was nothing devious in it.

She looked down at the blanket she was sitting on that was laid across the bottom of the bed. Out of any blanket available at whatever store she was in, she picked this beige blanket. Maybe it was a frivolous decision made on a whim, or maybe she'd taken the time to make her choice. She may never know.

A crease on the edge of the blanket caught her attention, and she reached out to smooth it. As her hand brushed at the fabric, a shock of memory hit her. She could remember scrunching the blanket up in her hands. She had been sitting on the floor at the end of the bed.

She slid down to the floor, and the blanket came with her. The same thing had happened in the memory. She could feel it. She had been crying. Sobbing. Something had overwhelmed her, but whatever it was, it wasn't part of what she remembered now. All she could remember now was the anguish as she squeezed the blanket close to her chest.

She remained on the floor, numb and in pain at the same time as though she were watching herself from another room. Then the grief faded, and she lifted her eyes to look around the room. It occurred to her how alone she was. With no friends to confide in, she was marooned in her own life. Her dad was there for her, but she didn't *know* him. She trusted him because she had no reason not to, but it was also out of necessity.

She pressed the heel of her hand against her chest that tightened at the thought that she was a stranger in her own home. Her eyes drifted around the room one more time and paused on the table beside her bed. It had a drawer in it like at the Palmers. She remembered the Bible that Clara kept in there and wondered if she had left anything precious in there herself.

When she pulled the drawer open, it looked empty but she caught sight of the edge of a folded piece of paper. She opened it and read the handwritten note:

*If I make my bed in Sheol, behold, You are there.*

"Sheol?" she mumbled. "What does that even mean?" It stuck to her tongue like she knew it. It reminded her of the agony she'd felt only a moment before. "Hell," she said as she traced her finger over the letters. "If I make my bed in hell."

She hurried to her desk for a pen and sat, rewriting the line below the first. When she finished, she tapped the pen on her lip, contemplating the two lines that were nearly identical.

She hadn't written those words for no reason. It had to be a clue. Or was it a riddle? But why would she write something so vague? Why write a clue at all? The only purpose it served was to taunt her with half-remembered ideas that remained out of reach. Even the ache she'd felt when she sat on the floor remained beyond grasping. It didn't matter how hard she dug into her mind, she had no idea what any of it meant.

"Find something?" Julian asked from the door.

Eva jumped up, closing her fist around the paper while she spun around. "You scared me."

"Sorry. You were taking a while. I wanted to make sure everything was okay."

"I'm fine. I found this, but I don't know what it means." She held out the paper as Julian approached. "It's in my handwriting. I checked."

"Where'd you find this?" Julian asked as he read it.

"In the drawer beside my bed."

His face remained neutral, but she could see a twitch in his face that suggested he wasn't happy about it. "It was just sitting there? Why'd you know to look in the drawer?"

"I didn't. I noticed the drawer and thought I'd see if I kept anything by my bed. See if I kept anything important in there."

"You don't remember writing it?"

"I don't even know what it means."

"It's from the Bible."

"Really? Do I read the Bible?"

"No. No, you never were one for fairy tales. You're far too practical."

"But I wrote that note."

He crumpled up the paper. "It could mean anything. Plenty of people quote the Bible for various reasons. It's only a scrap of paper. I'm sure it's nothing." He tossed it in a garbage can before heading for the closet, where he pulled open the door to reveal a large walk-in wardrobe.

He lifted a suitcase off the top shelf and laid it open

on the bed. "Once you're done looking around, you can put everything in here. If you need more cases, I'm sure we can find something, or I can send Tyler back later." Eva was looking at the floor. Julian walked over to her. "Hey, it won't be like this forever. Give yourself time to adjust."

"It's frustrating feeling like everything is just beyond a veil that I should be able to push aside. But the harder I try, the further away it gets."

"Then don't try. Let it rest for a bit. Once we get you settled in at my house, I want you to take the time to look after yourself. There is no need to hurry this. No one is rushing you. You've got all the time you need."

Eva looked across the room into the open closet. "I've got a lot of clothes."

Julian laughed. "You always did like clothes. Shoes too."

"I have no idea what to choose."

Julian raised his hands. "Don't come to me for advice. I can do a lot of things, but fashion is not my forte."

"But you're dressed well."

"I've got a guy for that. Try on as much as you want and see what you like."

"That's a good idea."

"I'll leave you to it. I've got a phone call to make. Come out into the living room when you're ready."

When Julian left the room, Eva went to the garbage and pulled out the note, stuffing it into her pocket. Maybe she didn't read the Bible, but she'd written that note for a reason. She might not remember doing it, but it felt important.

But Julian was right. It was time to take the pressure off herself. She walked into the closet and set her hands on her hips. A rack full of dresses took up the right side of the closet. She could come back for those if she needed them. Today, she'd choose the basics.

## Chapter 18

WHEN JULIAN ENTERED the living room, he looked back down the hall to make sure Eva hadn't followed him out, then he pulled his phone out and pressed it to his ear.

"Michael. Do you have an update on Ray? Is he ready?"

"He's not only ready, he's excited."

"Sounds like the student is becoming the master."

"When you enjoy the work you do, it's easy. People are so desperate to belong it's almost too simplistic. All you have to do is make them feel important and they're willing to do almost anything."

"Some of them *will* do anything."

"Like Ray."

"And you've explained to him the entire process of what we need from him?"

"I've gone through it multiple times, yes. He's ready. And Julian. I wanted to say thank you for entrusting this to me."

"You know I've been following your work at my company for a long time. I've probably made you wait longer than necessary, but the timing now couldn't be better. Being able to entrust you with this means I can spend more time with Eva."

"I must say, I am overwhelmed and very pleased at how everything has worked out."

"I think we all are."

"How's she doing?"

"Remarkably well. And I have some good news for you."

"Oh yeah?"

"You may recall the request you made of me a couple of years ago with regards to Eva." He kept his eyes on the hall while he spoke.

"I had put it out of my mind when things didn't go as expected."

"Yes, well, the thing is, her mind is completely wiped clean and I have a fresh start with her, but I want to minimize any chance of losing her again. That's where I could use your help."

"I'm listening."

"Eva was always strong-minded, but over this last day, I've noticed a change. She needs someone who can anchor her."

"I see."

"I need someone I can trust to work with me to keep her in place. I'd also appreciate an extra set of eyes keeping tabs on her in this very delicate time. She must feel secure in her new position and to keep her safe from wandering. If she is preoccupied with a new love, that would help while we renew her place within our ranks."

"And you believe I can do that?"

"You'll understand when you see her again. So the only question remaining is whether you are still interested in her, and if so, are you up to the task?"

"Julian, I would…relish the opportunity to build something with Eva."

"Good. But to begin, you'll need to tread lightly. I have seen your work and I know how good you are. She is incredibly moldable at the moment. She carries around a great deal of fear and anxiety that you can use, but don't push too hard too fast. This is a long-term solution and I need to know you are in this completely."

"You know I have committed myself to your work and doing so with Eva by my side is more than I could have ever asked."

"Except you did ask." Julian chuckled.

"True. You know I go for the things I want."

"It's one of the traits I like most about you. And it's why I know you're ready to handle my daughter. I'll be in touch soon. Keep up the good work with Ray and don't let up until his assignment is finished. I want everything to go off without a hitch. If we can get a win there, it will be a very successful couple of weeks for the foundation."

"It will indeed."

Julian put the phone in his pocket, took a moment to enjoy his recent successes, then focused on the next issue that needed handling.

He pulled open every drawer in the living room and

checked in, and under, everything else. He was lucky the note hadn't triggered a memory for Eva, but he couldn't be sure another one wouldn't.

After Eva had disappeared, they had searched her house for any clues that would lead them to those who Eva had been working with, making sure nothing was missed. It was an impossible thing that they would not have seen this note.

He moved to the bookshelf and pulled the books out, flipping through the pages. He had just pulled another off the shelf when Eva emerged from the hall.

"I'm ready," she said, lugging the case out. "Anything worth reading?"

He smiled and slipped the book back. "Not my kind of reading. Here, let me get that for you."

"No, it's fine. I'm strong enough to carry it."

"That's not the point." Julian took the case and walked with her to the elevator. "How'd you do? Find anything you liked?"

"All those clothes. I hardly knew where to start. Everything fancy I left behind. I don't expect to be going anywhere for a while."

"Don't put too big of a damper on your social calendar. You might recover faster than you expect."

"Then I can come back. For now, I'll stick with comfort. I won't impose on you for that long, and I don't want an entire wardrobe I have to lug back here later. Especially if I won't wear most of it."

"T-shirt and jeans it is then, I suppose?"

"Yup. But don't worry. I'm pretty sure they're all designer."

"They're definitely all designer." Julian laughed.

---

When they exited the elevator on the ground floor, Tyler was talking to Silverman. He stopped midsentence when he saw them and retrieved the suitcase from Julian.

"I think you better let me," Tyler said. "I'll use it to plow a path through those maniacs."

"The police haven't arrived yet," Silverman said. "Would you rather wait?"

"No," Julian said. "I'd rather get Eva home." He turned to her. "If you think you'll be okay once more through the crowd?"

"Yeah. I just want to get out of here."

"Best of luck, Miss Underwood," Silverman said. "I hope to see you soon. And again, I am so sorry about what has happened here today."

"That's okay," she said. "It's—It's good to see you too." She smiled shyly, then followed Julian to the door. He leaned toward her. "You handled that well," he whispered. "I told you you were good at public relations."

"An awkward goodbye is good PR?"

"You acknowledged Silverman and put his mind at ease even though yours is anything but. It came naturally to you?"

"I wouldn't say naturally, but it seemed like the right thing to do."

"Then it came naturally."

"You two ready?" Tyler asked with one hand on the door and the other lifting Eva's suitcase as a shield.

"After you," Julian said and Tyler pushed the doors open. Eva kept her head down as they shouldered through the crowd and pushed back through to the car.

Once Julian had Eva safely inside, he closed her in and jostled his way to the front seat, where he joined Tyler.

He lowered the privacy screen that had been blocking the front seats from the back. "Ready to go?"

"You're riding up front?"

"I've got some business to attend to that I don't want to disturb you with. Take the time to rest."

Eva nodded, then leaned her head back on the seat.

Julian put the screen up as Tyler got in beside him.

He waited until Tyler pulled onto the street before hissing at him, "I thought you went through her entire apartment."

Tyler looked at Julian before quickly refocusing on the road. "We did."

"She found something."

"What? Where?"

"In the drawer next to her bed."

"What did she find?"

"A piece of paper with a scripture written on it."

"Sir, that's impossible."

"And yet, there it was in the drawer beside her bed."

"Did you bring it with you? We can analyze the handwriting and see if we can identify who wrote it."

"She wrote it herself."

"That's impossible."

"You keep saying that, and yet..."

"Did she remember it?"

"No, luckily she had no idea what it meant or why it was there."

"Are you sure?"

"Yes."

"But she was always a very good lia—"

"Tyler, I must say, I'm not accustomed to all of this second-guessing I'm getting from you lately. If I recall correctly, you were the one I put in charge of finding Eva and disposing of her. You didn't complete that mission, and we now find ourselves in an unusual situation that I am taking advantage of. But if you're upset about the outcome, you have no one to blame but yourself. If you'd done that job I asked you to, we wouldn't be here right now."

"You're right."

"I know."

"Sir, if I may, it's my concern for you and your work that causes me to worry."

"Well, don't. It doesn't suit you. I don't keep you close because you worry. I keep you around because you're effective. But if you think that will be a problem going forward…"

"No, sir."

"Good, but I'd still like to know how that paper got in her drawer."

"Sir, you know that as soon as we confirmed her body was missing, we went straight to her apartment to make sure that if she wasn't dead and she returned, we'd be waiting. We went through everything, just like you asked. Her apartment was clean."

"There is no way you could have missed a scrap of paper in the drawer by her bed?"

"No. We were very thorough."

"If that's true, then someone put it there afterward, and I want to know who."

"Someone could have broken in and planted it."

"What exactly would that accomplish? And why use a vague scripture like that? Besides, she wrote it herself, so if someone left it, it had to be a note she'd written before falling in the river. Not to mention that it wouldn't be easy to break in there. That is a highly secure apartment."

"They are involved in that voodoo stuff. Maybe it was that."

"Voodoo stuff?"

"Yeah. They might not call it that. But whatever it is, it's supernatural. You know what they can do."

"Do I?"

"Remember that man we found out about early this year? We went after him and nearly had him, then he disappeared. One second he was there and the next he was gone."

Julian sighed. "Or that could have been incompetence."

"Sir, with all due respect, my men are highly trained."

"So highly trained Eva escaped you at the river?"

"That's what I mean. Eva's good, but she's not that good. She shouldn't have survived."

"So you're saying they're using magic?"

"I'm saying it's not natural."

"Tyler, they can use as much mojo as they like, but no one can deny now that the universe is on my side. If Eva survived because of some magic spell, then why is she sitting behind me right now? If any kind of sorcery saved her, it was an enchantment that worked in our favor. Otherwise, she'd be with them right now and not us. And look at how much we've accomplished so far. Even with the setbacks we've had, our triumphs have far outweighed our losses."

"But, sir—"

"Tyler, let them have their party tricks, if that's what it is. All the signs point to our victory. They're clutching at straws. They're desperate. The best they can manage is some unintelligible note that Eva handed over to me as soon as I asked her."

"That *is* a good sign."

"We have the upper hand, Tyler. We will win. But that doesn't mean we don't remain vigilant. I don't want them slipping any more notes into her drawers."

"It won't happen again."

"Make sure it doesn't. I want you to go through her apartment again and make sure we have surveillance on all points of entry."

"I'll get it done."

"Thank you."

"Can I assume that you don't intend to keep her in the dark forever? She's of no use to you if she isn't able to participate in your organization."

"No, that is correct. It's a delicate balance but we have time to give her the space she needs. She was my disciple once and she will be again. If she can't remember why she turned against me in the first place, then we have a good chance of putting her right back where she belongs sooner rather than later."

"I look forward to it."

---

Eva blinked up at the roof of the car. The memory of anguish she'd had in her room with the blanket had been intense but not overwhelming. Dr. Smith had said she might get parts of her memories back, but she wouldn't tell her dad about it yet. With little to say besides some strong feelings, she'd wait until she had something more concrete so she didn't get his hopes up unnecessarily. It was hard enough keeping her own emotions in check.

If she could piece together a few more snippets, if they ever came, perhaps they would eventually lead to a full thought. And one full thought could lead to another.

She'd spend the next few days at her dad's house, but if no new memories surfaced, she'd go back to her own home.

If she could eventually remember the group she was involved with, the one who gave her the tattoo, she might even be able to stop them from hurting anyone else.

She closed her eyes. It was a relief knowing she was safe from them for now. But how many more had they brainwashed? How many more were already caught up in their schemes? She couldn't hide from the possibility of helping others. She wouldn't allow herself to stay afraid forever.

# Chapter 19

JULIAN SLID the partition down as they approached a large wrought iron gate.

"Welcome home," he said.

Eva took in the wide expanse of the gate. She was grateful for the tinted windows as several news vans were parked nearby and multiple cameras were pointed at the limo as at passed through the gate. But no one was clamoring for a comment, and once they passed through the gate, Eva turned to watch it close behind them with a satisfying shudder.

She turned back around in her seat and sighed with a smile.

"I'm glad you approve." He winked.

Eva leaned toward the window to look up at the large trees that lined the driveway until the house came into view.

"This is your house?" She didn't hide her awe.

"It was yours, too, for a long time. You loved it here."

"It's as big as a castle." The green lawn spread out in waves until they hit a tall, perfectly groomed hedge. "It's beautiful."

"I'm glad you think so. I hope you find it a productive place to recover."

The car pulled around the circle drive and stopped.

Eva didn't wait for the door to be opened for her. She stepped onto the paved driveway and turned in a slow circle. How could she not remember this life? A house this imposing with a heavy, dark, double-front door shouldn't be so easy to forget.

Julian walked up beside her. "What do you think?"

"I don't know what to think. I'm overwhelmed."

"You are looking a little pale. It's been a big day. Let's get you settled in."

"It's been a big week."

Julian put his hand on her back and led her up the steps. The doors opened before they reached the top and a man in a tuxedo appeared, standing at attention after fixing the doors in place.

"Thank you, Donald," Julian said, leading Eva inside.

The grand entryway was lit by a crystal chandelier. Eva counted three archways leading farther into the house, along with an enormous staircase. "I don't remember this at all." Fresh flowers sat on tables around the circular area.

"It's so strange that nothing is familiar to you and yet, you are still you."

"Am I?"

"I'm pleased to say yes."

"It feels like a dream."

"Better a dream than the nightmare you were in with the Palmers. Oh, I forgot to tell you. The FBI contacted me earlier. They apprehended Franky."

"They did? Alive?"

"Yes. They didn't tell me how. But they did say that they found explosives and plans in the shed out back, so he'll probably never get out of prison."

"What about Clara?"

Julian's lips bunched together. "They haven't been able to locate her. When they entered the house, she was nowhere to be found. They believe she escaped. But you have nothing to worry about. There is no way she could get in here."

"No. She wouldn't try to find me."

"You sure about that?"

"Positive. Franky was the one who wanted to hurt me. She was there, but without him, she wouldn't do anything else."

"Then why is it that you seem sad?"

"Clara kept me alive. She nursed me back to health. She really was very kind to me."

"Until she threatened you."

"She was scared. Franky had her all turned around. If it weren't for him...She thought I was there to hurt her family. She thought she was protecting him."

Julian shook his head slowly. "You were always very generous with people. Always thinking the best of them."

"Was I? The whole thing was so awful."

"If we hadn't gotten you out of there, you'd probably be dead."

"I know. I just wish things didn't turn out how they did. I wish I would have been able to convince them I didn't want to hurt anyone."

"You could have lived with them, do you think? You would have been happy with that?"

"Not with Franky. I'm glad they got him, but I can't say I'm upset that Clara got away."

"As your father, I don't have any good feelings about Clara or Franky. But if she's the reason you're alive and not dead, then I suppose a part of me must be grateful, even if I don't like it. But really"—he took Eva's hands —"I'm most thankful to the FBI for getting you out of there in one piece."

"It wasn't the FBI who did it."

"What do you mean?"

"There was another man. He got there before they did."

"Another man? Who?"

"A guy who lives in town. His name's Ben. That's all I know. The store owner—Roger—he said Ben was in the special forces or something. Came home with PTSD and was hiding away in that little town. He must have found out about what happened and he came to rescue me. He saw me at the store when Roger did. He saw my tattoo."

"And?"

"It freaked him out. He must have come across the group I was involved with. He must know about them, but he helped me anyway."

"Ben, huh? Do you know Ben's last name?"

"No. The only other thing I know about him is that he lives near that town in a blue house by the river."

Julian looked at Tyler, who was expressionless. "We should find him and say thanks."

"I don't think that's a good idea," Eva said.

"Why not?"

"He's a loner. After he saved me, he disappeared. I don't know why. But I don't think he wants any attention for what he did."

"Okay, then we'll leave him alone."

"Thank you. Although, once I've settled, I'd like to go see him myself and say thanks. I wouldn't mind asking him about the tattoo and what he knows."

A figure appeared at the top of the stairs. "Julian, you've returned. And with a very special guest, I see."

"Bea. Yes, we've brought Eva home finally."

The woman hurried down the stairs. "Eva. I know you don't remember me, but it is wonderful to see you safe." She gave Eva a tight hug, then held her back at arm's length. "Look at you."

"Eva," Julian said. "I'd like you to meet Mrs. Beaman. She'll help you get settled in. Anything you need, you can ask her if I'm not around."

"Mrs. Beaman, it's nice to meet you again."

Bea's face squashed up in a fleshy smile. "Clever girl. If you'd like to follow me, we've got your old room ready."

"Thank you. I wouldn't mind having a rest."

"Dr. Smith gave you more of those sleeping pills?" Julian asked.

"Yeah. I'm set for the week at least."

"Good."

Eva headed for the stairs, but Julian put a hand on Bea before she could lead the way. "Make sure she doesn't run into Kaitlyn," he whispered. "I'd rather not have to explain the girl's presence in this house until Eva is ready to hear it all."

"I've locked off that wing, so there should be no problems with accidental encounters, although Kaitlyn is out of the house in training most of the time."

"How's she doing."

"You should visit soon and see for yourself. You'll be impressed. I know you're preoccupied at the moment, but she's been asking about you."

"I should have some time over the next couple days while Eva is recovering. Depending on how her rehabilitation goes, it's possible we'll be able to use her as a mentor for the girl."

Bea's hands clapped together. "That would be wonderful."

"I'll let you go, but make sure Eva takes her sleeping pills to rest. We don't want her having any dreams."

"Of course." Bea hurried up the stairs after Eva, who had wandered up to the second floor.

Julian waved at her and watched until Bea led her down the hall, then he turned to Tyler. "I need you to find out everything you can on this Ben that Eva mentioned."

A muscle in Tyler's cheek flexed.

"What is it?"

"Do you remember Ben Waite? You hired him a few years ago."

Julian's lips flattened. "How can I forget the man who blew up my facility? That set us back years and was a harsh lesson to never trust outsiders."

"Yes. As far as I know, he never got the tattoo, but he knew about it."

"Tyler, he died in the explosion."

"That's what we thought."

"Don't tell me you believe he faked his death and now this is the same Ben? That's far-fetched, even for you and your voodoo theories."

"Eva survived."

"An exploding building is completely different."

"But it seems odd, doesn't it? That a man named Ben saved Eva?"

"But that would mean he was living in the town where Eva randomly washed up. That would be impossible to plan."

"Maybe he didn't plan it. Maybe he took advantage of his circumstances."

"All right. Look into it."

"And if it's the same man?"

"If by some miracle Ben Waite survived, then I definitely want to have a chat with him. I'm still cleaning up after the mess he made."

"Sir, do I have your permission to put together a task force on this?"

"You think that's necessary?"

"Do you remember why you hired him in the first

place? If it really is Ben, we'll only have one shot at this. He's too good."

"Point taken. Okay, bring in whoever you need on this. I won't lose him again."

"Thank you, sir."

Tyler left, and Julian marched through one of the arches to his study, where he slid the doors closed and locked them.

He pushed aside the heavy curtains and looked out the window.

Ben had single-handedly blown apart an operation that had taken Julian decades to prepare for. He wouldn't miss the opportunity to deal with him. They had a new plan in place now, but Julian was getting older and he didn't want to miss what he'd spent most of his life striving for. There had been others who had begun preparing before him, but Julian was the one who'd taken the foundation to new heights.

A wry smile slid up his face, and he arched his head backward. He savored the moment and applauded himself on his patience. Men like him rose up to change the world for a reason. He would take his place among the greats because preeminence could not help but be drawn to him. His name would one day be enshrined and remembered as a man who changed the face of the world.

He looked at his watch, then moved to the cupboard where he poured himself a bourbon, finishing it in one gulp before he went to his desk and sat in the large leather chair.

He watched the second hand tick. They were

waiting for him to contact them, but they could wait a few seconds longer.

Once the hour hand struck two, he initiated the conference call on his computer and waited for everyone to join.

"Good afternoon and thank you all for your patience. As you are aware by now, Eva is back."

Applause and congratulations followed, then a man with short, jet-black hair asked what they were all wanting to know. "What exactly does that mean?"

"With regards to what, Xavier?" Julian leaned back in his chair, enjoying their agitation. He knew how far to take it.

"It was our understanding," Xavier said, "that you were going to take care of her. We expected to be informed of her demise, not her resurrection. Wasn't all that nonsense about a missing daughter a publicity stunt for when they discovered her body?"

"Your understanding did not account for the extraordinary turn of events that took place. Ladies and gentlemen, Eva Underwood has lost her memory, but not her training. I expect to have her back at my side in the near future."

"You're not serious," said a woman in the top left corner of the screen.

"Did I stutter, Senator?"

"I don't mean to be obtuse," she continued. "But how can that be possible?"

"You can call it a miracle if you like. But the bottom line is, Eva can't remember leaving our fold and, there-fore, she's safely back in it. I'll be honest. I expected you all to be more excited than this. You know how experienced she was and what she offered to this organization. It was a shame to have to remove her, but it seems we've been handed a gift. We're keeping a close eye on her, but it looks as though she's back with us for good."

"Don't mistake our surprise for disbelief," Xavier said. "Having her back is a rare gift. We have all pledged our loyalty to you and you can expect our full support."

"Thank you. I will assume the group shares your sentiments unless they tell me differently."

A few nods went around the screen, but the senator spoke. "Can you give us any guarantees that Eva truly is on our side?"

"I give you my word. I expect that is good enough."

"You don't think your judgment is clouded in any way?"

"Senat—Emilia, I appreciate your concern for my well-being. However, you know that I was up-front with all of you about Eva's turn and I have proven that I will do what is necessary for the good of all of us. My judgment is as reliable as it has always been. If I thought it would be more beneficial to the society if I disposed of her, she'd already be in the ground. My decision to take her back is not connected to any selfish motives."

"Okay," Emilia said. "Then I look forward to hearing of her progress."

"And I look forward to informing you of her progress, as I'm sure you will all be eager to have her with us again on a deeper level where she belongs. Now, as you can all appreciate, I have a lot to do today, so if we can move on to the main reason for this gathering, I'd like to know where we are at with the bill."

"We've turned the holdout," said a man with thick glasses.

Julian smirked. "That didn't take long, Bruce. You said you expected to need more time."

"I was looking forward to a good fight, but in the end, we found a skeleton."

"Not much sport in it, is there? Sometimes it's almost too easy. How confident are we that the bill will pass?"

Emilia spoke. "I'm still working on the speaker of the house. Once she's with us, it should be an open road."

Julian nodded. "Everything depends on this now. We've spent years preparing for this moment grooming would-be senators and others who have now risen to power. If we don't get it through now, we miss our chance. I want to make sure we are confident of a victory."

"We're close now. Very close," said Bruce. "Once it passes through the House and Senate, which it will. It's only the president left and if it passes by a large margin, he'll be on board. You know, Julian, you could do a lot if you sat in his chair."

"Who, the president's?" Julian laughed. "I have no interest in being tied down like that. But I'll tell you this, one day I will own him. Or her, as the case may be. I have several in mind who might take that job one day."

"That would make things easier," Bruce said.

"All in due time. For now, let me know when you

have further updates. I don't want a slim victory here. I want a landslide. I want the country to be convinced that this is what's best for them, and we don't do that on a narrow margin."

"The press will help with that," said Xavier.

"Yes, but we want the American people to see that the leaders of this country are on board as well. This is a time for unity, not division. I don't want the press getting so carried away they alienate people. But for now, I will leave it in all of your capable hands. I have to go spend some quality time with my daughter and remind her how much she cares about this family and its goals."

"Good luck, Julian," Xavier said.

"Luck has never had anything to do with it."

## Chapter 20

EVA STAYED in her room for most of the next twenty-four hours. She was alone except for a visit from her dad for coffee.

The anxiety she had at her apartment hadn't left her as she expected it to. It didn't matter that she was safer here from the press. Something else had followed her here. It had nothing to do with her accommodation. It went deeper than that.

She squeezed her eyes tight as another wave of fear gripped her. When she mentioned it to her dad, he suggested it would take time. Her fears were irrational. She kept telling herself that, but it didn't stop the chills from climbing her spine at unidentified noises, or shadows in the night. If it weren't for the sleeping pills, she wouldn't be sleeping. She knew that for sure. The dreamless sleeps were a refuge because even when the sun found its way to her window, it still felt as though her demise was creeping closer.

The image of the wolf haunted her. Its dripping

teeth were a permanent feature at the back of her eyelids until the pills took her off to oblivion. It was as though it was waiting for her to let her guard down before it pounced again.

She pulled the note from under her pillow and read it aloud. "If I make my bed in Sheol, behold, You are there." It was hard to tell if the fear retreated at the reading of the words, or if it was her imagination, but she'd take the comfort that it gave, whether it was real or imagined.

It wasn't simply the unknown terrors hiding just out of sight that made her edgy. The mark on her wrist burned into her thoughts and she ran a thumb across it, pressing down as though she could rub it away. Despite her dad's assurances that everything he taught her was for her safety, there had been a period of time in her life when she must have used her skills for terrible deeds. It was a small blessing that she lost her memory and could return to her family. But the activities she'd participated in before losing her memory were another shadow that hung in her peripheral vision, and no matter how hard she tried, she couldn't shake it.

All the fears rolled into a growing determination to visit Ben. If leaving the house didn't terrify her right now, she'd go see him immediately, but she'd have to wait until she had the courage to venture out and find out who it was that Ben had been afraid of. As someone who used to be in the special forces, he should have an idea about how to bring them to justice. She had her dad too. He would want to help if it meant getting back at the people who had stolen his daughter from him.

She wanted to know, too, why Ben had saved her life. What kind of bravery led a man to help her when he thought she might be the enemy? She could use a bit of that for herself.

A soft knock came at her door and she stuffed the note back under her pillow before opening it to find Julian standing with a giant smile on his face.

She couldn't help but smile back. "You're in a good mood this morning."

"You don't know how good it feels to come knock on your bedroom door knowing you'll answer."

"Yeah, well. One of these days, I'm going to have to venture out. I'm turning into a hermit."

"Still not feeling great?"

"I can't shake this anxiety. No matter what I do, it keeps hanging on. I know you keep telling me it will take time, but I had hoped for some relief."

"Is there anything in particular that you're struggling with?"

"I wish I could tell you. It's more of a vague sense of doom."

"Instead of giving you the same old pep talk about it taking time and try not to rush it, I have another piece of advice to offer this morning."

"I'm all ears."

"I believe that part of your problem is that you are spending too many hours on your own with your own thoughts. I know you don't want to leave your room, but I think you should. As your dad, I have been quite satisfied keeping you locked up and safe, but you need to have more human contact."

"I have had human contact."

"The kind that's not your parent."

"I take it you're here because you have something in mind?"

"I do. I thought you might like to join me for brunch. There's someone here who would like to see you, and I think it would do you good."

She took an involuntary step backward. "Who?"

"Eva, I know this is hard, but it's what is best for you. All you're doing in here is stewing on your fear. Venturing out can only do you good, and I promise you can retreat to your room anytime you feel too over-whelmed. Maybe you'll even spark a memory."

She bit the inside of her cheek. "What if I can't ever remember anything?"

"What about it?"

"I'm useless." Tears sprung into her eyes. She covered her face and sat back on her bed. "I'm sorry."

"Don't be." Julian pulled a chair over to sit close. "You're not useless."

"I've been so scared since being rescued. I wasn't this scared when I was held hostage. They beat me, but I still felt in control, which is crazy. But here, it feels like the whole world is about to collapse in on me. I go from being relieved that I can't remember anything to terrified I might never know anything about my past. I can't settle on anything. Everything is wrong. Everything feels wrong."

"Hey, listen to me. It will all be okay. No one has any expectation on you. If you never get your memory back, then we'll have a fresh start. You get to discover again all the things you love and maybe find something new and unexpected. And if you do remember, then we move forward with that. Whatever happens, we will make the most of it. There is no wrong answer for you right now. Whatever comes, comes."

"How can this not bother you at all?"

"Eva. I thought you were dead. I have you back. The thing that worries me the most is how upset you are. I hate to see what this is doing to you. You need to take the pressure off. Come downstairs and eat. Show your face to the sun and stop trying so hard to make everything right."

"But whoever is down there, I don't know them. All I'll do is make them feel bad."

He reached up and caught a tear that threatened to drip from her chin. "The only person you're hurting is yourself. I'll prove it to you if you come down and have something to eat. You've barely had anything since you've been back. Just give it a chance."

He stood and held out his hand for her to take. She looked at it, then put her own in his and he pulled her up. "You said I can run back up here if I can't handle it?"

"Yes."

"And no one will mind?"

"Not at all."

Julian walked Eva down the stairs where a man, not Tyler, stood guard.

"Tyler has the day off?" Eva asked.

"He's running an errand for me," Julian said as he

took Eva's arm and led her through one of the large archways and into an open library full of light.

A good-looking man in a suit with broad shoulders smiled at the pair as they entered.

"Hi," he said.

Eva's face warmed. He was the sort of man you didn't mind smiling at you. She was surprised by her response. Part of her wanted to retreat, but she didn't give into it. Instead, she enjoyed his smile and offered her own.

"Eva, this is Michael," Julian said. "Thanks for waiting, Michael."

"Not at all. It's good to see you, Eva."

"I guess you know me?" Eva said, smiling awkwardly.

"Michael Rosenbloom is your boss."

"At the PR company?"

"Yes," Michael said as he reached out a hand and took hers, giving it a gentle squeeze. "I'm really pleased to see you looking so well. Julian has told me everything that's happened and I'm here to give you my full support, however I can."

"Does that mean you're not freaked out that I have no idea who you are?"

"Freaked out? No. I'd say I'm more concerned about you and your well-being."

"Didn't I tell you, Eva?" Julian said. " You have nothing to worry about."

"That doesn't make it any less frustrating. It will be hard for me to keep my job if I don't even remember by boss. Did we know each other well?"

The side of Michael's mouth lifted in an ironic grin. "Pretty well, yeah."

"If you don't mind," Julian said. "I'll leave you two for a moment and check on brunch. We'll have it outside there on the patio." Julian nodded toward the large glass doors that led out to a covered paved area surrounded by a variety of plants.

"Shall we?" Michael swept his arm toward the doors. "It's a lovely morning."

Eva nodded and followed him out. The smell of freshly cut grass swirled around them and Eva closed her eyes, lifting her face to the sun. She took a deep breath. "This is what I needed. Don't tell my dad, but he was completely right. I've been hiding in my room, but this sun is wonderful." She looked at Michael, who was watching her, and she blushed again. "So," she said, retreating to a seat at a small round table. "What is it I used to do at work? Was I any good?"

"You were amazing. I had heard about you from Julian before we met. And I'll be honest, I was disappointed he gave you the job."

"Ouch."

Michael grinned. "I thought you got it because you were his daughter, not because you were any good. I didn't think it was a wise move for the company."

"I hope you're not about to tell me you were right."

"Not in the least. I should have known better. Julian doesn't work that way. He is an expert at recognizing potential in people and seeing them flourish under his guidance. He gave you the job because he knew you'd be brilliant at it."

"Sounds like you're sucking up to the boss's daughter." She laughed. The thrill of casual conversation, and perhaps a bit of flirting, was an irresistible balm to her stress.

"I must admit, I probably am a little. But I'm also telling you the truth."

"What did I do that was so brilliant?"

"You had a way of taking anyone's situation and turning it into whatever you wanted. You could make anyone—didn't matter who they were or what they did —into a hero or a villain, as the case may be. Whatever suited your purpose."

"I'm not sure I'm following."

"Well, for example, after an incident at the mayor's office, you entered the scene and changed what was not only a career-ending indiscretion, but also one that could have seen the mayor thrown into prison. By the time you were done with him, he was a hometown hero. And the whistleblower was out of a job and nearly thrown in jail himself."

"What was the incident?"

"Embezzling. Or at least, that was the charge."

"But was he?"

"Not by the time you were done with him."

She frowned. "What about before that? Was he embezzling before I got to him?"

Michael ran his tongue along his bottom lip. "You learn not to ask questions you don't want the answers to in this business. It's all about appearances. You don't remember, but you held on to that as much as the rest of us."

"So that's what I do? I keep people from being arrested for crimes they commit?"

"No." He reached a hand across the table and touched her fingers. "You help people to be the best person they can be. Kind of like your dad. Sometimes that means giving them a second chance. And you are a master at it."

"I *was* a master. I don't remember how to do anything anymore."

"I don't think it will take much to bring that back. It's in your blood."

A tremor curled through Eva's stomach. She couldn't talk about this anymore without feeling nauseated. If she made it back to work, she'd change how she did things. She didn't like the idea of being the reason people weren't held accountable for their actions. "How long have we known each other? Is there anything you can tell me about myself? Things I liked. Things I hated."

"You loved playing tennis."

"Really?"

"Yeah."

"Did we ever play?"

"All the time."

"Did I ever beat you?"

"All the time." Michael laughed. It was a nice sound.

"Okay, tell me something I hated."

"Eggs."

"Really?"

"You keep saying that. Is it that surprising to you? Don't tell me your palate has changed."

"Clara made me eggs at breakfast almost every morning. I really liked them."

"Clara?"

"The woman who found me." Eva dropped her eyes. "She saved my life."

"But didn't she and her son hold you captive?"

"Yes. But before that, she was very kind to me. It's crazy what fear does to people."

"There's something called Stockholm syndrome—"

"It's not that."

"But you know what it is?"

"It's amazing the random information I can remember. You'd be surprised."

"But you don't think it's that?"

"I feel sympathy for her. Maybe pity. Not so much for Franky, but Clara? Maybe it's because she looked after me and I know if she could have stopped Franky, she would have."

"I can't imagine how terrifying that must have been for you."

"It was strange, actually. Even tied to the chair, I knew I had some amount of control. Maybe it was the training my dad gave me, but it was more like I'd learned not to give up no matter what the odds. I don't know why I can't still feel that now. I guess it's all sort of caught up with me. Now that I'm safe, I don't have the defense mechanism to protect me."

"That's a good thing that you're not in fight-or-flight mode anymore. It will help you process everything that's happened. It won't be easy, but you have a lot of people around who care about you."

"Were you always this concerned for my well-being? Or is it because you don't want to lose me as your star employee?"

Michael pressed his lips together. "You weren't just my employee. In fact, it's weird to call you that."

"But my dad said you were my boss."

"I am. But we were in a relationship."

"Oh." Eva cleared her throat. "I did not see that coming."

"I take it that means seeing me hasn't stirred any feelings?"

"I mean, you're—" She swallowed. "No, I don't remember anything." One thing she now understood about herself was that she blushed easily.

"It's okay. I don't expect anything from you. It was pretty new."

"Everyone around me has memories of me, but... I'm sorry. You've lost your girlfriend. That must be horrible for you to sit here knowing that."

"Not lost. It just means I have the opportunity to woo you again."

Eva dropped her eyes into her lap. "Do me a favor and don't use that word again."

Michael laughed. "It is a terrible word, isn't it?"

"Shockingly."

"I look forward to the opportunity for us to get to know each other again."

"So do I."

"Really?"

"But if you could go easy on the wooing for today. I don't think I could handle it."

Michael laughed again, his straight white teeth gleaming in the sunlight. "I wouldn't dream of it. That was never my intention coming here. I only wanted to see that you were well."

"I'm glad you came. It's the first time I've been able to relax since I got here. The first time I've really laughed."

She fought the blush that threatened again by the look he gave her then. It was the first time she felt as though she had something to look forward to.

## Chapter 21

BEN HADN'T BEEN able to sit down all day. He built the fence around the garden at the back of his house, trying to forget about Felix's visit and his revelation that there was still work to be done. It was always the not knowing that caused the greatest anxiety. It would be better if something happened. Anything. Anything was better than waiting. For the first time, he was actually expectant instead of fearful that God would call him into action and so far all he'd asked of Ben was to wait.

In the kitchen, he pulled a glass from the cupboard, but put it back and stuck his head under the faucet, gulping down the water. Then a warning tightened in his chest and he shot up, wiping the dripping water from his face while he stood silently listening.

It was the silence that made the loudest sound. When he had been in the garden, the birds were chirping, but now there was nothing.

He crept toward the window and peered out, keeping his body hidden against the wall. The sun was nearly at its peak and his yard was clear, but something was out there and it wasn't just the shadows this time.

Movement in the trees had him heading toward his room to retrieve his gun from the safe. But after only a couple of steps, the front door exploded open.

Ben dove behind the couch as shots were fired. He looked up at where the bullets had lodged in the wall. Either his assailant was a terrible shot, or they weren't aiming to kill.

He crawled to the edge of the couch and peered around the side. A figure loomed over him, the barrel of a gun aimed at his head. Ben's arms shot up, grabbing the man and flipping him over and against the wall.

The man attempted to get up, so Ben elbowed him in the face and took his gun, firing on another man who had entered, before diving for his room, where he tipped his dresser in front of the door, barricading himself in.

He stayed hidden behind his bed in case anyone was at the window, then he pulled out his safe and retrieved his weapons.

"Benjamin Waite, you slippery little ghost," a voice called through the door. "You're supposed to be dead."

Ben held his breath and steadied himself before responding. "This is so embarrassing. You know who I am, but I don't know you."

"Have you forgotten me so quickly? I'm offended."

"I'm sorry to hear that. I am a terrible host. I would completely understand if you wanted to go."

"I'm afraid that's not an option."

Something in the man's voice triggered in his memory. He saw in his mind's eye the man with a blond ponytail get out of the car before Julian. He held back the tremble in his gut and focused on his loathing for the man. "Wait. Is that you, Tyler?"

"Aw, shucks. You do remember."

Ben had anticipated another visit from Felix before he was sent on his next assignment. He hadn't expected to be ambushed.

"It's been a long time," he yelled through the door as he checked to see how many rounds he had.

"Julian wanted me to extend his thanks. He is grateful for you saving his daughter, if not a little perplexed. Not sure what angle you were working there, but it was a job well done."

"Is that why you came all the way out here? You could have sent me a card. That would have been sufficient."

"Why'd you do it, anyway?"

He had no reason to lie to Tyler. Ben wasn't confident he'd make it out of here alive and he didn't have any secrets that needed keeping. But if this was it for him—if God was ready to take him home—Ben would take as many of them down as he could before going. "She was in trouble. She needed help, so I helped her."

"You're kidding."

"Why would I be kidding?"

"So you heard about some woman in trouble, and you saved her only to find out she's Julian's daughter?"

"That seems to sum it up pretty well." Ben took a peek at his window. It was clear, but Tyler was good at what he did. He'd have someone out there waiting. Probably more than one.

"Did you really not know that she was Julian's daughter?"

"What difference does it make?"

"I guess it's poetic in a way," Tyler said.

"I didn't know you were into literature."

"I'm a modern-day renaissance man. But you'll be interested to know that we were hunting her down to kill her before she fell into that river and lost her memory. She had joined the ranks of the traitors, such as yourself. Those who find Julian's vision too impossible to follow."

"Smart girl."

"But pointless. When I arrived with Julian on-site at the Palmers, we were there to make sure we finished the job we started."

"You were going to kill her in front of the FBI?"

"Ben, please. We expected Franky and Clara to do the job for us once we found out where she was. But when we discovered she'd been rescued, we would have operated discreetly. You know that. You know how these things work, don't you? Or have you forgotten?"

"So you almost killed her unnecessarily."

"Julian was overjoyed when he discovered her memory loss. You should see him. I haven't seen him this happy in a long time. He has his daughter back on his side. After everything that you did, things have worked out in our favor. She's a great asset to have back on the team."

"When you see him again, you can offer him my congratulations."

"You can tell him yourself."

"No thanks. I've got plans."

"He'll reach his goals, you know. No matter what anyone tries to do. He's rebuilt since that incident you caused and he's got a bigger and better plan. Thanks to you, he'll reach higher heights than any of us dreamed possible."

Ben's mind raced with uncertainty about his decision to leave Eva with the FBI. If he'd brought her back here, she'd be safe. But then why was he so certain of leaving her when he did? He thought God had made it clear that he'd done the right thing, but why would he want to send her back there? Especially when she didn't know what she was getting into. She had been free of Julian and God put her right back where she'd escaped from.

"How'd you find me, anyway?"

Tyler laughed. "That's the best part of all. Eva told Julian with her own lips that it was you."

Ben's teeth clenched. "How did she know who I was?"

"She didn't. She wanted to thank a guy named Ben who recognized her tattoo. I started to put the pieces together, although I found it hard to believe, but here we are."

"Luck appears to be on your side." And he meant it. Why was everything going Julian's way? Felix's words stumbled through his mind. *There is so much going on right now that you have no idea about.*

"I've got this place surrounded, Ben. Julian wants to have a word with you and probably mangle you beyond recognition, so he'd rather I didn't kill you, but I'll do what I have to do."

"And so will I." Ben crawled to the window and

spotted a man outside. He ducked out of the way. "How many guys you got out there?"

"Wouldn't you like to know? I haven't forgotten your abilities, so I made sure to bring a big enough team that you will likely see the value of surrendering."

"Not likely."

"There are only two ways out of here. You either surrender, or you're dead."

"But if I go with you, I'm dead."

"True, but I know about guys like you. Give you a little hope and there's no chance you'll give that away. Nevertheless, it's your choice."

Felix had said the same thing. Why was it that every choice he was offered was a terrible one?

Ben got another good look outside and spotted at least three more guys. "Wow, you must be afraid of me, bringing a team this big."

"I underestimated you once. I won't do it again."

"Good for you, you're learning. I'm actually surprised Julian has kept you around as long as he has, with your inability to get the job done. He must be going out on a limb, trusting you to bring me in." He moved back to the safety of his bed. It would take a miracle to get out of this, but maybe this really was the end. "Like with Eva. What happened there? You were supposed to kill her and she gets away? I know she lost her memory, but come on, that was a serious screwup. I didn't think Julian put up with such incompetence."

*Okay, God. You going to keep me in the dark again? If you've got a plan, it's time for you to do your thing. Or is this it for me? My final stand?*

Ben waited, counting off the seconds, but nothing happened and he couldn't hear any clear direction from above.

Tyler knocked on the door. "You fall asleep in there?"

*Come on. What do I need to do?* "Just a little nap before we get to the good stuff. Actually, this isn't a great time for me. Would you mind stopping by a little later?"

"You're recycling your wit. This has been a nice reunion, but I'm running out of patience. Are you coming out or do I give my guys the go-ahead to destroy your house with you in it?"

*God?* He let out a breath and really listened, clearing his mind of everything else. He needed to know what God was thinking here.

*Go with him.*

Ben looked at the gun in his hand and shook his head. "Go with him where? I can't go back there."

*Lay down your weapons and go.*

Ben licked his lips. He'd been trained to withstand torture, but that didn't stop the fear from paralyzing his limbs. "I can't do this," he whispered.

Shots were fired into the door. "Time's up."

"Wait," Ben said. He closed his eyes and let out a breath that could be his last. "I'm coming out."

He emptied his mind as he pushed the dresser out of the way. It was no wonder God wasn't telling him anything ahead of time. He couldn't force himself to be on board with whatever plan this was. Everything in his training screamed at him to dive for his gun and shoot Tyler when he entered the room.

He put his hands on his head and stood rigid until Tyler barged in with his gun.

"That wasn't so hard, was it?" Tyler said with a nasty sneer. "You made this almost too easy for me."

"Should we start over?"

Tyler moved out of the doorway to make room for Ben to walk out. "No, I think we'll just go. I don't want to leave Julian waiting."

Four other men were waiting in the living room with their guns aimed carefully. "Man, you really did come prepared, didn't you? I'm flattered that you are this intimidated by me. It's endearing."

"Tell me that when I'm bashing your kneecaps in."

"You mean when I'm tied to a chair and can't fight back?"

"Tie him up," Tyler said as he pushed ahead and walked out the door.

One of the men grabbed Ben. He still had time to fight back, but he'd been given his orders, so he allowed the man to yank his arms behind his back and restrain him.

Ben dragged his feet along the floor as they pulled him toward the door. He had pushed all his emotions aside and felt a numb calm. When he stepped outside, a cool breeze brushed his cheek and a voice whispered in his ear.

*Trust me.*

# Chapter 22

JULIAN LEANED back in the chair after finishing the small meal. He'd enjoyed watching the interaction between Eva and Michael. Eva was at ease for the first time since returning home.

It was a small gamble bringing Michael here. She didn't need to remember him. She only needed to remember a feeling, and it wouldn't have worked. But he saw the way she looked at him, and it was clear she was besotted. Michael was also performing admirably. He said all the right things. There wouldn't be many women who could resist his charms.

The glass door opened and Julian looked up as Tyler appeared. "Tyler, you're back. How was your trip?"

"It was excellent."

"How did you find everything?"

"As we expected. I brought you back a gift."

"A gift?" Eva said. "I didn't know bodyguards bought souvenirs for their bosses."

"There was something in particular that I wanted," Julian said. "Tyler was good enough to get it for me. Very thoughtful, thank you."

"Not at all, sir. It was my pleasure."

"I hope it wasn't too much trouble for you?"

"Easier than expected. When you're ready, it's in the conference room."

"Excellent. Thank you."

Tyler left and Michael pulled the cloth napkin from his lap, laying it on the table. "Looks like you have a busy afternoon ahead of you, Julian. And I should get back to work." He stood. "Eva, it's been a pleasure seeing you again. Thank you for agreeing to have a meal with me."

Eva smiled. "It's been nice getting to know you for the first time. You should come again."

"I'd like that." He squeezed her fingers lightly, then leaned forward and kissed her cheek.

Before heading for the door, he shook hands with Julian. "I'll see you again soon."

"Let me walk you out." Julian followed Michael to the door. "Eva, you take your time out here. Enjoy the outdoors."

Eva smiled and closed her eyes as she lifted her face to the sun.

---

"That went well," Julian said as they moved into the foyer.

"You said you were apprehensive. I'm glad you're pleased with the results from this morning."

"I didn't want to push. But you did a number on her. It was obvious she was completely taken by you. You handled that with the correct amount of pressure. I have to say, it was fun to watch."

"Yes, I couldn't believe it myself, to be honest. I hadn't expected her to be so open to me. She's different from the old Eva."

"That's because the old Eva knew you too well. She knew what you were capable of. I can't say I blamed her for being uninterested. You can be a cold and egotistical brute when it suits you."

"I'll take that as a compliment."

"You should. But I'll warn you to keep that side of yourself from her. If she didn't like it before, she won't like it now."

"This time I knew going in, so that won't be a problem."

"But you are right. She is a different person now. I think you two were too much alike back then. She's softer now. A pleasant change."

Michael chuckled. "Listen to you. You used to boast about how cold and calculated she was."

"I did, but it got in the way at times. And honestly, I think it's partly to blame for her leaving us. She was so hardheaded. Once she made up her mind, that was it. But I believe now she will be easier to guide. And with you by her side, she will have a firm hand to show her the way. We'll organize more time for you to spend together. Maybe a more intimate gathering next time if you can control yourself."

"You know I can. But did you see how she looked at me?"

"I did, yes. It won't be long before she's eating from your hand—Oh, before you go, there's someone else I'd like you to meet."

"Is this the *gift* that Tyler referred to?"

"No, that's another project related to the explosion that destroyed my building last year."

"Intriguing."

"It is. Once I find out how all the pieces fit together, I'll bring you in on it, but for now, I'll keep it to myself."

"So if it's not that, who is it you want to introduce me to?"

"Kaitlyn."

"Ah yes. I was wondering when I'd have the opportunity to meet her. How's she doing?"

"Come and see for yourself."

Julian led the way to a wide door that he unlocked and they walked down a short hall into an open living room where Mrs. Beaman sat reading a book.

Katy was kneeling on the floor at a low table, writing in a notebook.

"Good afternoon, ladies," Julian said.

Bea looked up in surprise. "Julian, we weren't expecting you."

Katy jumped up and ran to him, wrapping her arms around him. "Uncle Julian."

He gave her back a quick, rough scrub, then held

her away from him. "My word, Katy, I think you've grown another inch since yesterday."

"You say that every time."

"Only because it's true. Bea, has she been behaving herself?"

Bea pushed herself up off the couch. "Most of the time. Michael, this is a nice surprise. How long has it been?"

"Too long." Michael walked to Bea and kissed her on each cheek. "It's nice to see you. I take it this is the infamous Katy I've been hearing so much about?"

Julian crouched down next to the girl. "Katy, this is Michael. He is a very good friend of mine."

"Nice to meet you, Michael," she said, holding out her hand. Michael took it and gave it a little shake.

"Nice to meet you too. She's got lovely manners."

Bea nodded. "She's a quick study."

Katy spun around and ran across the room, jumping up on the couch. "Wanna see what I learned?"

"Do you think you should jump on the furniture?" Julian said, looking at Bea.

"Just this once. It's worth it. I promise."

"All right. Show me what you can do."

Katy turned around and faced the back of the couch, then bounced and jumped backward, doing a flip off the couch with a perfect landing.

Julian clapped. "Wow, that was magnificent. You were born to do this stuff."

"And that's not all," Bea said with a mischievous grin. She nodded at Katy.

"Are you sure?" Katy whispered loudly across the room to Bea.

"Show him what you've got."

Katy bit her lip, but walked up to Julian and blinked wide eyes at him. "You remember how you said I could have everything I wanted?"

"I do."

"I would like a dog."

"Oh really? I'm not thrilled with the idea of having animals in the house."

"But you said I could have anything and saying no would mean you would go back on your word and you would never do that. I know you wouldn't."

Julian's eyes lifted to Bea. "Did you coach her in this?"

"Not at all. She used what she's learned and came up with it all on her own."

Julian sighed. "Very well done, but here's another lesson for you. Guilt is a great way to engineer the outcome you're after, but it's not always the best way. In fact, guilt often has negative side effects. Even if you get what you want, you may alienate the person you're shaming. That's okay when you're in a tight spot, but the best way is to instill a desire in the other person to want to give you what you're asking for. Or better yet, make them think it was their idea. Isn't that right, Michael?"

"It works marvelously," he said with a wink.

Katy frowned, but then her eyes got a sparkle, and one side of her mouth lifted. "You're so smart. That makes a lot of sense. I will take that into consideration."

"Such big words. Did they teach you that in school?"

"I learn a lot in school, but I learn so much more from you. I thought if I had a dog I could learn a lot by training him so I could show you how clever I was. I may never influence your decisions, but I wanted to show you how well I could train a dog. I don't need one. You teach me more than enough."

Julian laughed and clapped his hands together. "Bravo, young lady. You are a quick study. I will give your request a great deal of consideration. You are a remarkable girl, Katy."

"Thank you, Uncle Julian."

"I've got an important meeting I'm going to be late for, but it has been an absolute pleasure."

Julian gave Katy a squeeze on the shoulder, then he led Michael back to the main part of the house.

"That was a sight to behold," Michael said when they reached the front door.

"I did not expect that. She has come a long way in a short period of time."

"I take it Eva hasn't met her yet?"

"No, Eva doesn't know she exists and I'll keep it that way until I'm able to explain what Katy is doing here. I haven't got the time or inclination to play around with half-truths right now. But the time will come."

Michael put a hand on Julian's shoulder. "I am truly happy for you. You've worked so hard over the years and I'm pleased to see how well things are going. No one deserves it more."

"That's kind of you, Michael. And I'm lucky to have someone like you to help me along the way. But for now, we both have work to do. I'll be in touch."

The two men shook, and Julian waited until his car was out of sight before he went to find Eva. When he entered the library, she was looking through a bookshelf.

"Hope you have more luck than I did at your place."

"There's a lot to choose from. What kind of books did I used to read?"

"I haven't got a clue, but I'm pleased you seem to be feeling better."

"Much." She took a book from the shelf and looked at it. "Thank you for dragging me out of my room."

"Sometimes parents do know what's best for their kids." He walked closer. "You enjoyed Michael's company?"

"I did. He was charming and respectful. It was a nice combination."

"I'm glad you felt at ease with him. There haven't been many who you've been able to settle with."

"I imagine it's part of his PR training, knowing how to handle a person. I guess you get good at manipulating a situation for your benefit."

Julian lifted his chin. "If I didn't know him so well, I'd be inclined to agree with you. However—"

"It was a joke, Dad. He appeared to be very genuine to me."

"Ah, right. I'm unprepared for your sarcasm, I guess." He chuckled. "I'll get used to it again once I'm not worried about you. You always were very witty."

"Was I?"

"Actually, no. You were more serious than you are now."

Eva laughed. "Let's hope it sticks around. If I ever

get my memory back, I will attempt to maintain my wit just for you."

"I believe you would. I don't think your memory would change things, though. You are exactly the person you should be, memories or not. Now, if you're happy to occupy yourself, I have some things I need to see to."

"Your gift from Tyler?"

"Yes."

"What'd he get you?"

"A token to remind me of the past. You wouldn't be interested—sorry, that came out wrong."

"No. You're right. If it's connected to the past, then there's no reason for me to get involved."

Julian scrunched up his face in an awkward cringe, the sole purpose of which was to endear himself to her and give him the opportunity to change the subject. It worked.

Eva laughed. "Stop it, Dad. Don't feel bad. You don't have to walk on eggshells with me."

"I know. So now that you're out of your room, you should explore the house and grounds. One wing is locked due to ongoing renovations, but the rest of the place is open for your exploration."

"Will we have dinner together?"

"If that's what you want, I would love that."

"Great, I'll see you at dinner."

"I look forward to it."

"Oh, one other thing. Is there a computer I could get onto?"

"Anything in particular you're looking for?"

"Just research. I wanted to see what's going on in the world. See if there're any gaps that Google can fill."

"You remember Google?"

She shrugged. "I guess so."

Julian smiled. He'd mention to Tyler that they would need to do a history search on the computer. "There is a computer in the room to your right. There's no password. All you have to do is turn it on."

"Great. I'll see you at dinner."

# Chapter 23

BEN TIPPED his head from one side to the other, cracking his neck as Julian entered the room. Tyler followed behind and stood to the side.

It surprised Ben how calm he'd felt since Tyler took him. God had given him the courage to remain confident and to remember not to trust in himself. It was more than he would have ever asked for. This was a moment he had been terrified of for so long, but now that he was here, even though he had no idea what would happen, he was able to trust completely in whatever plan God had. Even if that meant death.

Julian paced slowly in front of him in an attempt to be intimidating. He stopped, looked at Ben with a wicked grin, then continued his stride. All Ben could see was a sad, defenseless man who squandered his time in a fruitless attempt to rule. The world would never be his. His whole life was a waste.

"Ben Waite." Julian stopped again. The devious

smile widened. "When I discovered you were still alive, I was overcome with so many emotions."

"They've got pills for that." Ben's face was deadpan.

"Using humor to cope with your imminent pain. Clever, I suppose. But what I find more impressive is how you are still breathing. You're going to have to tell me how you carried off such an amazing feat."

"Breathing? It's down to the diaphragm, really. I can't take much credit. I do it without thinking most of the time."

"Funny."

"Why thank you."

"No one survived that explosion. How did you?"

"Oh that? That was a miracle."

"That's what you're going to go with?"

"That's what it was."

"Lucky guy."

Ben sighed. "That's not how miracles work."

"Maybe not, but it looks like you're short on them today."

"What makes you say that?"

Julian took a step sideways and leaned down to get a clear view of the rope that secured Ben to the chair. "You are tied to a chair."

"I am."

"And Tyler said you came with him without giving him too much hassle."

"He asked nicely. I was being polite."

"Is that so? Or is it that you expect someone to come and rescue you?"

Ben shrugged. "Anything is possible." He didn't

know what to expect. He was prepared for the torture and death, but he couldn't put the impossible past God. And that's what it would have to be. There was no way out of here otherwise.

"Then perhaps you would like to inform me who your associates are?"

"I've been holed up in that cabin that Tyler and his guys riddled with bullet holes—thanks for that, by the way, Tyler. That's going to take me months to fix—I don't work for anyone."

"Okay then, let me rephrase. Who were you working for when you blew up my facility?"

Ben scrunched his mouth up to the side in thought. "Hmm. Let me think. Oh, that's right, I was working for you. Not a bad job until I found out what I was actually doing."

"That's not the right answer."

"I'm sorry. I didn't realize you wanted me to lie. Is there anyone in particular that you'd like me to implicate? Or should I pick someone at random?"

"You risked your life to destroy my facility for no one but yourself? Not likely."

"Maybe not likely, but if you want the truth, that's the only one I've got. I found out you were stealing kids and brainwashing them, and I thought to myself, *Ben, this isn't really your cup of tea.* Then I did something about it."

"And you never told anyone?"

"Silly, I know. But anyone who is aware of what a sick villain you are did not hear it from me. What about Eva? Does she know what you're doing? I've heard she's having trouble remembering anything at the moment. Have you told her yet?"

"Ah yes. Eva. Talk about a miracle. Thank you for rescuing her, by the way."

"Tyler's already given me your gratitude. I don't need it twice."

"I'm so relieved to have her home. And having her memory gone means I don't have to kill her again."

"You've killed her once already, have you? Because she was alive when I found her." Ben was enjoying this. It had been a long time since he'd had the boldness to banter, but today was the perfect time for it to be restored. He'd always been calm like this when he was in the special forces. It helped the guys under his command. It kept them relaxed but focused, and it was doing the same for him now.

"She did survive her episode in the river, yes. A win for us in the end."

"Seems to follow you around, though, doesn't it? All the people you want dead won't die."

"That just brings another level of satisfaction, though, doesn't it? You didn't die in that bomb blast, and now I get to kill you myself. Eva didn't die in the river, so now she doesn't have to die at all. In the end, I keep winning."

"Things do appear that way, don't they?"

"They don't just appear that way, Ben. That is how things are. And I'm concerned you will die never fully accepting that."

"Does that bother you?"

"In a way. I pity you. It's depressing that someone of your caliber will die not reaching his full potential."

"But you're still enjoying this?"

"I am, yes."

"Good. I'd hate to know you're completely disappointed in me. There was a time when I looked up to you."

"Is that true?"

"It is. I thought you stood for all the good things I wanted to see in my lifetime."

"I do represent those things. Your problem is that you're too soft. You're not willing to do what's required to see the outcomes you say you want so much."

"No. The outcomes you and I want are very different."

Julian leaned close. "I don't think they're as different as you hope they are. I think the thing that scared you in the end was how alike we really are."

Ben burst out laughing. It was forced, but that was the point. "You really do make the perfect villain. Did you go to school for that? Do they teach you those lines? Or do you pick up that sort of thing in the movies?"

"I have another question for you, if you don't mind."

"Shoot."

"It's a little thing, really, but I find it quite a conundrum."

"Don't leave me in suspense."

"Why'd you save her?"

"Wasn't doing anything else that day."

Julian sighed and looked up at the ceiling. "You really are having a good time with this."

"Your hospitality goes above and beyond."

"Perhaps, but it's incredibly time-consuming and I am a very busy man. Tyler, would you mind?"

"Pleasure, sir." Tyler pushed off the wall and strutted over to Ben, punching him in the face and then in the stomach.

"Thank you. Now, Ben, hopefully that sobered you up a bit. I'd appreciate you be straight with me from here on out."

It took Ben a second to get his breath back. "I'm not sure what to say."

"I only want the truth."

"I rescued Eva because she needed rescuing. And I blew up your facility because it needed blowing up."

"You can blame no one but yourself for this. Tyler?"

Tyler attacked with relish. He hit Ben with mostly body blows and was panting for breath when Julian put a hand up to tell him to stop.

"Don't overdo it. I'm not done with him yet." Julian stood in front of Ben, his arms crossed. "You're making this harder than it needs to be. If you would come clean, I can put you out of your misery quickly."

Ben heard the words Julian spoke, but it took him a minute to make sense of them. His mind was cloudy, and he struggled to lift his head. But when his eyes met Julian's, he smiled.

Julian's lips pressed together in agitation. "If you don't share your motivation for saving Eva, I can only assume that you intended to use her against me."

Ben blinked away the fog before responding. "You think too much of me," he grunted. "I'm not that organized."

"I'll tell you what. I'll make you an offer you won't be able to refuse."

"I doubt it."

Julian chuckled. "You put on a brave face, but you destroyed my facility in order to save a bunch of nameless kids."

"They're not nameless to the people who care about them."

"That's sweet. Well, with that in mind, today there are another bunch of kids who all have names and parents who love them. They will attend story time at a public library not too far from here. What they don't know is that I have organized for a gentleman named Ray to enter the library while they are all sitting down to hear a story. He's going to blow up the building with them in it."

Ben knew Julian wouldn't bother bluffing about something like that. "Why?"

"I've got my reasons. My point is, if you tell me what I want to know, I won't do it."

Ben laughed. It hurt his chest.

"That's funny, is it?"

"You're such a joker."

"You think I'm lying?"

"It doesn't really matter because even if you're telling the truth, you'll do it again another time. In the meantime, you've killed me and I won't be able to stop it a second time."

"You say that like you can stop me now."

"Stranger things have happened."

"Ben, you may have survived that blast, but it damaged your brain."

"Then kill me now. I'm not going to tell you anything you want to hear."

"What is it you think I want to hear?"

"That I told the entire army about what you're doing. And I kidnapped Eva in order to torture her and make you suffer."

"That sounds closer to the truth."

"Well, it's not. So kill me."

"I'm a patient man, and I will put in as much time as is necessary in order to force you to tell me the truth."

"If that's what you want." *God, I'm going to need your help to endure this.*

Ben may have been trained to withstand torture, but that was a long time ago, and every man had a breaking point. He hoped his was death. It wasn't because he had anything important to give away to Julian. He wasn't lying about that. When he had survived the explosion, he did nothing but run and hide like a coward. He had convinced himself that no one would believe him and that Julian had people everywhere. But that didn't mean he wouldn't cave and say what Julian wanted to hear. And that could put people in danger.

But if he could die without giving Julian anything, he could plant a seed of paranoia that maybe God could use into the future. If this was the last assignment God gave him, then he welcomed it. It was an opportunity to die with honor. It was more than he deserved.

Eva made herself comfortable at the table against the wall in a small study and booted up the computer.

After opening up the search engine, she glanced up at the door before typing:

*If I make my bed in Sheol, behold, You are there.*

The results brought up the scripture that surrounded those words and Eva read them aloud.

"If I ascend to heaven, you are there; If I make my bed in Sheol, behold, you are there. If I take up the wings of the dawn, if I dwell in the remotest part of the sea, even there your hand will lead me, and your right hand will take hold of me." A flutter erupted in her chest and she felt light-headed. No memories accompanied the flood of emotion, but the feeling was familiar. This verse had caused the same feelings somewhere in her past. It was a sort of euphoria that gave her a fullness in her being.

After pushing back from the table, she closed her eyes, enjoying the freedom from everything she'd endured.

The scripture meant something to her. Did that mean that God meant something to her?

"God, if you're real," she whispered, "you have to help me with my memory here. Please. I want this memory back."

An image appeared behind her eyes. She saw a woman about forty who looked concerned. "We're running out of time." The woman's voice echoed in her mind. "They're already way ahead of us."

He own words formed from the past conversation. "But those who are for us are more than those who are against us."

A man yelled in pain, and Eva's eyes sprang open. They echoed through the thoughts she'd been having, but her reaction was separate from the vision she'd had. It was as though she'd heard the sound while sleeping, but it woke her up straining to hear it again.

The house was silent.

She blinked, then turned off the computer and walked into the foyer where she paused, listening.

*It's time to go.* The thought threaded through her mind.

"Time to go where?"

*You need to find him.*

"Find who?" She pressed the heels of her hands against her temples. "I think I'm losing my mind."

Another sound, faint, reverberated in the distance. She couldn't tell what it was. It could have been an animal or someone calling out somewhere off in the distance.

"Can I help you with something?"

Eva jumped. "Donald." She pressed a hand to her head and closed her eyes. "You scared me."

"My apologies. That was not my intention."

"No, I know. I thought I heard a noise."

"What kind of noise?"

"I don't know. It almost sounded like someone crying out in pain."

"This house is old and very large. I imagine there would be many noises that can sound…unusual."

"Like a man calling out?"

"Yes. I'm sorry I can't help you. But again, houses make strange noises that can be mistaken for other sounds. Like shadows that look like monsters in the night."

"You didn't hear anything?"

"No, but my hearing isn't what it used to be."

"I'm sure it's nothing. Just the house, like you said."

"Is there anything else I can help you with?"

"Do you know where my dad is?"

"I'm afraid I don't. Would you like me to find him for you?"

"No, that's okay. I'll see him at dinner."

"Very well."

Donald clasped his hands behind his back, but didn't move.

She couldn't escape the feeling that she'd done something wrong. "He suggested I explore the house in order to get familiar with it."

"Indeed."

"I think I'll have a look around."

"Very well."

# Chapter 24

EVA WENT THROUGH THE HOUSE, checking every door that would open. She found a large door leading into what she assumed was the wing her dad had mentioned. It was locked, along with another room off the foyer.

She tiptoed around, waiting for another sound she could identify, but the house was silent. It must have been in her head.

She went up the stairs to return to her room, but when she got to the second floor, the idea of spending the rest of the day on her bed was a suffocating prospect.

The sun had lifted her spirits earlier, so she trotted back down the stairs where Donald was still standing.

"I was thinking of going outside," she said as though asking his permission.

"Very well."

She gave a curt nod, unsure if there was anything

else that was required of her, but Donald wasn't even looking at her anymore.

Outside, she followed the gardens that hugged the edge of the house and went around to the backyard past the pool.

The sun was hot, and the sparkling blue water looked inviting. She dipped a toe in and found the water icy cold. Too cold for her.

As she continued her trek, a gap in the garden alerted her to the door camouflaged in the wall. It wasn't hidden, but if she hadn't been paying attention and focusing on the surrounding details, she could have missed it.

The door had no handle, and when she pushed on it, it didn't give, but she noticed a box halfway up the side of the doorframe. When she lifted the panel, she found a keypad lock. She studied it, wondering if she knew the combination after growing up here.

It would be a harmless thing to try a random number and see if her muscle memory knew the code. Her mouth curled up in a grin. Not very adventurous to gain access to what she guessed was a storage room, but it was oddly entertaining and more interesting right now than reading a book. She lifted her arm and allowed her fingers to dance across the terminal.

After pushing numbers at random, a light blinked red. She squinted at it, focusing her thoughts, but that only made her mind blanker. She tried again, but still got the red light.

Her fingers moved to the crease along the doorframe.

If she could get in, she would bring something that was stored there and show it to Julian at dinner. She'd set it on the table without saying a word. It was a stupid amusement, but she was enjoying having a family who cared for her. And she was sure Julian would get a kick out of it.

With renewed determination, she went back to the buttons and closed her eyes. After taking a deep breath, she let it out slowly while her finger drifted. She let them slide across the numbers without overthinking.

With her eyes still closed, her fingers depressed wherever they pleased. The door clicked and when her eyes opened, she saw the green light.

Laugher burst from her in triumph. "I can't believe that worked."

A lip had appeared at the edge of the door that previously had been flush with the wall. She pushed on it, shoving it open.

Inside, a staircase led down. It was lit by a soft, red glow. She could see to the bottom of the stairs, but then it turned a corner.

"Wine cellar?"

On the inside of the door was a handle. She held the handle and let the door close softly so it didn't click closed, then she crept down the stairs. Voices drifted from somewhere inside, but they were muffled.

At the bottom step, Eva stopped. It was ridiculous, but she felt Donald's disapproving gaze on her. Julian had put no restrictions on her wanderings. He'd encouraged her to explore anywhere she wanted except for the wing that was being renovated. He wouldn't have expected her to get down here, but if it was off-limits, he could have said.

She straightened her shoulders. If she was in the wrong, she'd apologize. It's not like anything untoward was going on that she would be forbidden from seeing. Maybe her dad was down here selecting what wine he wanted to serve at dinner.

Her foot planted on the floor at the bottom of the stairs and she didn't hesitate to continue, turning the corner and walking down the long corridor.

Someone was talking again. It was still muffled, but she thought now that it sounded like her dad. She just couldn't tell what he was saying.

When she turned another corner, she screamed and jumped back when she found a gun pointed close to her head.

Her hands shot up toward the ceiling. "Don't shoot," she said to Tyler, who kept the gun pointed in her face.

She didn't move, but looked past him to where Julian stood with his hands on his hips, in front of a man tied to a chair. She gasped when she realized the man was Ben. "What's going on?"

"Tyler," Julian said. "Lower the gun. I'd rather you didn't shoot my daughter."

Tyler did as he was commanded, but kept the gun in his hand and an eye on her.

Eva lowered her arms and waited for her legs to give out, but they remained strong. She looked at Ben. His face was bloody, but she knew it was him.

"Eva," Ben said softly. "It's good to see you again."

She walked slowly into the room. "Why do you have Ben tied up? Is this the *gift* that Tyler got you?"

"It's complicated," Julian said. "How'd you get down here?" His face was unreadable, but his voice was calm.

"I found the door outside as I was taking a walk around the house. I thought I'd try punching in whatever numbers came to me."

"That's all you did? Just punched in a bunch of random numbers and you got it right?"

"I had to clear my mind first, but yes. I thought it was storage. Obviously, I was wrong."

"That's incredible. And you don't remember being down here on any previous occasions?"

"No. I take it I have been?"

"It's just like your training. It's still in there." Julian bit his lip and looked like he was considering what to say next. "Your reaction to walking in on our interrogation is surprising."

"Interrogation? Of the man who saved my life?"

"But you're not horrified to see him tied up like this? I would have expected you to run away. It's encouraging that you aren't affected by it in that way."

"I may not have run away, but I am upset. Why would you do this to the man who I told you had rescued me? You need to let him go."

Julian was unfazed by her concern. "I don't blame you for believing that he saved you."

"I was there. He saved my life. I don't know what it is you think he's done."

"He did rescue you, and for that I am grateful to

him. I've even told him that. But it's his other motivations that I'm concerned about."

"What other motivations?"

"The reason he saved you in the first place."

She looked at Ben. She had wondered the same thing herself, but obviously wasn't as skeptical about his intentions as her father.

"Did he tell you why he saved me?" she asked.

"He's given me a couple variations."

"And what are they?"

"He said you needed rescuing, but he also said he wanted to kidnap and torture you in order to make me suffer."

She stiffened. "But he brought me to the FBI once I was free."

"Only because he had no choice. They arrived before he could get you out of there. He had to hand you over or be hunted down."

She looked at Ben. "Is that true?"

Ben smiled at Julian. "You must be enjoying this."

"Answer my question," Eva said.

"It's true that I said that, yes."

"But why?"

Julian shifted on his feet. "Why don't you tell Eva how you used to work for the Underwood Foundation? *My* foundation."

"You used to work for my dad? You didn't tell me that."

"That's why I was upset to see your tattoo."

Eva looked at her wrist. "This has nothing to do with him."

Ben looked at Julian. "Would you like to tell her, or should I?"

"He has a rather dangerous delusion," Julian said. "About me and everything I stand for. He worked for me for a time and was very good at what he did. But we had a misunderstanding, and that has caused a rift I have been unable to rectify. I'd like to understand what's going on inside his head, but he's not being cooperative."

"Is that true?" she asked Ben, stepping closer to him. The way he angled his head sparked something in her memory. But she couldn't place it.

"He must have found out that you were in town," Julian said. "Decided to kidnap you from the Palmers for himself. He's already destroyed extensive property that I owned, killing some of my employees in the process. Torturing my daughter is a logical next step."

"You murdered people because you don't like my dad?"

Ben opened his mouth to respond, but then closed it again before finally saying, "Yes."

"Just to destroy his property?"

"I blew up a facility he owned, yes."

"Why?"

"That's what I'd like to know," Julian said, stepping back. He leaned against a table and crossed his arms.

"To stop your father," Ben said.

"To stop my father from what?"

He closed his eyes. It was obvious he was in pain. "It doesn't matter."

She took another step closer. "Oh, I think it does matter."

Ben opened his eyes and looked directly into hers. His deep-blue eyes seemed to plead with her to understand. She had another shock of what felt like a memory, but she still couldn't identify it.

"Ask your dad what your tattoo means," Ben said.

"This," Eva said, holding up her arm. "This tattoo that you're so afraid of?"

"Tell her what it means, Julian."

"You're changing the subject," Eva said.

"Same subject. Ask him."

"You're a trained professional. I can only presume that you're using tactics to turn the attention away from you in order to avoid the truth that my father is right about you. You were trying to kidnap me. You worked for my dad and you knew who I was. Maybe you even know the truth about the tattoo and you used my loss of memory to manipulate me into thinking this tattoo was related to my family. But it won't work. We're not here to talk about me. We're here to talk about you."

"That's my girl," Julian said under his breath. "Keep pushing."

She was energized. The feeling of control. Making a man break. She knew this. This is what she was made for, and she was dizzy swimming in a lust for it. "Maybe you wanted to kidnap me so you could send me home to my father, piece by piece."

"You always were the best interrogator," Julian said. "Bravo. You still have it."

It was the first time she'd felt comfortable in her own

skin. She had been pretending before, but this was her. This is where she'd come from. This is what she knew.

She turned her head and saw a knife sitting on a nearby table. When she picked it up, Tyler lifted his gun. Julian put his hand up and he dropped it again. After tucking his gun away, he stepped back into the shadows.

Julian grinned. "Shall I leave it with you, daughter?"

"What information do we need from him?"

"I'd like to find out if he is working with anyone now, or did back then. And whether anyone is planning anything further."

She circled around behind Ben and stopped. Her brow pushed together. She looked up at Julian, who gave her a sharp nod of encouragement.

Her step faltered for a moment as she moved again. She'd been here before. Not as a memory of things she'd done in the past, but in this actual moment. She had been afraid and desperate.

She continued around until she stood in front of him again. She looked into his deep-blue eyes.

"You don't know what you're doing," Ben said.

If she hadn't fully given in to the desire that had arisen inside of her, her face would have registered the shock as she realized where she was.

# Chapter 25

EVA SWALLOWED BACK HER PANIC. This was her nightmare. It was the fever dream she had when she was sick at the Palmers. She had thought back then that it was a memory of some horrible thing she'd done. But it was a vision of what was yet to come, and she'd just experienced the same thrill that had sickened her in the dream.

She glanced down at the knife in her hand. Her fingers flexed around it. It was the same.

"Make him pay," Julian said. "He was ready to hurt you. He wanted to."

She lifted the knife and her muscles tightened as they had in her dream. She knew where to cut a man to make him bleed but not die immediately. This was the moment before she'd ripped from her sleep in horror, but she wouldn't wake from it this time.

"That's my girl," Julian said. "Make him afraid."

She glanced up at the knife. There was no turning back. She had no options left but to move forward.

She plunged the knife toward Ben, but at the last moment, she twisted around behind him and cut his bonds. She didn't think about her next move, just dove toward Tyler, who was pulling his gun. Her body slammed against his arm and the gun fell from his hand as she smashed it against the wall.

He swung his fist to catch her in the ribs, but her elbow dropped to block it. He went in again. This time his fist connected and he knocked all the breath out of her. He grabbed her head, intending to slam it down onto his knee. But before he could, Eva threw her arms up and knocked his away, then threw her head up and caught him under his chin. The force shoved his head back, and it connected hard with the wall behind him. When he slumped to the ground, she lunged for the gun and pointed it at Tyler until she could confirm he was unconscious. Then she turned toward her father.

---

It only took Ben a fraction of a second to recognize that Eva had cut him free. He didn't dwell on it when she threw herself at Tyler. He jumped from the chair to go for Julian, pushing aside the pain and ignoring the change in blood pressure that threatened to make him pass out or throw up. He couldn't afford either option. He had to maintain control if he was going to stop Julian, and he didn't have the time to equalize. With his vision dimming, he brought his elbow up as he leaped for Julian with enough force that the impact sent him to the floor.

A gun poked out of Julian's jacket and Ben snatched it, pointing it at him as he stumbled backward. "Don't move." He took deep, slow breaths to clear his head, using all of his energy to hold the gun steady.

"Don't," Eva said from across the room. Ben turned to her and saw she had a gun pointed at him.

"Eva. What are you doing?"

"Don't kill him."

"Eva," Julian said. "I'm sorry. It was too much for you, but Ben's the enemy here, not me." Eva's face scrunched up in uncertainty. "Take the gun from him so we can sit down and talk about this. We don't even have to tie him up again, if you're not ready for that."

Ben kept his gun aimed at Julian, but he kept a close eye on Eva. "Don't listen to him," he said. "You take the gun from me and he'll kill me then probably you."

"He's lying. He's a madman," Julian said. "He's dangerous and you need to get that gun from him. Otherwise he'll kill me and you'll never forgive yourself."

Eva pressed the heel of her hand against her temple. It was clear she was confused. If Ben didn't do something fast, he might lose her. Moments ago her eyes were full of confidence and strength. Now she looked like a scared little girl, just like when he'd rescued her from the Palmers.

He lowered the gun a fraction and stood slowly. "Eva, why did you cut my rope?"

"I don't know."

"I think you do."

Julian spoke. "You don't have to answer his questions. Get the gun from him and then we'll take some time to talk through this—"

"Stop," Eva said. "You wanted me to hurt him. To kill him. And I guess there was a time when I would have, but today…I just knew I couldn't. I can't be that person anymore. I won't let it happen."

Ben could shoot Julian. Eva was in a haze of confusion, and it wouldn't be difficult to pull the trigger on Julian and then disarm her. But it wasn't right. She needed to be protected, and that would do the opposite. He also couldn't ignore the warning he felt in his spirit that he had to leave both Julian and Tyler alive.

"Eva, we need to go. I can get you out of here."

"Don't do it." Julian shifted on the ground. "Don't leave me. You can't go with him. He'll use you against me. He doesn't care about you. He only hates me."

"Eva, look at me." She did. "We need to get out of here. You're not safe. Your dad is not who he pretends to be."

"Why did you save me?" Eva said. "I want the truth. Was it really to hurt my dad?"

"It's complicated."

"I told you," Julian said.

"So Dad was right? I just saved the man who wanted to torture me to hurt him?"

"No. That's not what's complicated."

"But you admitted you said those exact words."

"I did. I said that because I knew that was what Julian wanted to hear, but I didn't mean it. My only purpose was to get you safely out of that house. I didn't have a plan beyond that."

"You don't just save someone because they need saving. You ran away from me at the store and then you came back. Why?"

Ben let out a heavy breath and looked at Julian. "I don't have time to explain. You cut me free, so let me go. You don't have to come with me, but I am telling you, you're not safe here."

"Careful, Eva," Julian said. "If you go with him, you're leaving with the enemy. Let him go if you have to, but don't leave me. Please. You're all I have."

Ben scrubbed a hand down his face. They didn't have time for this stalemate, and he couldn't compete with Julian's influence. Tyler would wake up soon and complicate everything.

"I had hoped that the reason you cut me free was because you trusted me. Or at the very least, that you remembered who your father is."

"I can't remember anything."

"Then we're going to keep going around in circles. I can't explain why I rescued you and you can't explain why you cut me free."

"I dreamed about it."

"What?" both Ben and Julian said at the same time.

"Wait," Ben said. "You dreamed about this. About me being here tied up."

"Yes. I didn't remember at first."

"And in your dream, you cut me free?"

Eva's lips pinched closed. "No. But I didn't have control then. I have control now."

Ben sent a silent prayer up to heaven. They were running out of time. Someone was going to die soon.

*Psalm 139.*

The scripture reference sprang to his mind, and he was ready to try anything, even if he was making it up. He was desperate.

"Psalm 139?" he said quickly.

"What?" Eva paled.

"Psalm 139. 'If I go up to the heavens, you are there.'"

Julian cursed under his breath. "Eva, this is your last chance. He'll kill you."

She stared at Ben. "If I make my bed in Sheol, behold, You are there."

"Eva," Julian threatened.

She lifted her gun to point it at Julian. "Stop talking." She looked back at Ben. "How do you know that verse?"

"I know a lot of verses."

"But why choose that one?"

Here goes nothing. "God told me. Just like he told me to rescue you."

Eva winced in indecision. "I don't know what to do."

"Anything is better than staying in Julian's house. But we need to go now. You're going to have to trust me."

"But I don't."

"Then pretend."

Eva frowned. "I don't have any other choice, do I?"

"Of course you do," Julian said. "I've protected you and cared for you."

Eva shook her head and tucked the gun into the back of her pants.

"Eva, don't do this to me. Not again," Julian growled.

Ben stepped over and knocked him across the head with the gun. Eva clamped her hands over the scream that erupted from her mouth.

"He's not dead," Ben said. "But we couldn't have him following us out. Let's go."

Once they were outside, Ben scanned the area. "You don't happen to know the best way out of here?"

"I've only come in through the gate."

"Then I guess we're going to have to climb over it."

"There are security cameras."

"I'm more worried about making it down the driveway in one piece." They heard a voice yelling from down the stairs. "Sounds like Tyler woke up. We're going to have to run and pray." Ben grabbed her arm and pulled her toward the front of the house, but Eva stopped him.

"Wait." She turned and looked across the lawn at the high bushes. "There's a way through there."

"Are you sure?"

"I, uh, yeah. Yeah, I'm sure." She sprinted across the lawn and he had no choice but to follow.

Eva dropped to her knees when she reached the hedge and wriggled through the branches. She had an easier time getting through than he did. His adrenaline dulled most of the pain, but he had to drag his body through the thick branches that ripped at his bloody shirt.

Once they were concealed behind the bush, he shifted around to look back at the house. Tyler had just stumbled out of the door. After looking around, he staggered toward the front of the house with his phone pressed against his ear. Ben could see blood coating the back of his head.

"Here," Eva said, unlatching a small door and pushing it open.

Ben judged the opening to be big enough to fit, but once he got his head through, he had to squeeze his shoulders and almost got stuck. Pain shot down through his legs and he groaned. Eva grabbed him by the armpits and helped to pull him out.

"You're hurt. Is it bad?" she asked once they were both through.

Ben sat in the scraggly underbrush where they were hidden by a copse of trees that opened onto a park. He closed his eyes to wait for the pain to dull. "I don't think anything is broken, but I'm pretty sore."

Eva had been standing, but she dropped down to sit next to him while he recovered some strength. "I didn't make a mistake, did I? My poor dad. I know what he did to you was wrong, but—"

"No. Don't feel bad for Julian. He's not who you think he is."

"Everyone has their breaking point. Even Clara. She truly looked after me until she was scared and then she made a bad choice."

"You believe Clara actually cared about you, fine. Maybe she did. But that's not your father. Julian uses his kindness to manipulate people. All he wanted to do was control you. I'm sorry to have to tell you this, but he is a very bad man. That's why I was afraid when I saw your tattoo."

"But it doesn't have anything to do with my dad. It was the group I was involved with after."

"What group?"

"I have no idea. I thought you would know."

"That tattoo is connected to the Underwood Foundation. If Julian told you differently, he was lying. It's the mark that those who are truly loyal give to themselves to show their devotion."

"Give to themselves?"

"Yes. You do it to yourself."

"But I didn't see it on anyone else."

"Not everyone has it on their wrist."

"Do you have one?"

"No. I didn't get that far. I wouldn't have. I've given my life to Jesus, not a cause."

Eva sucked her bottom lip into her mouth and closed her eyes. "I wanted to hurt you."

"None of us is above temptation."

"Temptation? How can you call it that?"

"Because that's what it was. Extreme, maybe. But you didn't give in to it. You made the right choice in the end."

"I can't think about this right now."

"Then don't."

"But what do we do? Where do we go?"

"We'll find somewhere safe where you can process all of this, but there's something else we need to do first."

Eva looked suspicious. "What?"

"In order to get information out of me, Julian told me his plans."

"What plans?"

Ben hesitated. He couldn't be sure how she'd respond to the reality of what a terrible man her father really was. "To blow up a library. We need to stop it."

"A library? Why would he do that? Did he tell you why?" Ben looked at the ground and Eva stiffened. "What? He told you. What is it?"

"It will be filled with kids from local schools."

Eva stood. "No. That can't be true."

"I'm sorry, but that's the kind of man your father is."

"But why? What is he trying to accomplish?"

"He didn't say. I can only speculate, but Julian will do anything to see his vision come to life no matter what the cost."

"But this? You're sure?"

"I'm confident. Yes. I've seen firsthand what he's capable of. This is not beyond him."

"What if he was bluffing?"

"Julian's not one to bluff. Besides, we can't take that chance." He pushed up from the ground. The pain had subsided enough that he would ignore it. "We have to do everything we can to stop it."

"Okay. You're right. What library is it?"

"No idea. But there will be only one that has local schools visiting today. It shouldn't be too hard to discover."

Ben looked through the trees to the park beyond where a few people were walking their dogs. The street on the other side of the road was lined with brown-stones. "Any idea where we are?"

"No."

"All right, then we better start walking."

Eva grabbed his arm after he took a step. "You can't walk out there looking like that. And certainly not into a library. You'll need to clean yourself up or you'll draw unwanted attention."

Ben plucked at his stained shirt. "Good point." He watched her as she scanned the area. "Eva."

"Yeah?"

"Are you okay with this? It must be a lot to take in all at once."

"Almost everything that's happened since I lost my memory has been so…awkward. I've tried to embrace the simplicity of living a normal life, but this"—she swept her hands toward the park—"looking for the best possible route to remain undetected is what feels normal. Threatening you with a knife was normal. Being tied to a chair at the Palmers was normal." She frowned. "It's terrible. But stopping a bombing in a library also feels normal."

"Maybe, but he's still your father. And until a short time ago, he was a man you trusted."

"I can't think about that right now. Can we please just focus on saving those kids? We have work to do."

Ben knew from personal experience that allowing yourself to become absorbed in your work was the best way to push aside the things you couldn't deal with. But she couldn't escape it forever. He'd learned that from personal experience as well.

## Chapter 26

EVA AND BEN kept out of sight where they could. When it was impossible to remain concealed, Eva would scout ahead to get Ben through unnoticed.

"There's a gas station up the road," she said after returning from her reconnaissance. "But you'll have to cross the street."

Ben rubbed his hand down his shirt. "If we act naturally, we should get away with it. I won't be exposed for long."

"It's not just the shirt I'm worried about." She pulled off the buttoned blouse she'd been wearing over a tank top. "Sorry, you're not going to like this."

She spit on the sleeve and scrubbed at his face. Ben flinched when she hit the cut on his lip, but didn't complain.

"That was a first," he said when she finished. "How do I look?"

She stepped back and winced. "It'll have to do. We only have to make it across the street."

. . .

Ben kept his head down and waited behind the gas station while Eva got the key to the bathroom.

"You're going to need a new shirt. Clean your face properly and I'll be right back."

Ben had expected worse when he looked in the mirror. Eva had done a good job of getting most of the blood off and because Tyler's blows had been directed at his trunk, his face only carried a cut to his lip and a couple of bruises, but there was minimal swelling.

When Eva slipped back into the bathroom, she handed him a T-shirt. "I hope this fits."

"Did you nick it?"

"I forgot my purse. We can come back later once either of us has any money if it bothers you."

He held up the shirt. "Superman?"

"My options were limited. I don't know why you're complaining. It doesn't have blood on it, so it's an improvement."

He hung the shirt over her shoulder and pulled off his blood-soaked one.

"Whoa," Eva said, reaching out to touch a large purple bruise on Ben's ribs. "That looks bad."

Ben flinched when her fingers touched the skin. "It's nothing."

"You sure nothing's broken?"

"Yeah. I know what a broken rib feels like."

She moved to his other side, making note of the bruises that covered his torso. "Ben, this looks really painful."

"I told you, I'm fine."

"Doesn't it hurt?"

"Yeah." He grabbed the clean shirt from her shoulder. "But we've got more pressing matters." He pulled it over his head and tugged it carefully over his injured body. "I feel like an idiot," he said, yanking on the hem.

"Cheer up. You're about to save people. It's appropriate."

"I'm not trying to be a superhero. I'm trying to remain incognito."

"It stands out less than blood."

"Fine."

"Did my da—Did Julian give you an idea of when it would happen?"

"No. We could be too late."

"Or we might walk in right as the whole place goes up." She let out a shaky breath.

"Eva, I told you, you don't have to do this. I can go on my own."

"I'm not afraid to die."

"Then what is it?"

"You want to know what terrified me the most about losing my memory?"

"What?"

"While I was at the Palmers, I would get snippets of my past that hinted at this terrible person I used to be. I was scared to death of finding out who I truly was, or worse, becoming that person again. Julian convinced me it was only training and that I never used it to hurt anyone. But he lied. He had trained me for the specific purpose of hurting people. And now I know I am the person I feared the most."

"You can't know that for sure. You don't remember."

"I don't have to. Ben, I was ready to kill you. Being in that room with you tied to a chair and feeling the thrill—I wasn't scared, I was excited."

"But you saved me."

"If that had happened a year ago, I would have killed you and enjoyed it."

He put his hands on her arms. "I never met you when I worked for Julian, so I can't speak to who you were then, but that's not who you are now. You have to let go of that. Besides, you knew that scripture, remember?"

"I know one part of one scripture and that's supposed to prove something?"

"Eva—"

"Stop. Please. Don't try to fix it. I'm not running from it anymore. I'm tired of hiding and hoping it won't jump out and devour me. This is my chance to do the right thing while I still can. If I can help save those kids, then at least I have an opportunity to make up for all the bad things I've done. And if I die in the process, then it's no more than what I deserve."

"Saving those kids won't fix anything. It won't make you feel any better."

"Are you trying to make me feel worse?"

"What I mean is, that's not how you find freedom from your past. It won't work. You'll save those kids and then look for the next thing to do because it will never be enough."

"That's why I'm not afraid to die. But you have to promise me something."

Ben sighed. "What?"

"If we live through this, and my memory returns, and I become—" Her voice cut off, and she squeezed her eyes shut. "If I go back to the person I used to be, you have to promise me that you'll make sure I can never hurt another person."

"You won't turn back into that person."

"You don't know that. Please, Ben. Promise me you'll do whatever it takes to make sure I can't hurt anyone ever again."

He couldn't do it. Not what she wanted.

When he'd first discovered Eva's true identity, he thought he'd never forgive her. But Felix had been right. God had been right. Whoever she had been once, that was not the person she was created to be.

But if she ever got her memory back and *did* turn into the person she feared the most, he'd do everything in his power to remind her of who she was right now. Even if he died trying. "I'll do whatever it takes."

"Thank you."

———

Eva called it luck, but Ben knew it was God. On their way out, she had mentioned to the gas station attendant that she'd heard about one of the local libraries hosting schoolkids in the area. The man knew which one it was and it wasn't far.

The kids were still piling out of buses when they arrived.

"He won't blow it until everyone is inside," Ben said as they climbed the stairs, scanning everyone in the area. "We have time."

"We should split up," Eva said, joining him at the top of the steps. "Find anyone that looks suspicious."

She headed for the door, but Ben grabbed her arm, pulling her to a stop. "I'm not letting you do this on your own. We need to stay together."

"I know what I'm doing."

"You have skills you don't fully remember or understand."

"I don't need my memory for this. I defended myself against you at the store, if you recall."

"That's different."

"Why?"

"Because I could have taken you down if I'd wanted to. I was trying not to hurt you."

"I handled myself with Franky and he's bigger than you. And what about Tyler?"

"We're sticking together. We don't know what we're dealing with."

"You don't trust me."

"That's not the word I would use."

"What word would you use?"

He put his hands on his hips. "Eva."

"What word?"

"I'm trying to protect you."

"I don't need protecting. In fact, if you hadn't shown

up at the Palmers, I probably would have gotten out of there on my own."

"Don't do this. Why are you doing this?"

"What?"

"You're giving in to the anger. You're embracing it because you think it makes you stronger. But that's not who you are."

"You don't know who I am."

"Yes, I do. Now let's go. We don't have time to argue, and you're not leaving my side."

"Fine."

They walked into the main part of the library, where teachers were gathering with their students.

"It should be easy to spot the odd one out in here," Ben said.

"I don't see anyone. You?"

"No. Let's keep going."

They wandered around, checking in every room. After turning a corner, they almost ran into a woman with short curly hair and wide glasses. "Oh!" she said, almost dropping the pile of books she was carrying.

"Sorry," Ben said as they tried to dodge around her, but she shifted and cut them off.

"Can I help you find something?" she asked, hugging the books against her chest.

"No, we're new in town," Eva said, taking Ben's hand. "Newlyweds. We love books, so the first thing we wanted to do was check out the local library. It's busy in here."

The librarian hooted. "Busy is an understatement. It's a zoo in here this afternoon. Normally it's much quieter, but today we've got kids from five surrounding primary schools joining us."

"That's fantastic," Eva said.

The woman beamed. "Yes, it is. Now, the children will be confined to the kids' area back the way you came, so you can steer clear of that. Unless you're interested in the kid's area? Maybe dreaming of the future?"

The librarian was looking so expectant that Ben couldn't help himself. "We do want a lot of kids."

"We do?" Eva said.

"Yes. At least five."

"Wow," the librarian said. "That's wonderful. I look forward to having them visit with us one day…soon?"

"No," Eva said. "I'm not ready for kids yet. Certainly not five." She glared at Ben.

"Oh. Well, I guess you two have some things to discuss. Down there behind me, you'll find adult fiction. But if it's nonfiction you're after, you'll find those upstairs. We have several copies of *The Five Love Languages*. Also *Men Are from Mars. Woman Are from Venus*, if you think that will help."

"We don't read much science fiction," Eva said and Ben snorted.

"Okay. There are computers on all the floors if you need to use the internet or do a catalog search. Or one of us would be more than happy to help you find something."

"Is there a basement?" Ben asked.

"Sure is, but it's not open to the public. You won't find anything down there but dusty books in need of repair and a lot of old furniture. And we had a gas leak too."

Ben's eyebrows raised.

"Nothing to worry about," the librarian continued. "It was fixed, and we got the all clear, so you're safe up here."

"Right, thanks for your help. We'll make sure to check upstairs." Ben pulled Eva forward.

"Fantastic. Enjoy yourselves and don't be afraid to ask any questions."

"Thanks." He kept hold of Eva's hand as they walked away and hesitated to let go when they'd reached the end of a hall where the bathrooms were.

"I think we should check the basement," he said, finally releasing her hand.

"Five kids?"

"I couldn't help it. She was so excited about our future prospects. *You* could have been more excited."

"I wasn't prepared for your ruse."

"You started it, wifey."

"Whatever."

"Why are you so flustered?" He laughed, making it worse. The flush that travelled up her neck surprised him.

"We need to stay on topic. If I wanted to plant a bomb, you're right. The basement is where I'd do it. Should we tell someone? Should we evacuate the building?"

"I thought of that. The problem is, we don't really know what Julian's up to or how he's going to do it. What if we get everyone out and he sets something off outside? If we find the bomb downstairs, then we can get everyone out of here."

"Then let's go."

It didn't take them long to find the basement door. Ben looked up the hall to make sure the coast was clear. Before he opened the door, screaming erupted from back down the hall.

Ben and Eva looked at each other, then ran down the hall.

# Chapter 27

BEN PRESSED himself against the wall that led into the main kids' area, then quickly jutted his head around the corner to assess the situation.

"Is that our guy?" Eva asked.

"Looks like it."

"Only one?"

"Yeah."

"Shut up!" the man screamed at the room of students. The wailing stopped, but there was still scattered whimpering.

"Everybody sit down on the floor and cover your head with your hands."

"Why is he having them do that?" Eva whispered. "Why not blow the place up now?"

"Julian doesn't want just casualties. He's after more. I expected it."

"You!" the guy shouted at someone. "Call all the news stations."

"News stations?" The woman's voice wavered.

"Do you not speak English! Yes, the news stations! All the media. I want them here. Tell them if they don't get here soon, I'll blow the whole place up."

"So he's after publicity," Ben said, more to himself than Eva. "But why?"

"Does it matter? The important thing is that it gives us time to stop him. Any ideas? Or do we run out and jump him?"

Ben scooted around Eva and headed back up the hall toward the bathrooms.

"You need the toilet?" Eva asked as they entered the men's room.

"Nope." Ben pulled off his shirt and wrapped it around his elbow. "I need a better view."

He jammed his elbow into the mirror, cracking it.

"Your bruises look worse."

"Will you stop worrying about my injuries?" He levered out a small piece. "There. Now we can see what's going on. Hold that."

He handed Eva the mirror shard and put his shirt back on.

"The Superman shirt came in handy after all," she said.

"I didn't take you for one of those types who likes witty banter when their life is on the line."

Eva shrugged. "We haven't known each other that long."

Ben took the mirror from her. "If the shirt gave me x-ray vision, that would have been better."

. . .

Once they were back down the hall, Ben crouched down and reached his arm around the bottom part of the wall, angling the mirror so he could get a clear view of the man Julian had called Ray. He'd taken off his coat to expose the bomb that was wrapped around his chest.

Ben pulled the mirror back. "He's got the trigger in his hand, so we'll have to take him out before he has time to push the button."

"How do we do that?"

"King hit?"

"What?"

"If we knock him out in one hit, he won't have time to react."

"But that means we have to get close to him. How do we do that without being seen?" Ben's lips bunched together in a grimace. "You look like you have an idea, but I'm not going to like it."

"Well…You might like part of it."

"Tell me."

"How's that right hook of yours?"

"You want me to do the punching? I thought you were trying to protect me."

"I would do it myself, but I think he'd be less suspicious of a woman."

"I'm pretty sure he'd be wary of anyone who appeared from around the corner."

"Not necessarily."

***

Eva shoved Ben forward. "Get out there," Eva yelled.

"I'm going." Ben stumbled out into the open.

"I wish I had a gun," Eva mumbled. "He's not gonna buy it."

"He will. Trust me." Ben had his arms raised as they came around the corner.

"Who are you?" The bomber held the trigger out in front of him. "I'll blow it."

"Whoa, Ray," Eva said. "You can't blow that until I'm clear. That's the deal."

"Who are you?" Ray poised his finger over the button. "How do you know my name?"

Eva shoved Ben hard, and he turned to her. "You're enjoying this."

"Maybe a little. Go sit down." She turned to Ray. "Don't tell me they didn't tell you."

"Who didn't tell me what?"

"You really don't know who I am?"

"Should I?" His thumb settled to the side of the button.

"I'm Eva. Julian's daughter? He didn't tell you I would be here?"

"I didn't talk to Julian. I only talked to Michael."

Eva swallowed. "Michael Rosenbloom?"

"Yeah. He's a good friend of mine."

It shouldn't surprise her that Michael was involved, but she couldn't hide the shock. "I...I don't know why Michael wouldn't have mentioned it. I saw him earlier today."

"You did?"

"Yeah, we had brunch. He told me about you. I don't know how it could have slipped his mind."

"But why are you here? Michael explained everything to me. I know what I'm doing."

"I'm sure you do. But my dad sent me down here to see how things are going. This is your first time out, right?"

"Yeah."

"He wanted to make sure things went smoothly. Don't take it personally. He's a control freak like that."

"You can tell him I've got this. I've done everything Michael asked. Everything."

"That's great." She moved closer to him, nodding at the bomb vest. "Did you make that yourself?"

"Yeah." His back straightened. "Why?"

"It's good work."

"Thanks."

"You ever do this before? I don't mean the vest part. Obviously there's no coming back from this job, but have you blown anything up before?"

"Animals and stuff."

"Fertilizer bombs?"

"Yeah."

She nodded as she took another step. "Pipe bombs?"

"Yeah. I know a lot about this stuff. That's why Michael trusted me with such a big job."

"I can tell you know your stuff. Which trigger did you choose for this one? Looks like you have to push it?"

"Yeah, I do."

"Didn't want to go the other way? Where the bomb goes off when you release it?"

"I would have, but this was a last-minute thing. They

had someone else lined up, but Michael said they couldn't trust her like they trust me."

"Last minute? And you were ready to give up your life?"

"I choose to give my life for this. It is an honor. Besides, it was kind of my idea." His arm lowered a fraction. "Michael said Julian was impressed." He wasn't focused on the trigger anymore.

Eva took another step closer. "I bet he was. I know I'm impressed. I can tell you've got a head for this stuff." With one last step, she swung her arm hard. With her other hand, she made a grab for the trigger, protecting it as Ray fell.

Ben was beside her in a moment. "That was very well done. You have amazing reflexes."

"I tried not to think about it too much. Just let my muscles do their thing."

"But even that act you put on. He was completely disarmed. I would have gone in straight for the punch, but your way was better."

"Was it?"

"Yeah." Ben turned to the room. A few of the teachers had stood. Some were inching toward the door.

"I don't want anyone to panic," he said. "But please, move in an orderly fashion to the door. There are probably police out there by now, so exit with your arms raised and do whatever they tell you."

The librarian they'd bumped into earlier approached, but still kept her distance.

"Thank you so much, you two. Aren't we lucky you

moved into our town? Do you really think he would have blown us all up? Even with all these kids here?"

"There's no way to know for sure. Why don't you head out with the others?"

The librarian stretched out her neck to look at Ray, unconscious on the floor. "I should have known."

"You couldn't have," Eva said. "How could any of you have expected this to happen?"

"But when he came in from the gas company yesterday, shouldn't I have been able to tell something was wrong?"

"Gas company?" Ben said.

"Yes, the gas leak, remember? He was here yesterday to fix it. Or at least that's what he said. But I guess... Does that mean there wasn't one?"

Ben looked at Eva, then back at the librarian. "Can you make sure everyone gets out of here?"

"Sure." She nodded and hurried off to direct traffic, calling out for people to stop pushing.

"I'll go have a look," Ben said under his breath.

"I'll come too."

"No, you have to stay here with Ray. I don't know what to do with this vest, and we can't risk him waking up and setting it off."

"You're right. Just be careful."

Ben raced through the hall and down the basement stairs. He found a light switch on the wall and turned it on, but stopped when he saw what a huge space there was. A bomb could be anywhere.

Then he noticed all the dust. Scuff marks were visible along the floor. He followed them, but it took some backtracking. Ray must have changed his mind about where to set up the secondary bomb.

The trail ended in the back corner where a timer blinked with ninety seconds left. Ben took an involuntary step backward as his chest twisted. He thought he'd be ready to face anything, but a surge of fear incapacitated him as he stared at the descending numbers.

"This can't be happening." He wiped sweaty hands down his pants. "I can't do this again, God. I can't do this." He stood frozen until a thought pushed into his mind. Eva, among others, was still upstairs. If he didn't stop this, she would die too.

He pushed aside his stupor and knelt beside the weapon. As he looked at the wires, he rubbed his clammy hands together. He'd learned about creating and disarming bombs while in the special forces. With only three wires, this one should be simple, but it wasn't because all his knowledge was locked away by fear and it refused to surface. The most he could bring to mind was that he needed to pull the right wire. That meant they had a 33 percent chance of surviving.

"God, please."

Fourteen seconds.

He put his fingers on one wire, then another.

Ten seconds.

"God." His heart pounded loud in his ears.

Five…four…three…

He went back to the first wire and yanked, sucking in what could be his last breath.

The timer stopped on two. His head dropped, and a whimper escaped his throat.

"Thank you. Thankyouthankyouthankyou."

He stood on shaky legs and stared at the digital read-out. Then he thought of Julian, who would be watching and waiting. He had to get Eva out of there.

---

He found her arguing with a police officer.

"I'm not ready to go yet."

"Ma'am, that is a live bomb. We need to evacuate everyone before the bomb squad can proceed."

"Then you'll have—" She yanked her arm out of the officer's grasp when she saw Ben. "Hey. There you are."

"Sir, what are you doing still in the building? We need to evacuate everyone. Ma'am, you two need to come with me."

"Officer, you need to let the bomb squad know there's another one downstairs. I've disarmed it." Ben saw the officer's hand go to his gun. "I'm ex-special forces. Her too. That's why we were able to apprehend the suspect. We'll give a full statement when you're ready."

"I'll need you to come outside with me."

"Sure." Ben nodded to Eva, then whispered, "Julian will have someone around. We need to get out of here."

The officer spoke into the walkie-talkie at his

shoulder to inform whoever was in charge about the second bomb.

"You two head over there." He pointed to an area beyond where they'd cordoned off the library. News vans were everywhere.

"Got it. Thanks for your help." He grabbed Eva's hand and pulled her closer. "Keep your head down. We don't need our faces on the news."

An officer met them at the bottom of the stairs. "If you could join the group over there, there are paramedics ready to assist if you're injured or feeling unwell."

"Great, thanks."

They edged themselves across the fringe of the group to the outside, but too many people were crowded around.

"What do we do now? Should we tell the police what we know?"

"Won't do any good."

"Why not?"

"Julian has control over too many powerful people."

"So there's no way to stop him?"

"Not by human means."

"What's that supposed to mean?"

"I'll explain later. Right now, we have to figure out how to get out of here."

"I don't see how we can."

"We've come this far…" He believed the words he'd spoken to Eva a moment ago. If they were going to get anywhere, it wouldn't be with their own strength.

"So, there *was* a bomb in the basement?" Eva said, scouting the area around them for a means of escape.

"I disarmed it with two seconds left."

"Are you serious?"

"Yeah. It was close."

"Why would Ray give himself so little time?"

"Maybe it wasn't Ray. Maybe Julian or Michael had control over the second bomb in case things didn't go their way."

Eva smirked. "They didn't plan that very well. I guess they weren't counting on us being here."

Ben swallowed. They were close to succeeding. His eyes drifted around the scene, and he spotted a man standing on the other side of the crowd in a trench coat.

"Felix."

"What?" Eva said.

"Nothing."

Felix was looking directly at Ben and gave him a small nod.

Ben grabbed Eva's hand. "You ready to make a break for it?"

"Yes, but—" A horn blasted from the far side of the library. It was loud and everyone looked. Everyone except Ben and Felix.

Even Eva was diverted until Ben jerked her sideways and she stumbled along with him.

"What was that?" she said once they were out of sight.

"That was a distraction."

"Wait a second. You did that? How?"

"You wouldn't believe me if I told you."

"Try me."

"Later."

"No, now. How'd you do it?"

Ben sighed. "You sure you want to know?"

"Yes. Why wouldn't I?"

"I didn't do it. It was God."

"Ben, seriously. How'd you do it?"

"I told you you wouldn't believe me."

"Fine. It was God. But I expect more details later. What do we do now?"

"Now comes the tricky part."

"Stopping a bomber wasn't tricky?"

"No, finding a safe place to go is. We can't go back to my house and neither one of us knows anyone safe to stay with."

"I might know somewhere."

"Really? Even with no memory?"

"Yeah. But you're not going to like it."

## Chapter 28

THEY WAVED at the truck driver when he dropped them off on the side of an empty road.

"You really think this is a good idea?" Ben asked as they headed for the trees.

"It's all I've got. If you've got a better one, I'm all ears."

She stopped once they were among the trees.

"What's wrong?" Ben said.

"I don't actually know where I'm going."

Ben cut in front of her. "I guess I'll lead the way."

They stayed close to the road, but remained concealed in the trees. It slowed the journey, but they couldn't afford to take any risks. Julian would know about the failed bombing by now and he'd have everyone out looking for them.

After a couple of miles, Ben turned to go deep into the forest.

"I really hope you know where you're going," Eva said after they'd been walking for an hour.

"Do I look like I don't?"

"Hard to tell."

A clearing opened up ahead. "Do you still think we're lost?"

"Do you want a medal?"

"That would be really nice, actually."

She held back her smile as she brushed past him, but he put a hand on her shoulder. "Wait here. I want to make sure there aren't any surprise guests."

"There won't be."

"Just let me do my thing."

"If it makes you feel better."

"It does."

Eva crouched down and watched Ben sneak around the edge of the property. The house was dark, and everything was quiet, but she'd let him indulge himself if it made him feel better.

She picked up a stick off the ground and drew a line in the dirt at her feet. Then a gun cocked in her ear. She closed her eyes and steadied her breathing. They couldn't have been followed. They'd been so careful.

She stood slowly and breathed deeply. She had the training to deal with this situation, but her dad knew now what she was capable of, and whoever he'd sent would be hard to subdue. Her only hope was that Ben hadn't been found yet.

"What do you think you're doin' here?" The familiar drawl sent a flood of relief through Eva's tense muscles.

"Clara." She turned slowly, with her hands up. "I'm so glad it's you."

"My, haven't we changed our tune in such a short period of time?"

"I didn't think you'd be here. I thought you'd escaped through the hatch."

"No one pushes me outta my home."

"I really need your help."

"Because of you, my son is in prison."

"You're lucky he's not dead."

Clara jerked the gun forward and squinted. "You itchin' for me to shoot you?"

"I'm sorry. But he deserves to be in prison. I wasn't lying to you when I said he'd attacked me and I was defending myself."

"That why you sent the FBI?"

"I didn't."

"I think it would be better if you walked away now before someone gets hurt."

"If I had anywhere else to go, I wouldn't have come here. I know neither one of us is happy about this reunion, but I had no choice."

"There's always a choice."

"Okay. Well, you can choose to shoot me dead or help me, because I'm not leaving."

"Why are you even here?"

"I'm trying to stop an evil man."

"Who?"

Eva pulled her sleeve back. "The tattoo. You were right about it."

Clara's eye twitched. "You got your memory back?"

"No. But my dad is the one who brought the FBI

here to get me back. He runs an organization, kind of like a cult. He's trying to kill me."

"Your dad, huh?"

"Yeah."

"That's rough. He the reason you fell in the river?"

"I think so."

"So I was right?"

"You were."

"And you're not trying to sweet-talk me?"

Eva couldn't help the smile. "No. I promise."

"How do I know this ain't some ploy to get me to trust you again?"

"You don't."

"But you do know how to fight. There ain't many in this world who could take Franky down like that."

"My dad taught me all of that. Clara, I was a bad person. I did terrible things that I can't remember."

"If you can't remember nothin', then how do you know?" Clara's voice was still rough and skeptical.

"I just know. But when Franky attacked me—"Clara shoved the gun in Eva's face. It would have been easy to disarm her, but she didn't want to force Clara to help. "I'm sorry, but it's true. He attacked me. That's why I had to fight him off. Not because I'm a bad person, but because I was protecting myself."

"Well...I'm sorry about that. That's probably my fault, keeping him at home when he should have gone off and found himself a wife."

"No, it's not your fault. He's a grown man. He has to take responsibility for his actions."

"I don't know."

"Just like I have to take responsibility for mine."

"Still…"

"Clara, you said when you found me you had been called to do the Lord's work, and I believe that's still true. I'm only alive now because God used you to protect me. And now I need your protection again."

Clara made a sound between a harrumph and a laugh. "Now I know you're sweet-talkin' me. But I'm also likely the only one who'd be crazy enough to believe a story like yours."

"And it does you credit."

She lowered the gun. "All right. Come inside." She led Eva toward the house.

Eva looked around for Ben as they crossed the yard. She waved so he knew it was safe, but she couldn't see him anywhere. "There's one other thing."

"Why am I not surprised there's more?" Clara pulled on the door.

"I'm not here alo—" Ben was standing inside when the door opened. He swiped the rifle from her hands and spun her around, pinning her against the wall with the barrel of the gun pressed against her neck.

"Ben, stop." Eva put her hand on his shoulder, pulling him back. "She's helping us."

Ben eased back, but he kept the gun pointed at her. "Is that right? Eva, you said the house would be empty."

Clara's eyes were fiery with anger, but there was a little fear there. "So your plan was to be squatters in my house, young man?"

"Ben, please put down the gun." She rested her fingers on top of the barrel, pressing down lightly.

Ben's shoulders twitched in indecision, but he finally lowered the weapon.

Clara held out her hand. "Can I have my gun back?"

"No."

Eva tsked. And snatched the gun from Ben, handing it to Clara. "If she wanted us dead, I, for one, would already be dead."

Ben glared at Eva. "Could I have a word with you?"

"While you two get your story straight," Clara said, "I'm going to go make myself a cup of tea."

Ben stepped out onto the porch. "It wasn't that long ago that she was ready to kill you."

"No, she wasn't. How many times do I have to say it? Franky was the one who was dangerous. She was confused. She didn't know what to think. All she knew was that she had to look after her family and that was what she was doing as best she could."

"I can't believe you can dismiss her actions like that."

"If I can't make excuses for her behavior, how am I ever going to be able to get over mine? With Franky gone, I truly do not believe she is dangerous. Besides, you should be happy because she believes in God."

"I think there are a lot of things she believes in."

Eva threw her arms up in the air. "Well, she's all we've got."

"But I don't trust her."

"Do you trust me?"

He gritted his teeth. "Yes."

"Then trust me when I tell you she's safe. Without Franky here, she can think for herself."

"Think for herself? Are you kidding? She hasn't got all her marbles."

"So? I'm a murderer and you're what? Perfect?"

"Why would you even say that about yourself when you can't remember killing anyone?"

"I've already explained it to you. I'm not going to do it again. It makes me sick."

Ben put his hands on his hips and sniffed. He hadn't trusted Eva in the beginning either. And God hadn't given him any other bright ideas about where to hide out. "I guess we have nothing to lose."

She punched him lightly on the chin. "That's the spirit."

"Tea's ready," Clara called from the kitchen.

"Would you like some tea?" Eva smiled and went into the house without waiting for Ben, but he followed her in.

When they entered, Clara had already put three cups on the table. "You two gonna fill me in on the whole story?" she said while she poured everyone a drink.

"We can tell you the parts we know," Eva said. "But before we get into that, I'd like to know why you stayed here."

"Where else am I gonna go? This is my home."

"You hid in the bunker?"

"I did. It's the one good thing my husband left me. I've been sleeping in there ever since the FBI raided my home with their dirty boots. Safer in there. I don't need to sleep with one eye open in case someone comes snoopin' around."

"What about Franky? Why didn't he hide?"

She scowled. "'Cause he's an idjit. That's why. Had it in his head that he was gonna show them. In the end, look where it got him. Locked up. It's a miracle he didn't blow us all up. Don't know why he didn't. I told him they weren't worth it, but he wouldn't listen. So there you have it. Now I wanna know what's goin' on with you two." She smiled. "I can't tell you how satisfying it is to find out I was right all the time. I mean, I knew I was right. But to hear it coming from the likes of you? Very satisfying."

"You weren't right about everything," Ben grumbled.

"Which parts?"

"There aren't aliens."

Clara blew a raspberry. "I'm not one of those crazies who believe in aliens. I'm not bonkers. But the government is spying on us, right? Using their satellites, creating super soldiers, big brother, chemtrails. And what about New Coke?"

"New Coke?" Ben asked.

"Yeah, Coke changed their formula to drive up demand of the original product. All part of the New World Order."

"I don't think we can comment on any of those," Eva said.

"I knew it." Clara slapped her hand on the table, nearly spilling their drinks. "So it *is* true."

"No, I don't mean 'no comment' like that. We don't know anything about any of that."

"What *do* you know about?"

"Not much of anything. Ben, you probably know more than I do. You blew up that facility for a reason."

"Ahh." Clara's voice was high-pitched in expectation of this new revelation. "You're a bomb-maker, are you? Like my son."

"No," Ben said before sending Eva something close to a death stare. "Not like him. But I don't really want to get into it."

"Why not?" Clara said. "You got skeletons in your closet?"

"You've got enough theories to keep you busy. You don't need me to add to them."

"Come on, Ben," Eva said. "She's opened her home to us. "

"You want my help? You gotta come clean. My hospitality only extends so far. I won't put my life on the line without knowing what I'm getting into."

"She's got a point."

Ben sucked air through his teeth. "Fine. Julian created a program that was introduced into schools nationwide. It gave him access to test results and student files and made it possible for him to identify anyone who showed promise for recruitment from a young age."

"Is that true?" Eva said. "Is that what he was doing?"

"Until I blew up the building and destroyed all the hardware, yes."

"I had no idea. But what did he do once he'd identified someone for recruitment?"

"It depended on what level he expected them to rise to."

"And?"

Ben stared at a spot on the table. "Some parents were addicts. That made it easy because he'd give them all the drugs they wanted in exchange for their kids."

"You mean he'd just take them?"

"Yeah."

"And what if the parents weren't interested in giving up their kids?"

"It doesn't matter. The point is—"

"It does matter," Eva said.

"He didn't want to draw attention to himself, but for a top performer, if necessary, he went as far as making them orphans."

Both Clara and Eva gasped.

"Monster," Clara said. Eva just shook her head.

"I helped him do it until I realized what was going on."

"How could you not know?"

"He never gave me all the information." Ben's voice lowered. "He'd tell me what I needed to hear in order to get me to do the job."

"And I was a part of that too," Eva said with her head bowed.

"I don't know how involved you were in that program. I never met you while I was there."

"And what about the dental scheme?" Clara asked.

"Was that part of it? Or was he going to add that on later?"

"Dental scheme?"

"Yeah, you know, so he could put tracking devices into their teeth."

Ben closed his eyes and took a breath to keep from saying what would make the situation worse. "There was no dental scheme."

"You sure?"

"The program itself was bad enough, trust me. I risked my life to destroy it."

Clara leaned toward Ben. "People like to bandy that phrase around—*risked my life*. It's not something that should be applied lightly."

"I should be dead. I brought the bomb into the building, and Julian's guys figured out what I was doing. They wouldn't let me out alive, so I had to blow it while I was inside."

Eva's eyes widened. "You blew the building while you were inside?"

Ben looked into his lap. "Yeah."

"How are you alive?"

"I shouldn't be."

"Wait, so it was my fault."

"What?"

"I told Julian about you saving me. I gave you away. Did he think you were dead?"

"Yeah."

"So I'm the reason they picked you up. You were safe until I told them where you were. I'm so sorry. I didn't know what I was doing."

"It served its purpose."

"How can you say that? What if I had killed you?"

Ben shrugged. "You didn't."

"But look at you. You're injured, and that's my fault."

"The bruises will heal. It all served its purpose. When Tyler came for me, I went with him by choice."

"Why?"

"Because we wouldn't be here right now if I hadn't gone with him. You'd be at home with your dad with no idea about what was going on."

"But you couldn't have known that."

"I didn't." He reached out a hand and rested it on hers. "Eva, if things hadn't happened exactly as they did, you'd be at Julian's house right now, hearing about a library full of kids that had been blown up."

"What's that?" Clara said.

Eva licked her lips. "Before coming here, we stopped a library full of kids from being blown up."

Clara puffed out her cheeks and fell back against her chair. "My, my. You two have been busy. What's this Julian guy have against kids, anyway?"

Eva pushed back from the table. "I need to clear my head."

# Chapter 29

BEN FOLDED his hands on the table after Eva left the house. He wanted to follow her out but knew she needed some time to process. If it were him, he'd want some space before he'd be ready to talk.

"You hungry?" Clara said.

"Not really."

"Well, I am. All this conspiracy really works up the appetite."

Ben watched her as she moved through the kitchen.

"Why did you do it?" he asked. She turned.

"Do what?"

"Hurt Eva." He was surprised by the pain that appeared in her eyes.

"I didn't want to." She turned away from him and kept preparing herself a meal, but continued to talk. "I liked her. I believed in her. I guess I'd always wanted a daughter, too, and when I brought Eva home and discovered the pain she'd suffered, all I wanted to do was care for her."

"Then why?"

"'Cause Franky's all I've got. He's my blood."

"But you had Eva."

Her head dropped. "She wasn't mine. I don't know if you noticed, but there's a wildness about her that can't be tamed."

"That doesn't give you the right to tie her up."

"I found an injured bird once. I looked after it till it was better. I thought it was tame. It was a lovely, gentle bird, but as soon as it could fly away, it did. That's Eva. I knew that as soon as she was better, she'd be gone. I guess a dark part of myself wanted to force her to stay. I didn't want her to get hurt. I didn't really think Franky had it in him to treat someone like that, but I was wrong. That's why I let you go when you came for her."

"You think you let us go?"

"There was a moment when I had a clear shot, but I couldn't do it." She shrugged. "After that, I went to hide in the bunker."

"And Franky tried his luck with the FBI."

"I was angry when they arrested him, but then I heard the FBI talking after they went through his shed." She picked up a dish towel and twisted it. "Franky was planning something very bad. I didn't know he had gotten to that point. Or maybe I didn't want to know." She looked down at her white knuckles. "Listen, you should go after Eva. She's looking a little pale."

Ben nodded and left Clara to her regrets. But he didn't think he had any comfort to give to either woman.

He found Eva sitting on the steps of the porch. He

stood in the door until she looked back at him. "You just gonna stand there and stare?"

"I didn't want to intrude."

"It's okay. You can sit."

"You okay?"

"It's so strange being back here."

"I bet. I, uh…I talked to Clara. I believe she's genuine. She might be a bit mixed up, but like you said, none of us are perfect."

"Yeah."

"You want to tell me what's bothering you?"

"Should I make out a list?"

"There is a lot right now. How about you just tell me what's hurts the most?"

Eva twisted her fingers together. Her eyes searched the space in front of her for a response. Finally, she said, "I have this horrible emptiness inside of me."

"Because of your memory loss?"

She shook her head. "You believe in God. I don't know what I believe in, but I can't deny that there is a power that is beyond you and me and beyond Julian. It has woven us through everything that's happened today. But there is still so much evil. And I feel as though I'm in some kind of purgatory."

"You can't put so much pressure on yourself. It will take you time to adjust."

She scoffed. "Julian said the same thing."

"Even the bad guys get it right now and then."

"The thing is, with everything I've learned in this small space of time, I know that I became an enemy of Julian's. But I have no memory of that decision. And with that scripture that I know, it suggests that I may have made a choice in the recent past to believe in the same God you do, but I can't remember it."

"It doesn't give you peace knowing that you might have?"

"No. Whatever led up to that decision is gone. What if I've lost my chance because I can't remember?"

"You can choose him again."

"Can I? The doctor said it was likely that if I regained memories, they would come back in pieces. What if the only pieces I get back are the ones where I'm committed to Julian?"

"What if you do? What are you afraid of?"

"That I'll lose my humanity, and it will be too late to get it back."

"Lose your humanity?"

"I'm afraid it will be more than I can live with. More than any of us can."

"What do you mean?"

"What if I remember and I turn on you?"

"That's not going to happen."

"You don't know."

He took her hand and threaded his fingers through hers. "Eva, you have got to stop doing this to yourself."

"How can I? I can't ignore the freight train that might be barreling down on us right now."

"And a plane could crash into the house tonight. You're worried about something that is highly unlikely to happen. You just need time to heal. You'll get through this."

"But how do you heal from a wound you can't identify? How will I ever know if that part of myself has been cured and I'm safe from it? How can I ever be certain I won't hurt you?"

"Do you want to hurt me now?"

"I—"

"Look at me."

Eva looked.

"Deep down inside right now. What are you feeling? Do you want to hurt me?"

She shook her head.

"What do you want?"

Her lips parted as though she was going to respond, but only a small sigh escaped and she leaned toward him.

He held his breath. He wanted it to happen, but knew it shouldn't. It would cross a line he wasn't prepared for and neither was she.

"Dinner's up if you're hungry!" Clara called out.

Eva pulled back and separated her hand from his. "We should eat." She jumped up and hurried inside, but Ben stayed where he was, staring out into the yard that was hazy with dusk.

---

Eva swept through the kitchen without acknowledging Clara and locked herself in the bathroom. She leaned against the wall and steadied her breathing. The pull she'd felt toward Ben had her feeling completely unhinged. With Michael, it had been different. She'd been attracted to him, but he'd taken advantage of her vulnerability and used it to draw her in. That was clear now. She had wanted the security of someone besides her father caring for her. Michael had said all the right things to charm her, and she'd fallen for it at the time. But there was something else with Ben that touched a deeper place inside of her and it terrified her.

She pushed out a decisive breath and went to the sink to wash her hands. She couldn't afford to be unguarded anymore. There was too much at stake. Neither one of them could afford to get distracted. He must know that as well as she did. She'd be grateful to have a friend, someone she could rely on and feel at home with, but that was all.

She held her breath, then shook everything aside and went to eat dinner with Clara.

The woman's presence was the perfect steadying factor because, in a way, she kept them all off-balance and focused on what really mattered.

They'd come to the right place.

---

Ben rubbed at his eyes to dislodge the memory of the look Eva had given him. Until that moment, he hadn't thought of her in that way. Not consciously anyway. She was a beautiful woman and it must have been simmering under the surface, waiting for an opportunity. But violence and uncertainty weren't a good breeding ground for a relationship.

"How're you holding up?"

Ben jumped away from the figure who had appeared beside him. "Why would you do that? You shouldn't turn up unannounced," he said once he'd settled.

Felix shrugged. "You were distracted."

"No, I wasn't. How long have you been here?"

"Just turned up. Although, you know God's with you all the time."

Ben looked up at the dark sky and grimaced. He didn't want to think about God's opinion on what almost happened. "You know, if someone comes out here, they'll think I've lost my mind talking to the air."

"They'd see me if they came out."

"Really?"

"I'm not invisible. But no one's coming out."

"What'd you do, put them to sleep?"

"No, I just picked my timing. I wanted to tell you personally what a great job you've done so far. I know it hasn't been easy."

Ben took a deep breath. "No, it hasn't. But you know, it's strange."

"What is?"

"I was so afraid to get involved, but now that I am" —he shook his head—"I don't know. It's like the fear has gone. I was afraid of the idea of doing something, but now that I'm doing it…"

Felix nodded. "That, my friend, is the treachery of fear. As a weapon of the enemy, he will speak all kinds of lies to keep us bound by it. Humans have a way of looking at fear as their protector when all it does is hold you captive. But once you come out from under the veil, you find freedom."

"Don't get me wrong, I've still got plenty of issues."

"He'll take you as you are."

Ben laughed, but then sobered. "And what about Eva?"

"What about her?"

"Is she going to be okay?"

Felix looked at Ben and locked his eyes on him. "He didn't send you on this assignment to fix her."

"I didn't say he did."

"Ben. Listen to me. *He* is the only one who can help her. That is not for you to do. If you try, you will fail and you'll pull each other apart."

"I got it."

"Are you sure?"

"Yes."

"Good."

Ben picked at his fingers. "Will she ever get her memory back?"

"I don't know."

"Would you tell me if you did?"

"I don't do hypotheticals."

"Of course you don't. By the way, thanks for your help at the library."

"You looked like you could use a hand."

"I don't know how we would have gotten out of there without you. But we only stopped one thing. Julian's not done."

"Then you better get busy."

"Doing what exactly?"

"You have to stop him from getting control."

"Of what? Are we talking about end times here?"

"Not end times. You said yourself you can have no impact on the end result. The Bible is clear that He is holding back the Antichrist until his time is ready. And when that time comes, there will be no stopping him."

"Then what are we stopping?"

"The devil knows he hasn't got much time left. He is doing everything in his power to snatch sheep while he still can."

"Julian's doing a good job helping him do that."

"He is."

Ben leaned forward, resting his elbows on his knees. "You said a lot had been asked to help, but had refused."

"Yes."

"Is there anything I can do? Julian has people everywhere. We need as many as we can get."

"You know the story of the loaves and fishes?"

"Of course."

"He can do miraculous things with small portions. Like with Gideon and his army. But that doesn't mean you stop praying for the harvest workers." Felix put a hand on Ben's shoulder. "Don't worry. There are more that He's preparing. There are more coming. Be patient."

"But time is short."

"He is not slow in keeping his promise, as some understand slowness. Instead, He is patient with you, not wanting anyone to perish, but everyone to come to repentance."

"Then we'll wait for his instruction. And we'll be ready to act."

To be continued …

## Enjoy the book?

Book reviews are the most powerful tool I have as an author to grow my readership. If I had the sway of a New York publisher, perhaps it would be easier to gain attention, but a simple reader review is way better than what any top publisher can offer…

Readers like yourself are what make the biggest difference to an author, and if you've enjoyed this book and wouldn't mind spending a few minutes leaving a review, it would help me out immensely.

## Free Bonus Chapter

One of the best things about being a writer is that I get to build relationships with my readers. And one of the best ways to do that is through a newsletter. I'm not a prolific emailer, but I will occasionally send out a newsletter with details on new releases, special offers, other projects I've been working on and anything else I have that might be of interest.

When you sign up, you'll get the bonus chapter that tells the story of Ben's encounter in the field when he's trying to overcome the darkness in Chapter Five from Felix's perspective.

### GET YOUR FREE CHAPTER NOW

Or visit: subscribepage.io/chapterfive

# Also by Shawna Coleing

## Underwood Series

Christian Thriller

UNDER THE VEIL (book 1)

UNDER FIRE (book 2)

UNDER SIEGE (book 3)

## Shadow Alliance Series

Christian Romantic suspense

SHADOW GAME (book 1)

SHADOW LINE (book 2)

SHADOW BREAK (book 3)

SHADOW TRACE (book 4)

SHADOW POINT (book 4)

## Hidden Alliance Series

Christian Romantic Suspense

HIDDEN TRIAL (book 1)

HIDDEN DEPTHS (book 2)

HIDDEN ASCENT (book 3)

HIDDEN CHANCE (book 4)

## Inspired by Judges Series

Contemporary Christian Romantic Suspense

SAMSON

GIDEON

JEP

JAEL

## Bristol Kelley Duology

A clean romantic suspense

SLEIGHT OF HAND (book 1)

SMOKE AND MIRRORS (book 2)

## Erin Hart Duology

A clean romantic suspense

OUT ON A LIMB (book 1)

CUT TO THE CHASE (book 2)

# About the Author

Shawna Coleing is the author of the Shadow Alliance Series. You can find her on her website or feel free to contact her by email at: shawnacoleing@pgturners.com

Otherwise you can connect with her here:

 Formatted with Vellum

Made in the USA
Monee, IL
10 June 2026